EERIE EAST ANGLIA

EERIE EAST ANGLIA

Fearful Tales of Field and Fen

Edited by
EDWARD PARNELL

This collection first published in 2024 by
The British Library
96 Euston Road
London NW1 2DB

Selection, introduction and notes © 2024 Edward Parnell
Volume copyright © 2024 The British Library Board

The Editor asserts his moral right to be identified as the Editor of the work in relation to all such rights as are granted by the Editor to the Publisher under the terms and conditions of their Agreement.

"Dearth's Farm" © 1923 The Estate of Gerald Bullett.

"Ringing the Changes" reproduced by permission of Artellus Ltd. Copyright © 1955 Robert Aickman.

"If She Bends, She Breaks" © 1984 The Estate of John Gordon.

"Dr. Matthews' Ghost Story" © 1990 Penelope Fitzgerald. Reproduced as an extract from *The Gate of Angels*, published by HarperCollins.

"Possum" by Matthew Holness previously published in *The New Uncanny* (Comma Press, 2008) ed. Sarah Eyre and Ra Page. Reprinted by permission of the author.

"Blood Rites" © 2016 Daisy Johnson. Reproduced from *Fen*, published by Penguin Random House.

Every effort has been made to trace copyright holders and to obtain their permission for the use of copyright material. The publisher apologises for any errors or omissions and would be pleased to be notified of any corrections to be incorporated in reprints or future editions.

Cataloguing in Publication Data
A catalogue record for this publication is available from the British Library

ISBN 978 0 7123 5571 1
e-ISBN 978 0 7123 6897 1

Frontispiece illustration by Sandra Gómez.

Illustrations on pages 6 and 320 by James McBryde, from the first edition of M. R. James's *Ghost Stories of an Antiquary* (Edward Arnold, 1904).

Cover design by Mauricio Villamayor with illustration by Sandra Gómez
Text design and typesetting by Tetragon, London
Printed in England by CPI Group (UK) Ltd, Croydon, CR0 4YY

CONTENTS

INTRODUCTION	7
FURTHER READING AND ACKNOWLEDGEMENTS	12
A NOTE FROM THE PUBLISHER	13
"Oh, Whistle, and I'll Come to You, My Lad" M. R. JAMES	15
Father Maddox's Tale R. H. BENSON	41
The Dust-Cloud E. F. BENSON	55
The Man with the Roller E. G. SWAIN	73
The True History of Anthony Ffryar INGULPHUS	87
Dearth's Farm GERALD BULLETT	97
The Seventeenth Hole at Duncaster H. R. WAKEFIELD	113
The Crown Derby Plate MARJORIE BOWEN	131
Miss de Mannering of Asham F. M. MAYOR	149
The House on the Marsh FREDERICK COWLES	179
Stivinghoe Bank R. H. MALDEN	191
Ringing the Changes ROBERT AICKMAN	207
If She Bends, She Breaks JOHN GORDON	245
Dr. Matthews' Ghost Story PENELOPE FITZGERALD	263
Possum MATTHEW HOLNESS	273
Blood Rites DAISY JOHNSON	295
A Vignette M. R. JAMES	307

INTRODUCTION

East Anglia. A slippery label that defines an area of the east of England. Perhaps even as slippery as the eels that once so commonly slithered through the region's rivers and dykes... Historically, the term refers to the Kingdom of the East Angles, formed in the sixth century after the arrival in Britain of the Angles, a Germanic people from the Jutland peninsula. Though quite where, exactly, you place contemporary East Anglia's boundaries is open for debate. Certainly, the counties of Norfolk and Suffolk should be included—as well as Cambridgeshire (though this, too, might start to get contentious with some purists); I would also bring in Essex, and could be tempted to embrace a sliver of the Lincolnshire Fens. Others may justifiably advocate the inclusion of some portions of the Home Counties, but all of that is an argument for another day... In this anthology of ghostly tales, I'll stick to Norfolk, Suffolk, Essex and Cambridgeshire, which will give us more than enough pleasing terrors to be getting on with.

Is there a defining quality to the East Anglian landscape? Again, the answer isn't straightforward—for a relatively small expanse it is more varied than a comparable area you might find in, say, the Corn Belt of the USA. But it does have a reputation—not helped by Noël Coward—of being very flat. This isn't entirely fair—there are plenty of gently rolling hills in Norfolk and Suffolk, and a couple of spots in Essex and Cambridge that reach almost 150 metres in height. But it is true there are a lot of flat fields, particularly when we get into the Fens, in the north-east corner of the region; the neighbourhood was, after all, under water (or at best marshland) for much of its recent history, until the arrival of the Dutch engineers who drove forward the drainage of those lands for agriculture from the seventeenth century onwards.

So, were I to try to describe the essential qualities of the East Anglian landscape, what would I include? Well, despite my protestations to the contrary, it would indeed be mostly flat, with the odd gently wooded hill on the horizon, a line of tall poplars following a dyke in the foreground, and some rougher freshmarsh, grazed by cattle and geese in the middle distance. There might be a windmill, and a round-towered church. Possibly even an impressive Queen Anne-style house somewhere in the scene. Above, certainly, would be an all-engulfing sky, seeded with just the occasional grey-tinged cloud. Were we to shift our view coastwards, we would notice some wide, meandering channels, wildfowl-strewn saltmarshes, and crunching shingle spits, with perhaps a strange sea fret now moving imperceptibly inland towards our imagined vantage point. You get the picture.

Away from the topography and natural features, we've already noted a few stone-built reminders of people's endeavours—and certainly the region is rich in its human traditions, particularly from the medieval period onwards when wool and foreign trade brought prosperity and the construction of so many magnificent churches, abbeys, and grand places of residence. Going back further we have, below the crumbling cliffs of Happisburgh in north-east Norfolk, much earlier evidence of our ancestors, in a set of 800,000-year-old hominid footprints uncovered in 2013—the most ancient marks of primitive humanity found to date outside Africa. This pressing sense of history, of course, is fertile territory for the ghost story.

In attempting to choose the different tales for this collection, there was one figure whose name kept cropping up, and who casts a tall, spectral shadow over it all. Montague Rhodes James—or Monty as he was known to many of his closest friends (though he usually signed himself as "MRJ")—was born in Goodnestone, a small Kent village midway between Canterbury and Deal where his father was curate, in August 1862. After three years the family moved to Great Livermere in Suffolk, six miles from the town of Bury St Edmunds, when Herbert James took up the rectorship of St Peter's Church.

Initially schooled at home (including in Greek and Latin by his father—classical scholarship would loom large throughout his life), aged 11 the young Monty was sent to Temple Grove prep in southwest London, whose surroundings were to inspire "A School Story" (published 1911); he was to make a lifelong friend here in Arthur Benson (see later in this anthology for tales by two of the younger Benson brothers). Eton followed Temple Grove, and then King's College, Cambridge, with those prestigious academic institutions dominating the rest of his days: he would go on to become provost at both. "About these places have been woven cords of affection which bind together the most diverse natures and stretch over the whole world: cords which run through a man's whole life and do not part at the supreme moment of death," he was to remark in a sermon delivered in King's College Chapel.

At Cambridge, the ghost stories that James wrote and read aloud for the amusement of his peers and the King's choristers became a local tradition of sorts. Clearly they had an impact on those who heard them, as a number of the writers in this anthology who were present at those candlelit, college-room readings went on to produce their own uncanny tales: the Benson brothers, R. H. Malden and E. G. Swain. More than half of the others included here, too, had connections with Cambridge. Certainly—and I write this as someone born in the same long stretch of Fenland flatness—the landscape encircling that ancient place of learning can appear strange to visitors: there's something bleak and unnerving about those endless vistas.

The region still feels cut off from the rest of the world—transport links are generally average at best—despite its proximity to London. And it remains a rural area, with reminders of its bucolic traditions everywhere. The semi-surrounding North Sea adds another liminal element into the proceedings, pressing its cold, grey waters up against the retreating land; even this is not a solid border, as the East Anglian coastline is one of the most rapidly eroding in northern Europe.

Also feeding the imagination of those writers drawn to the region as a backdrop for eerie fiction is its wealth of folklore and superstition. For example, we have the strange story of the Green Children of Suffolk's Woolpit, who seemingly emerged from the ground in the Middle Ages; the speechless wild man washed up at Orford beach and later imprisoned in its tower; or the devil-dog Black Shuck whose terrifying appearances herald chaos. More recently, a newer mythology has developed around "the most haunted house in England", Borley Rectory, formerly located on a ridge of lonely land just across the Essex side of the border with Suffolk; it's gone now, consumed by a fire in 1939, though ghosthunters still visit the village's graveyard for illicit souvenirs, or perhaps in hope of a glimpse of the phantasmal Reverend Bull. And Norfolk shouldn't be left out—it has its own piece of recent ghostly lore in the celebrated photograph of the Brown Lady of Raynham Hall, purportedly captured on film as she floated down the Hall's stairs in 1936.

But we circle back, once more, to M. R. James, as his influence extends past the printed page and onto celluloid—perhaps another key factor in East Anglia's dark hold over so many of our imaginations... Jonathan Miller's 1968 adaptation of the opening story in this collection for the BBC arts series *Omnibus* curtailed its title to *Whistle and I'll Come to You*. The stripping out of the flourish of the original's name is mirrored in the film's pared-down, black-and-white scenes, filmed on

INTRODUCTION

the cliffs at Suffolk's Dunwich and in the marram-guarded dunes of Waxham on the north-eastern edge of the Norfolk coast.

The first in the BBC's annual "Ghost Story for Christmas" strand, *The Stalls of Barchester*, was shot on location at Norwich Cathedral, with the following year's adaptation *A Warning to the Curious* taking the Suffolk setting but filming it mainly around Wells-next-the-Sea (with a few scenes at Happisburgh—the site of those early footprints) on the north Norfolk coast. Wells Woods manages to look both beautiful and menacing in Lawrence Gordon Clark's film, captured in 16mm grainy colour beneath a wintry sun that causes the near-sculptural trees to cast long, sinister shadows. As for the night-time set piece, it rivals *The Blair Witch Project* for the creepiness of its glimpsed torchlit horrors among the shadowed trunks. Although its seemingly unending expanse of sandy beach—which features in the opening sequence and again, briefly, to devastating effect at its climax—is now, even in the heart of the winter, a busy tourist destination, the belt of dune-strengthening, Victorian-planted Corsican pines can be disconcerting once you get away from the crowds. It's almost as if there is a figure there somewhere, lurking at the corner of your sight…

I hope you enjoy this anthology of East Anglian-set tales that I've chosen here. They take us from the beginning of the twentieth century up to the present—you'll be pleased to see that this outpost of eastern England continues to exert its ghostly pull over the imagination of contemporary writers. If this small selection only whets your appetite for additional chills, there is a short list on the following page of stories featuring the region that can be found in other titles from the *Tales of the Weird* series.

EDWARD PARNELL, 2024

FURTHER READING

"The Four-Fifteen Express" (1867) by Amelia B. Edwards. In *Spirits of the Season: Christmas Hauntings* (2018).

"The Ash-tree" (1904) by M. R. James. In *Evil Roots: Killer Tales of the Botanical Gothic* (2017).

"Bone to His Bone" (1912) by E. G. Swain. In *Haunters at the Hearth: Eerie Tales for Christmas Nights* (2022).

"The Bad Lands" (1925) by John Metcalfe. In *Roads of Destiny: And Other Tales of Alternative Histories and Parallel Realms* (2023).

"The Corner House" (1928) by E. F. Benson. In *The Outcast: And Other Dark Tales* by E. F. Benson (2020).

"A Tale of an Empty House" (1928) by E. F. Benson. In *Our Haunted Shores: Tales from the Coasts of the British Isles* (2022).

"Between Sunset and Moonrise" (1943) by R. H. Malden. In *Haunters at the Hearth: Eerie Tales for Christmas Nights* (2022).

ACKNOWLEDGEMENTS

Thanks to Mike Ashley, Jon Dear, Frank and Rob Gordon, Matt Holness, Daisy Johnson, Rosemary Pardoe, Ray Russell and Mark Valentine for answering my various questions and requests so generously. And to Tom Killingbeck and Euan Thorneycroft at A. M. Heath for their advice. Finally, to Alison Moss and the rest of the team at the British Library—with a special thanks to Jonny Davidson—for all their sterling work in putting together *Eerie East Anglia*.

A NOTE FROM THE PUBLISHER

The original short stories reprinted in the British Library Tales of the Weird series were written and published in a period ranging across the nineteenth and twentieth centuries. There are many elements of these stories which continue to entertain modern readers; however, in some cases there are also uses of language, instances of stereotyping and some attitudes expressed by narrators or characters which may not be endorsed by the publishing standards of today. We acknowledge therefore that some elements in the stories selected for reprinting may continue to make uncomfortable reading for some of our audience. With this series British Library Publishing aims to offer a new readership a chance to read some of the rare material of the British Library's collections in an affordable paperback format, to enjoy their merits and to look back into the worlds of the past two centuries as portrayed by their writers. It is not possible to separate these stories from the history of their writing and therefore the following stories are presented as they were originally published with one edit to the text and minor edits made for consistency of style and sense. We welcome feedback from our readers, which can be sent to the following address:

British Library Publishing
The British Library
96 Euston Road
London, NW1 2DB

1904

"OH, WHISTLE, AND I'LL COME TO YOU, MY LAD"

M. R. James

Montague Rhodes James (1862–1936) is arguably the foremost English writer of ghost stories—and East Anglian locations feature as a backdrop to around a third of his tales.

Given the quality of James's output, choosing a single East Anglian-set story to include here has proved challenging—so much so that I've decided to additionally incorporate "A Vignette", the last supernatural piece he was to write. I also seriously considered "A Warning to the Curious" (1925), the action of which takes place in Seaburgh, a counterfeit copy of the upmarket Suffolk resort of Aldeburgh, where the young James enjoyed visits to his paternal grandmother. The fictional Essex country house of Anningley Hall, whose sinister history is sketched out in "The Mezzotint", was a strong contender, too, along with "The Ash-tree" and its vengeful Suffolk witch, Mrs. Mothersole (a common family name on the gravestones of Livermere's St Peter's, Monty's local childhood haunt). But in the end, I turned towards another tale (like that latter-mentioned pair) from James's first—and best—collection, 1904's *Ghost Stories of an Antiquary*.

Probably written in the previous year (we know a version was read at King's College, Cambridge during Christmas of 1903), the title of "'Oh, Whistle, and I'll Come to You, My Lad'" (note the speech marks that form part of it) comes from a light-hearted 1793 love song of the same name whose lyrics are by Robert Burns. In James's story it is not a lover who is coming, but an apparition swathed in bedsheets—an archetypal image of the ghostly rendered here, for all of its seeming familiarity and physical impotence, as terrifying as any of the revenants and medieval demons that haunt his other tales. Events unfold after the arrival of Parkins, a neat young Cambridge professor, who is to spend his vacation in Burnstow—a place modelled on the south Suffolk resort (and today port) of Felixstowe.

"Who is this who is coming?" Read on to find out…

"I suppose you will be getting away pretty soon, now Full term is over, Professor," said a person not in the story to the Professor of Ontography, soon after they had sat down next to each other at a feast in the hospitable hall of St. James's College.

The Professor was young, neat, and precise in speech.

"Yes," he said; "my friends have been making me take up golf this term, and I mean to go to the East Coast—in point of fact to Burnstow—(I dare say you know it) for a week or ten days, to improve my game. I hope to get off tomorrow."

"Oh, Parkins," said his neighbour on the other side, "if you are going to Burnstow, I wish you would look at the site of the Templars' preceptory, and let me know if you think it would be any good to have a dig there in the summer."

It was, as you might suppose, a person of antiquarian pursuits who said this, but, since he merely appears in this prologue, there is no need to give his entitlements.

"Certainly," said Parkins, the Professor: "if you will describe to me whereabouts the site is, I will do my best to give you an idea of the lie of the land when I get back; or I could write to you about it, if you would tell me where you are likely to be."

"Don't trouble to do that, thanks. It's only that I'm thinking of taking my family in that direction in the Long, and it occurred to me that, as very few of the English preceptories have ever been properly planned, I might have an opportunity of doing something useful on off-days."

The Professor rather sniffed at the idea that planning out a preceptory could be described as useful. His neighbour continued:

"The site—I doubt if there is anything showing above ground—must be down quite close to the beach now. The sea has encroached tremendously, as you know, all along that bit of coast. I should think, from the map, that it must be about three-quarters of a mile from the Globe Inn, at the north end of the town. Where are you going to stay?"

"Well, *at* the Globe Inn, as a matter of fact," said Parkins; "I have engaged a room there. I couldn't get in anywhere else; most of the lodging-houses are shut up in winter, it seems; and, as it is, they tell me that the only room of any size I can have is really a double-bedded one, and that they haven't a corner in which to store the other bed, and so on. But I must have a fairly large room, for I am taking some books down, and mean to do a bit of work; and though I don't quite fancy having an empty bed—not to speak of two—in what I may call for the time being my study, I suppose I can manage to rough it for the short time I shall be there."

"Do you call having an extra bed in your room roughing it, Parkins?" said a bluff person opposite. "Look here, I shall come down and occupy it for a bit; it'll be company for you."

The Professor quivered, but managed to laugh in a courteous manner.

"By all means, Rogers; there's nothing I should like better. But I'm afraid you would find it rather dull; you don't play golf, do you?"

"No, thank Heaven!" said rude Mr. Rogers.

"Well, you see, when I'm not writing I shall most likely be out on the links, and that, as I say, would be rather dull for you, I'm afraid."

"Oh, I don't know! There's certain to be somebody I know in the place; but, of course, if you don't want me, speak the word, Parkins; I shan't be offended. Truth, as you always tell us, is never offensive."

Parkins was, indeed, scrupulously polite and strictly truthful. It is to be feared that Mr. Rogers sometimes practised upon his knowledge of these characteristics. In Parkins's breast there was a conflict now raging, which for a moment or two did not allow him to answer. That interval being over, he said:

"Well, if you want the exact truth, Rogers, I was considering whether the room I speak of would really be large enough to accommodate us both comfortably; and also whether (mind, I shouldn't have said this if you hadn't pressed me) you would not constitute something in the nature of a hindrance to my work."

Rogers laughed loudly.

"Well done, Parkins!" he said. "It's all right. I promise not to interrupt your work; don't you disturb yourself about that. No, I won't come if you don't want me; but I thought I should do so nicely to keep the ghosts off." Here he might have been seen to wink and to nudge his next neighbour. Parkins might also have been seen to become pink. "I beg pardon, Parkins," Rogers continued; "I oughtn't to have said that. I forgot you didn't like levity on these topics."

"Well," Parkins said, "as you have mentioned the matter, I freely own that I do *not* like careless talk about what you call ghosts. A man in my position," he went on, raising his voice a little, "cannot, I find, be too careful about appearing to sanction the current beliefs on such subjects. As you know, Rogers, or as you ought to know; for I think I have never concealed my views—"

"No, you certainly have not, old man," put in Rogers *sotto voce*.

"—I hold that any semblance, any appearance of concession to the view that such things might exist is to me a renunciation of all that

I hold most sacred. But I'm afraid I have not succeeded in securing your attention."

"Your *undivided* attention, was what Dr. Blimber actually *said*,"[1] Rogers interrupted, with every appearance of an earnest desire for accuracy. "But I beg your pardon, Parkins: I'm stopping you."

"No, not at all," said Parkins. "I don't remember Blimber; perhaps he was before my time. But I needn't go on. I'm sure you know what I mean."

"Yes, yes," said Rogers, rather hastily—"just so. We'll go into it fully at Burnstow, or somewhere."

In repeating the above dialogue I have tried to give the impression which it made on me, that Parkins was something of an old woman—rather henlike, perhaps, in his little ways; totally destitute, alas! of the sense of humour, but at the same time dauntless and sincere in his convictions, and a man deserving of the greatest respect. Whether or not the reader has gathered so much, that was the character which Parkins had.

On the following day Parkins did, as he had hoped, succeed in getting away from his college, and in arriving at Burnstow. He was made welcome at the Globe Inn, was safely installed in the large double-bedded room of which we have heard, and was able before retiring to rest to arrange his materials for work in apple-pie order upon a commodious table which occupied the outer end of the room, and was surrounded on three sides by windows looking out seaward; that is to say, the central window looked straight out to sea, and those on the left and right commanded prospects along the shore to the north and south respectively. On the south you saw the village of Burnstow. On the north no

---

[1] Mr. Rogers was wrong, *vide* "Dombey and Son," chapter xii.

houses were to be seen, but only the beach and the low cliff backing it. Immediately in front was a strip—not considerable—of rough grass, dotted with old anchors, capstans, and so forth; then a broad path; then the beach. Whatever may have been the original distance between the Globe Inn and the sea, not more than sixty yards now separated them.

The rest of the population of the inn was, of course, a golfing one, and included few elements that call for a special description. The most conspicuous figure was, perhaps, that of an *ancien militaire*, secretary of a London club, and possessed of a voice of incredible strength, and of views of a pronouncedly Protestant type. These were apt to find utterance after his attendance upon the ministrations of the Vicar, an estimable man with inclinations towards a picturesque ritual, which he gallantly kept down as far as he could out of deference to East Anglian tradition.

Professor Parkins, one of whose principal characteristics was pluck, spent the greater part of the day following his arrival at Burnstow in what he had called improving his game, in company with this Colonel Wilson: and during the afternoon—whether the process of improvement were to blame or not, I am not sure—the Colonel's demeanour assumed a colouring so lurid that even Parkins jibbed at the thought of walking home with him from the links. He determined, after a short and furtive look at that bristling moustache and those incarnadined features, that it would be wiser to allow the influences of tea and tobacco to do what they could with the Colonel before the dinner-hour should render a meeting inevitable.

"I might walk home tonight along the beach," he reflected—"yes, and take a look—there will be light enough for that—at the ruins of which Disney was talking. I don't exactly know where they are, by the way; but I expect I can hardly help stumbling on them."

This he accomplished, I may say, in the most literal sense, for in picking his way from the links to the shingle beach his foot caught, partly in a gorse-root and partly in a biggish stone, and over he went. When he got up and surveyed his surroundings, he found himself in a patch of somewhat broken ground covered with small depressions and mounds. These latter, when he came to examine them, proved to be simply masses of flints embedded in mortar and grown over with turf. He must, he quite rightly concluded, be on the site of the preceptory he had promised to look at. It seemed not unlikely to reward the spade of the explorer; enough of the foundations was probably left at no great depth to throw a good deal of light on the general plan. He remembered vaguely that the Templars, to whom this site had belonged, were in the habit of building round churches, and he thought a particular series of the humps or mounds near him did appear to be arranged in something of a circular form. Few people can resist the temptation to try a little amateur research in a department quite outside their own, if only for the satisfaction of showing how successful they would have been had they only taken it up seriously. Our Professor, however, if he felt something of this mean desire, was also truly anxious to oblige Mr. Disney. So he paced with care the circular area he had noticed, and wrote down its rough dimensions in his pocket-book. Then he proceeded to examine an oblong eminence which lay east of the centre of the circle, and seemed to his thinking likely to be the base of a platform or altar. At one end of it, the northern, a patch of the turf was gone—removed by some boy or other creature *ferae naturae*. It might, he thought, be as well to probe the soil here for evidences of masonry, and he took out his knife and began scraping away the earth. And now followed another little discovery: a portion of soil fell inward as he scraped, and disclosed a small cavity. He lighted one match after another to help him to see of what nature the hole was, but the wind was too strong for them all. By tapping and scratching the sides with his knife, however, he was able to make out that it must be an artificial hole in masonry. It was rectangular, and the sides, top, and bottom, if not actually plastered, were smooth and regular. Of course it was empty. No! As he withdrew the knife he heard a metallic clink, and when he introduced his hand it met with a cylindrical object lying on the floor of the hole. Naturally enough, he picked it up, and when he brought it into the light, now fast fading, he could see that it, too, was of man's making—a metal tube about four inches long, and evidently of some considerable age.

By the time Parkins had made sure that there was nothing else in this odd receptacle, it was too late and too dark for him to think of undertaking any further search. What he had done had proved so unexpectedly interesting that he determined to sacrifice a little more of the daylight on the morrow to archæology. The object which he now had safe in his pocket was bound to be of some slight value at least, he felt sure.

Bleak and solemn was the view on which he took a last look before starting homeward. A faint yellow light in the west showed the links, on which a few figures moving towards the clubhouse were still visible, the squat martello tower, the lights of Aldsey village, the pale ribbon of sands intersected at intervals by black wooden groynings, the dim and murmuring sea. The wind was bitter from the north, but was at his back when he set out for the Globe. He quickly rattled and clashed through the shingle and gained the sand, upon which, but for the groynings which had to be got over every few yards, the going was both good and quiet. One last look behind, to measure the distance he had made since leaving the ruined Templars' church, showed him a prospect of company on his walk, in the shape of a rather indistinct personage in the distance, who seemed to be making great efforts to catch up with him, but made little, if any, progress. I mean that there was an appearance of running about his movements, but that the distance between him and Parkins did not seem materially to lessen. So, at least, Parkins thought, and decided that he almost certainly did not know him, and that it would be absurd to wait until he came up. For all that, company, he began to think, would really be very welcome on that lonely shore, if only you could choose your companion. In his unenlightened days he had read of meetings in such places which even now would hardly bear thinking of. He went on thinking of them, however, until he reached home, and particularly of one which catches most people's fancy at some time of their childhood. "Now I saw in my dream that Christian had gone but a very little way when he saw a foul fiend coming over the field to meet him." "What should I do now," he thought, "if I looked back and caught sight of a black figure sharply defined against the yellow sky, and saw that it had horns and wings? I wonder whether I should stand or run for it. Luckily, the gentleman behind is not of that kind, and he seems to be about as far off now as when I saw him first. Well, at this rate he won't get his dinner as soon as I shall; and, dear me! it's within a quarter of an hour of the time now. I must run!"

Parkins had, in fact, very little time for dressing. When he met the Colonel at dinner, Peace—or as much of her as that gentleman could manage—reigned once more in the military bosom; nor was she put to flight in the hours of bridge that followed dinner, for Parkins was a more than respectable player. When, therefore, he retired towards twelve o'clock, he felt that he had spent his evening in quite a satisfactory way, and that, even for so long as a fortnight or three weeks, life at the Globe would be supportable under similar conditions—"especially," thought he, "if I go on improving my game."

As he went along the passages he met the boots of the Globe, who stopped and said:

"Beg your pardon, sir, but as I was a-brushing your coat just now there was somethink fell out of the pocket. I put it on your chest of drawers, sir, in your room, sir—a piece of a pipe or somethink of that, sir. Thank you, sir. You'll find it on your chest of drawers, sir—yes, sir. Good-night, sir."

The speech served to remind Parkins of his little discovery of that afternoon. It was with some considerable curiosity that he turned it over by the light of his candles. It was of bronze, he now saw, and was shaped very much after the manner of the modern dog-whistle; in fact it was—yes, certainly it was—actually no more nor less than a whistle. He put it to his lips, but it was quite full of a fine, caked-up sand or earth, which would not yield to knocking, but must be loosened with a knife. Tidy as ever in his habits, Parkins cleared out the earth on to a piece of paper, and took the latter to the window to empty it out. The night was clear and bright, as he saw when he had opened the casement, and he stopped for an instant to look at the sea and note a belated wanderer stationed on the shore in front of the inn. Then he shut the window, a little surprised at the late hours people kept at Burnstow, and took his whistle to the light again. Why, surely there were marks on it, and not merely marks, but letters! A very little rubbing rendered the deeply-cut inscription quite legible, but the Professor had to confess, after some earnest thought, that the meaning of it was as obscure to him as the writing on the wall to Belshazzar. There were legends both on the front and on the back of the whistle. The one read thus:

$$\text{FUR} \quad \begin{array}{c} \text{FLA} \\ \text{FLE} \end{array} \quad \text{BIS}$$

The other:

$$\text{✠ QUIS EST ISTE QUI UENIT ✠}$$

"I ought to be able to make it out," he thought; "but I suppose I am a little rusty in my Latin. When I come to think of it, I don't believe I even know the word for a whistle. The long one does seem simple enough. It ought to mean, 'Who is this who is coming?' Well, the best way to find out is evidently to whistle for him."

He blew tentatively and stopped suddenly, startled and yet pleased at the note he had elicited. It had a quality of infinite distance in it, and, soft as it was, he somehow felt it must be audible for miles round. It was a sound, too, that seemed to have the power (which many scents possess) of forming pictures in the brain. He saw quite clearly for a moment a vision of a wide, dark expanse at night, with a fresh wind blowing, and in the midst a lonely figure—how employed, he could not tell. Perhaps he would have seen more had not the picture been broken by the sudden surge of a gust of wind against his casement, so sudden that it made him look up, just in time to see the white glint of a sea-bird's wing somewhere outside the dark panes.

The sound of the whistle had so fascinated him that he could not help trying it once more, this time more boldly. The note was little, if at all, louder than before, and repetition broke the illusion—no picture followed, as he had half hoped it might. "But what is this? Goodness! what force the wind can get up in a few minutes! What a tremendous gust! There! I knew that window-fastening was no use! Ah! I thought so—both candles out. It is enough to tear the room to pieces."

The first thing was to get the window shut. While you might count twenty Parkins was struggling with the small casement, and felt almost as if he were pushing back a sturdy burglar, so strong was the pressure. It slackened all at once, and the window banged to and latched itself. Now to relight the candles and see what damage, if any, had been done. No, nothing seemed amiss; no glass even was broken in the casement. But the noise had evidently roused at least one member of the household:

the Colonel was to be heard stumping in his stockinged feet on the floor above, and growling.

Quickly as it had risen, the wind did not fall at once. On it went, moaning and rushing past the house, at times rising to a cry so desolate that, as Parkins disinterestedly said, it might have made fanciful people feel quite uncomfortable; even the unimaginative, he thought after a quarter of an hour, might be happier without it.

Whether it was the wind, or the excitement of golf, or of the researches in the preceptory that kept Parkins awake, he was not sure. Awake he remained, in any case, long enough to fancy (as I am afraid I often do myself under such conditions) that he was the victim of all manner of fatal disorders: he would lie counting the beats of his heart, convinced that it was going to stop work every moment, and would entertain grave suspicions of his lungs, brain, liver, etc.—suspicions which he was sure would be dispelled by the return of daylight, but which until then refused to be put aside. He found a little vicarious comfort in the idea that someone else was in the same boat. A near neighbour (in the darkness it was not easy to tell his direction) was tossing and rustling in his bed, too.

The next stage was that Parkins shut his eyes and determined to give sleep every chance. Here again over-excitement asserted itself in another form—that of making pictures. *Experto crede*, pictures do come to the closed eyes of one trying to sleep, and often his pictures are so little to his taste that he must open his eyes and disperse the images.

Parkins's experience on this occasion was a very distressing one. He found that the picture which presented itself to him was continuous. When he opened his eyes, of course, it went; but when he shut them once more it framed itself afresh, and acted itself out again, neither quicker nor slower than before. What he saw was this:

A long stretch of shore—shingle edged by sand, and intersected at short intervals with black groynes running down to the water—a scene, in fact, so like that of his afternoon's walk that, in the absence of any landmark, it could not be distinguished therefrom. The light was obscure, conveying an impression of gathering storm, late winter evening, and slight cold rain. On this bleak stage at first no actor was visible. Then, in the distance, a bobbing black object appeared; a moment more, and it was a man running, jumping, clambering over the groynes, and every few seconds looking eagerly back. The nearer he came the more obvious it was that he was not only anxious, but even terribly frightened, though his face was not to be distinguished. He was, moreover, almost at the end of his strength. On he came; each successive obstacle seemed to cause him more difficulty than the last. "Will he get over this next one?" thought Parkins; "it seems a little higher than the others." Yes; half climbing, half throwing himself, he did get over, and fell all in a heap on the other side (the side nearest to the spectator). There, as if really unable to get up again, he remained crouching under the groyne, looking up in an attitude of painful anxiety.

So far no cause whatever for the fear of the runner had been shown; but now there began to be seen, far up the shore, a little flicker of something light-coloured moving to and fro with great swiftness and irregularity. Rapidly growing larger, it, too, declared itself as a figure in pale, fluttering draperies, ill-defined. There was something about its motion which made Parkins very unwilling to see it at close quarters. It would stop, raise arms, bow itself toward the sand, then run stooping across the beach to the water-edge and back again; and then, rising upright, once more continue its course forward at a speed that was startling and terrifying. The moment came when the pursuer was hovering about from left to right only a few yards beyond the groyne where the runner lay in hiding. After two or three ineffectual castings hither and thither it came to a stop, stood upright, with arms raised high, and then darted straight forward towards the groyne.

It was at this point that Parkins always failed in his resolution to keep his eyes shut. With many misgivings as to incipient failure of eyesight, overworked brain, excessive smoking, and so on, he finally resigned himself to light his candle, get out a book, and pass the night waking, rather than be tormented by this persistent panorama, which he saw clearly enough could only be a morbid reflection of his walk and his thoughts on that very day.

The scraping of match on box and the glare of light must have startled some creatures of the night—rats or what not—which he heard scurry across the floor from the side of his bed with much rustling. Dear, dear! the match is out! Fool that it is! But the second one burnt better, and a candle and book were duly procured, over which Parkins pored till sleep of a wholesome kind came upon him, and that in no long space. For about the first time in his orderly and prudent life he forgot to blow out the candle, and when he was called next morning at eight there was still a flicker in the socket and a sad mess of guttered grease on the top of the little table.

After breakfast he was in his room, putting the finishing touches to his golfing costume—fortune had again allotted the Colonel to him for a partner—when one of the maids came in.

"Oh, if you please," she said, "would you like any extra blankets on your bed, sir?"

"Ah! thank you," said Parkins. "Yes, I think I should like one. It seems likely to turn rather colder."

In a very short time the maid was back with the blanket.

"Which bed should I put it on, sir?" she asked.

"What? Why, that one—the one I slept in last night," he said, pointing to it.

"Oh yes! I beg your pardon, sir, but you seemed to have tried both of 'em; leastways, we had to make 'em both up this morning."

"Really? How very absurd!" said Parkins. "I certainly never touched the other, except to lay some things on it. Did it actually seem to have been slept in?"

"Oh yes, sir!" said the maid. "Why, all the things was crumpled and throwed about all ways, if you'll excuse me, sir—quite as if anyone 'adn't passed but a very poor night, sir."

"Dear me," said Parkins. "Well, I may have disordered it more than I thought when I unpacked my things. I'm very sorry to have given you the extra trouble, I'm sure. I expect a friend of mine soon, by the way—a gentleman from Cambridge—to come and occupy it for a night or two. That will be all right, I suppose, won't it?"

"Oh yes, to be sure, sir. Thank you, sir. It's no trouble, I'm sure," said the maid, and departed to giggle with her colleagues.

Parkins set forth, with a stern determination to improve his game.

I am glad to be able to report that he succeeded so far in this enterprise that the Colonel, who had been rather repining at the prospect of a second day's play in his company, became quite chatty as the morning advanced; and his voice boomed out over the flats, as certain also of our own minor poets have said, "like some great bourdon in a minster tower."

"Extraordinary wind, that, we had last night," he said. "In my old home we should have said someone had been whistling for it."

"Should you, indeed!" said Parkins. "Is there a superstition of that kind still current in your part of the country?"

"I don't know about superstition," said the Colonel. "They believe in it all over Denmark and Norway, as well as on the Yorkshire coast; and my experience is, mind you, that there's generally something at the bottom of what these country-folk hold to, and have held to for generations.

But it's your drive" (or whatever it might have been: the golfing reader will have to imagine appropriate digressions at the proper intervals).

When conversation was resumed, Parkins said, with a slight hesitancy:

"Apropos of what you were saying just now, Colonel, I think I ought to tell you that my own views on such subjects are very strong. I am, in fact, a convinced disbeliever in what is called the 'supernatural.'"

"What!" said the Colonel, "do you mean to tell me you don't believe in second-sight, or ghosts, or anything of that kind?"

"In nothing whatever of that kind," returned Parkins firmly.

"Well," said the Colonel, "but it appears to me at that rate, sir, that you must be little better than a Sadducee."

Parkins was on the point of answering that, in his opinion, the Sadducees were the most sensible persons he had ever read of in the Old Testament; but, feeling some doubt as to whether much mention of them was to be found in that work, he preferred to laugh the accusation off.

"Perhaps I am," he said; "but—Here, give me my cleek, boy!—Excuse me one moment, Colonel." A short interval. "Now, as to whistling for the wind, let me give you my theory about it. The laws which govern winds are really not at all perfectly known—to fisher-folk and such, of course, not known at all. A man or woman of eccentric habits, perhaps, or a stranger, is seen repeatedly on the beach at some unusual hour, and is heard whistling. Soon afterwards a violent wind rises; a man who could read the sky perfectly or who possessed a barometer could have foretold that it would. The simple people of a fishing-village have no barometers, and only a few rough rules for prophesying weather. What more natural than that the eccentric personage I postulated should be regarded as having raised the wind, or that he or she should clutch eagerly at the reputation of being able to do so? Now, take last night's wind: as it happens, I myself was whistling. I blew a whistle twice, and the wind seemed to come absolutely in answer to my call. If anyone had seen me—"

The audience had been a little restive under this harangue, and Parkins had, I fear, fallen somewhat into the tone of a lecturer; but at the last sentence the Colonel stopped.

"Whistling, were you?" he said. "And what sort of whistle did you use? Play this stroke first." Interval.

"About that whistle you were asking, Colonel. It's rather a curious one. I have it in my—No; I see I've left it in my room. As a matter of fact, I found it yesterday."

And then Parkins narrated the manner of his discovery of the whistle, upon hearing which the Colonel grunted, and opined that, in Parkins's place, he should himself be careful about using a thing that had belonged to a set of Papists, of whom, speaking generally, it might be affirmed that you never knew what they might not have been up to. From this topic he diverged to the enormities of the Vicar, who had given notice on the previous Sunday that Friday would be the Feast of St. Thomas the Apostle, and that there would be service at eleven o'clock in the church. This and other similar proceedings constituted in the Colonel's view a strong presumption that the Vicar was a concealed Papist, if not a Jesuit; and Parkins, who could not very readily follow the Colonel in this region, did not disagree with him. In fact, they got on so well together in the morning that there was no talk on either side of their separating after lunch.

Both continued to play well during the afternoon, or, at least, well enough to make them forget everything else until the light began to fail them. Not until then did Parkins remember that he had meant to do some more investigating at the preceptory; but it was of no great importance, he reflected. One day was as good as another; he might as well go home with the Colonel.

As they turned the corner of the house, the Colonel was almost knocked down by a boy who rushed into him at the very top of his speed, and then, instead of running away, remained hanging on to him and panting. The first words of the warrior were naturally those of reproof and objurgation, but he very quickly discerned that the boy was almost speechless with fright. Inquiries were useless at first. When the boy got his breath he began to howl, and still clung to the Colonel's legs. He was at last detached, but continued to howl.

"What in the world *is* the matter with you? What have you been up to? What have you seen?" said the two men.

"Ow, I seen it wive at me out of the winder," wailed the boy, "and I don't like it."

"What window?" said the irritated Colonel. "Come, pull yourself together, my boy."

"The front winder it was, at the 'otel," said the boy.

At this point Parkins was in favour of sending the boy home, but the Colonel refused; he wanted to get to the bottom of it, he said: it was most dangerous to give a boy such a fright as this one had had, and if it turned out that people had been playing jokes, they should suffer for it in some way. And by a series of questions he made out this story: The boy had been playing about on the grass in front of the Globe with some others; then they had gone home to their teas, and he was just going, when he happened to look up at the front winder and see it a-wiving at him. *It* seemed to be a figure of some sort, in white as far as he knew—couldn't see its face; but it wived at him, and it warn't a right thing—not to say not a right person. Was there a light in the room? No, he didn't think to look if there was a light. Which was the window? Was it the top one or the second one? The seckind one it was—the big winder what got two little uns at the sides.

"Very well, my boy," said the Colonel, after a few more questions. "You run away home now. I expect it was some person trying to give you a start. Another time, like a brave English boy, you just throw a stone—well, no, not that exactly, but you go and speak to the waiter, or to Mr. Simpson, the landlord, and—yes—and say that I advised you to do so."

The boy's face expressed some of the doubt he felt as to the likelihood of Mr. Simpson's lending a favourable ear to his complaint, but the Colonel did not appear to perceive this, and went on:

"And here's a sixpence—no, I see it's a shilling—and you be off home, and don't think any more about it."

The youth hurried off with agitated thanks, and the Colonel and Parkins went round to the front of the Globe and reconnoitred. There was only one window answering to the description they had been hearing.

"Well, that's curious," said Parkins; "it's evidently my window the lad was talking about. Will you come up for a moment, Colonel Wilson? We ought to be able to see if anyone has been taking liberties in my room."

They were soon in the passage, and Parkins made as if to open the door. Then he stopped and felt in his pockets.

"This is more serious than I thought," was his next remark. "I remember now that before I started this morning I locked the door. It is locked now, and, what is more, here is the key." And he held it up. "Now," he went on, "if the servants are in the habit of going into one's room during the day when one is away, I can only say that—well, that I don't approve of it at all." Conscious of a somewhat weak climax, he busied himself in opening the door (which was indeed locked) and in lighting candles. "No," he said, "nothing seems disturbed."

"Except your bed," put in the Colonel.

"Excuse me, that isn't my bed," said Parkins. "I don't use that one. But it does look as if someone had been playing tricks with it."

It certainly did: the clothes were bundled up and twisted together in a most tortuous confusion. Parkins pondered.

"That must be it," he said at last: "I disordered the clothes last night in unpacking, and they haven't made it since. Perhaps they came in to make it, and that boy saw them through the window; and then they were called away and locked the door after them. Yes, I think that must be it."

"Well, ring and ask," said the Colonel, and this appealed to Parkins as practical.

The maid appeared, and, to make a long story short, deposed that she had made the bed in the morning when the gentleman was in the room, and hadn't been there since. No, she hadn't no other key. Mr. Simpson he kep' the keys; he'd be able to tell the gentleman if anyone had been up.

This was a puzzle. Investigation showed that nothing of value had been taken, and Parkins remembered the disposition of the small objects on tables and so forth well enough to be pretty sure that no pranks had been played with them. Mr. and Mrs. Simpson furthermore agreed that neither of them had given the duplicate key of the room to any person whatever during the day. Nor could Parkins, fair-minded man as he was, detect anything in the demeanour of master, mistress, or maid that indicated guilt. He was much more inclined to think that the boy had been imposing on the Colonel.

The latter was unwontedly silent and pensive at dinner and throughout the evening. When he bade good-night to Parkins, he murmured in a gruff undertone:

"You know where I am if you want me during the night."

"Why, yes, thank you, Colonel Wilson, I think I do; but there isn't much prospect of my disturbing you, I hope. By the way," he added, "did I show you that old whistle I spoke of? I think not. Well, here it is."

The Colonel turned it over gingerly in the light of the candle.

"Can you make anything of the inscription?" asked Parkins, as he took it back.

"No, not in this light. What do you mean to do with it?"

"Oh, well, when I get back to Cambridge I shall submit it to some of the archæologists there, and see what they think of it; and very likely, if they consider it worth having, I may present it to one of the museums."

"'M!" said the Colonel. "Well, you may be right. All I know is that, if it were mine, I should chuck it straight into the sea. It's no use talking, I'm well aware, but I expect that with you it's a case of live and learn. I hope so, I'm sure, and I wish you a good-night."

He turned away, leaving Parkins in act to speak at the bottom of the stair, and soon each was in his own bedroom.

By some unfortunate accident, there were neither blinds nor curtains to the windows of the Professor's room. The previous night he had thought little of this, but tonight there seemed every prospect of a bright moon rising to shine directly on his bed, and probably wake him later on. When he noticed this he was a good deal annoyed, but, with an ingenuity which I can only envy, he succeeded in rigging up, with the help of a railway-rug, some safety-pins, and a stick and umbrella, a screen which, if it only held together, would completely keep the moonlight off his bed. And shortly afterwards he was comfortably in that bed. When he had read a somewhat solid work long enough to produce a decided wish for sleep, he cast a drowsy glance round the room, blew out the candle, and fell back upon the pillow.

He must have slept soundly for an hour or more, when a sudden clatter shook him up in a most unwelcome manner. In a moment he realised what had happened: his carefully-constructed screen had given way, and a very bright frosty moon was shining directly on his face. This was highly annoying. Could he possibly get up and reconstruct the screen? or could he manage to sleep if he did not?

For some minutes he lay and pondered over the possibilities; then he turned over sharply, and with all his eyes open lay breathlessly listening. There had been a movement, he was sure, in the empty bed on the opposite side of the room. Tomorrow he would have it moved, for there must be rats or something playing about in it. It was quiet now. No! the commotion began again. There was a rustling and shaking: surely more than any rat could cause.

I can figure to myself something of the Professor's bewilderment and horror, for I have in a dream thirty years back seen the same thing happen; but the reader will hardly, perhaps, imagine how dreadful it was to him to see a figure suddenly sit up in what he had known was an empty bed. He was out of his own bed in one bound, and made a dash towards the window, where lay his only weapon, the stick with which he had propped his screen. This was, as it turned out, the worst thing he could have done, because the personage in the empty bed, with a sudden smooth motion, slipped from the bed and took up a position, with outspread arms, between the two beds, and in front of the door. Parkins watched it in a horrid perplexity. Somehow, the idea of getting past it and escaping through the door was intolerable to him; he could not have borne—he didn't know why—to touch it; and as for its touching him, he would sooner dash himself through the window than have that happen. It stood for the moment in a band of dark shadow, and he had not seen what its face was like. Now it began to move, in a stooping posture, and all at once the spectator realised, with some horror and some relief, that it must be blind, for it seemed to feel about it with its muffled arms in a groping and random fashion. Turning half away from him, it became suddenly conscious of the bed he had just left, and darted towards it, and bent and felt over the pillows in a way which made Parkins shudder as he had never in his life thought it possible. In a very few moments it seemed to know that the bed was empty, and then, moving forward into the area of light and facing the window, it showed for the first time what manner of thing it was.

Parkins, who very much dislikes being questioned about it, did once describe something of it in my hearing, and I gathered that what he chiefly remembers about it is a horrible, an intensely horrible, face *of crumpled linen*. What expression he read upon it he could not or would not tell, but that the fear of it went nigh to maddening him is certain.

But he was not at leisure to watch it for long. With formidable quickness it moved into the middle of the room, and, as it groped and waved, one corner of its draperies swept across Parkins's face. He could not, though he knew how perilous a sound was—he could not keep back a cry of disgust, and this gave the searcher an instant clue. It leapt towards him upon the instant, and the next moment he was halfway through the window backwards, uttering cry upon cry at the utmost pitch of his voice, and the linen face was thrust close into his own. At this, almost the last possible second, deliverance came, as you will have guessed: the Colonel burst the door open, and was just in time to see the dreadful group at the window. When he reached the figures only one was left. Parkins sank forward into the room in a faint, and before him on the floor lay a tumbled heap of bedclothes.

Colonel Wilson asked no questions, but busied himself keeping everyone else out of the room and in getting Parkins back to his bed; and himself, wrapped in a rug, occupied the other bed, for the rest of the night. Early on the next day Rogers arrived, more welcome than he would have been a day before, and the three of them held a very long consultation in the Professor's room. At the end of it the Colonel left the hotel door carrying a small object between his finger and thumb, which he cast as far into the sea as a very brawny arm could send it. Later on the smoke of a burning ascended from the back premises of the Globe.

Exactly what explanation was patched up for the staff and visitors at the hotel I must confess I do not recollect. The Professor was somehow cleared of the ready suspicion of delirium tremens, and the hotel of the reputation of a troubled house.

There is not much question as to what would have happened to Parkins if the Colonel had not intervened when he did. He would either have fallen out of the window or else lost his wits. But it is not so evident what more the creature that came in answer to the whistle could have done than frighten. There seemed to be absolutely nothing material about it save the bedclothes of which it had made itself a body. The Colonel, who remembered a not very dissimilar occurrence in India, was of opinion that if Parkins had closed with it it could really have done very little, and that its one power was that of frightening. The whole thing, he said, served to confirm his opinion of the Church of Rome.

There is really nothing more to tell, but, as you may imagine, the Professor's views on certain points are less clear cut than they used to be. His nerves, too, have suffered: he cannot even now see a surplice hanging on a door quite unmoved, and the spectacle of a scarecrow in a field late on a winter afternoon has cost him more than one sleepless night.

1907

FATHER MADDOX'S TALE

R. H. Benson

Robert Hugh Benson (1871–1914) was the youngest of six siblings: four boys and two girls. On Christmas Day 1882 their father, Edward White Benson, had been offered, and accepted, the position of archbishop of Canterbury—a promotion that led to the family leaving Truro, where he had been bishop; M. R. James happened to be visiting his Eton and Cambridge friend Arthur (A. C. Benson) in Cornwall when the offer of the archbishopric came through. The Bensons were a remarkable, gifted and generally tight-knit family—who would go on to move in the highest of circles, including Queen Victoria and William Gladstone, and count themselves friends of Robert Browning and the Tennysons—yet emotional, physical and mental health troubles stalked them all.

Known as Hugh, R. H. Benson followed his brothers Arthur and Fred to university in Cambridge, afterwards entering the Anglican Church before converting a few years later to Catholicism; he went on to become private chamberlain to Pope Pius X. This was a scandalous choice for the son of an archbishop, though by the time of the betrayal his father was no longer alive to suffer any embarrassment.

In addition to his religious roles, R. H. Benson was an author. He wrote a number of novels including the apocalyptic *Lord of the World* (1907), as well as around 30 supernatural tales in two collections: *The Light Invisible* (1903) and *A Mirror of Shalott* (1907). The majority of these stories make a point of referring to his Catholic faith—M. R.

James thought them "too ecclesiastical"—but alongside this evangelicalism, here in the excellent, understated "Father Maddox's Tale", you can see his familiarity with the Fens and its fine old houses from his time at Cambridge.

R. H. Benson died in October 1914 from an underlying heart condition and pneumonia.

"This is a most disappointing story," began old Father Maddox, with a deprecating smile. "You will find it as annoying as the 'Lady and the Tiger'; there is no answer. Or rather there are two, and you may take your choice, and no one can contradict you or satisfy you that you are right."

There was a moment's pause as the priest elaborately placed a pinch of brown powder on his thumb-nail and inhaled it noisily through first one nostril and then the other, with an indescribable grimace. He flicked the specks away, wiped his nose with a magenta cotton handkerchief, replaced his snuff-box, folded his hands, cocked one knee over the other, and proceeded. Father Maddox had looked so profound just now that Canon Maxwell had turned and challenged him; and here was the result. As he talked I watched his large, flat foot, creased across the toes, as if an extra two inches had been added subsequently. Its size and shape seemed the very embodiment of common sense.

"About fourteen or fifteen years ago," he began, "I was at a mission in the Fens—quite a little place—you would not know its name—about ten miles from Ely. I was very much pleased to hear one day that an old friend of mine had taken a house about seven miles away at a place called Baddenham—because, you know, the life of a priest at such a mission is apt to be very lonely, and I looked forward to his company now and again. The neighbouring Protestant clergy would have nothing to say to me."

The old man smiled at the company in his deprecating manner and went on:

"About a week later my friend, Mr. Hudson—a bachelor, by the way, and a Fellow of one of the Cambridge colleges, and a great recluse—my friend wrote and asked me to spend a Monday to Wednesday with him. There was a novelist coming to stay with him—I think I had better not mention his name; we will call him Mr. Baxter—and this—er—Mr. Baxter wished to meet a Catholic priest for a particular reason that you shall hear presently. I was very much pleased at this, for I had often heard the writer's name, as all of you have, Reverend Fathers"—he smiled slily—"and I liked his books. He was always very kind to us poor Papists, though I believe he was a man of no religion himself.

"Well, I gave out that there would be no Mass on Tuesday or Wednesday—and I said, too, where I was going, in case there was a sick-call, though that was not likely; and on the Monday afternoon I walked up with my bag from Baddenham station to the Hall.

"It was a very fine old house, very old—built, I suppose, about the beginning of the sixteenth century—and it stood in the middle of a little park of about a hundred acres. It was L-shaped, of red brick, with a little turret at the north end and had a little walled garden on the south.

"Mr. Baxter was not come yet; he would be there for dinner, my friend told me; and, sure enough, about half-past seven he came.

"He was a little man—not at all what I expected—with black hair a little grey at the temples, clean-shaven, with spectacles. He was a very quick man—I could see that. He talked a great deal at dinner; and it seemed, from what my friend said, that he was come down there from town to make a beginning at his new book, which was to be on the days of Elizabeth."

Father Maddox stopped, and looked round smiling.

"No, gentlemen, you cannot guess from that. The book was never written, as you shall hear."

There was a murmur of disappointment, and Father Brent, who had sat forward suddenly, sank back again, smiling too.

"Well, it seemed that Mr. Baxter wished to meet a priest, because he was anxious to hear a little of how Catholics managed in those days, what it was that priests carried with them on their travels, and so forth; but it appeared presently that Catholics were not to be the principal characters of the story, though he thought of bringing them in.

"'I must have a priest, Father Maddox,' he said. 'There might be some good side-scenes made out of that. Please tell me everything you can.'

"Well, I told him all I could, and about the missal and altar-stone at Oscott, and so on; and I told him, too, the kind of work that priests had to do, and their dangers, and the martyrdoms.

"'Did many give in?' he asked.

"'Apostatise?' I said. 'Oh, a few—very few.'

"He seemed very thoughtful at that, and after we had smoked a little he asked if we might go round the house. He liked to know what sort of a place he was sleeping in, he said. He seemed to get very much excited with the house: it was certainly an interesting old place, with several panelled rooms, uneven floors, diamond-paned windows, and all the rest. There was a curious little place, too, in the turret: a kind of watchtower, it seemed, with tiny windows, or rather spy-holes, all round. I never remember having seen anything like it elsewhere; and it was approached by an oaken stair from the room below. It was so small that two people could hardly turn round in it together.

"Well, we saw everything, going with candles, and came down again at last to the old parlour, and there we sat till nearly midnight, Mr. Baxter asking me all sorts of questions, many of which I could not answer.

"When our host took up his candle to go to bed, Mr. Baxter said he would sit up a bit, so we left him and went upstairs.

"I am always a poor sleeper, particularly in a new house, and I tossed about a long time. It was winter, by the way—or rather, late autumn—so I had a fire in my room, which was at the top of the stairs, the first door on the right. Then, when I did go to sleep at last, I dreamed that I was still awake. I don't know whether any one else has ever had that; but I often do. I remember what I dreamed, too. It was that I was back again in the parlour with the other two, and that I was trying to sleep in my chair, but that Mr. Baxter would not be quiet; he kept walking up and down the room, waving his hands and talking to himself, and that the other man—ah! wait." The priest paused. "I have not explained properly. At first, in my dream, the third man was certainly Mr. Hudson—at least, I supposed so—but after a while it seemed not to be; it was some one else, I did not know who, and I could not remember his face. This third man, apparently, was not trying to sleep; he was standing in the corner of the room, in the shadow, watching Mr. Baxter as he went up and down. Well, this went on a long while, and then at last I awoke, wide awake, and lay much annoyed. I was hardly fully awake before I heard Mr. Baxter come upstairs. I heard his bedroom candle clink as he lit it in the hall below, and then I heard the creak of one of his shoes, which I had noticed before. He came upstairs, past my door, walking rather quickly as his way was; and I heard him shut the door of his room, which was at the further end of the landing. Then I went to sleep."

Father Maddox paused, took another pinch of snuff, looking round on us.

"Is that all clear, so far?" he asked.

There was a murmur of assent, and he went on:

"Well, Mr. Baxter was very late at breakfast. He did not come down till we had finished, and I thought he looked very tired. He was plainly rather excited, too, and as he helped himself at the sideboard he turned round.

"'My dear Hudson,' he said, 'what a house this is of yours! It has really inspired me. I sat up till nearly three, and I believe I have got a first-rate idea.'

"Of course we asked what it was, and as he ate his porridge he told us.

"He was going to bring in an apostate priest—a man, sincere enough in his faith, who gave way under torture. He was to be the son of a family who remained good Catholics, and he was to come home again to the very place where he had been caught, and where his mother was still living. It would be a good situation, thought Mr. Baxter—the apostate son, believing all the time, and his mother, who of course loved him, but who hated the thought of what he had done—and these two should live together in the house where they had said good-bye two months before, when the mother thought her son was going to his martyrdom. It seemed to me quite possible, and I said so; and that pleased Mr. Baxter very much.

"'Yes,' he said. 'And, Hudson, would you mind if I took this house as the scene of it? It seems to me just made for it. That little turret-room, you know, would be the place from which the priest saw the constables surrounding the house; and the room underneath could be the chapel. And think what he would think when he saw them again! Do you mind?'

"Mr. Hudson, of course, said that he would be highly honoured, and all the rest; and so it was settled.

"Presently Mr. Baxter was off again.

"'It is quite extraordinary,' he said, 'how vivid the whole thing is to me—the character of the priest, his little ways, the weakness in his face, and all the rest; and the mother too, a fine silent old lady, intensely religious and intensely fond of her son, and knowing that he had only yielded through pain. He would limp a little, from the rack, and not be able to manage his knife very well.'

"I asked him presently how he worked out his characters—and how far—before he began to write.

"'Generally,' he said, 'I leave a good deal to the time of writing. I first get the idea, and perhaps the general appearance of each person, and of course the plot; then I begin to write; and after about a chapter or two the people seem to come alive and to do it all themselves, and I only have to write it down as well as I can. I think most writers find it happens like that. But this time I must say it is rather different: I don't think I have ever had anything so vivid before. I am beginning to think that my Catholics will have to be the principal people after all. At any rate, I shall begin with them.'

"He talked like this a good deal at breakfast, and seemed quite excited. It all seemed to me very odd, and particularly so when he said that, when he was once in the middle of the book, his characters seemed almost more real than living people; it was a kind of trance, he said; the real world became shadowy, and the world of imagination the real one. Since then I have asked one or two other writers, and they have told me the same.

"Well, when we met at lunch I began to understand how true it all was. He was actually in a kind of waking dream; he had been writing hard all the morning, and it seemed as if he could pay no attention to anything. He didn't talk much—hardly a word, in fact—and finally Mr. Hudson said something about it.

"'My dear man,' said the other, 'I really can't attend. I am very sorry; but it's a kind of obsession now. I tell you that this book is the only thing that matters to me in the least. They are all waiting for me now in the study—Mr. Jennifer the apostate, his mother, and an old manservant of the house. I can't possibly come out this afternoon; this chapter has got to get done.'

"He really was quite pale with excitement, and he rushed out again as soon as he had finished.

"Well, Mr. Hudson and I went out together, and we got back about four, just as the evening was beginning to close in. We had tea alone; Mr. Baxter had ordered it for himself, it seemed, when our host went in to see if he was coming.

"'He is working like a madman,' he said, when he came back. 'I have just given him the keys of the turret; he says he is going up there before it is quite dark to see how far away the priest could have seen the constables round the house.'

"After tea I went upstairs to put on my cassock and change my shoes, and as I went into my room I heard the study door open and Mr. Baxter come out. I watched him, from inside, go past, and heard him cross the landing to get to the turret-room and the stairs.

"Now I must explain."

Father Maddox paused; then he leaned forward, drew up the little table by his side, and began to arrange books in the shape of an L.

"This is the first floor, you understand. This small book stands for the horizontal of the L. My room was here, in the angle, at the top of the stairs. Mr. Baxter's room was on the right, past mine, at the end of the horizontal. Just opposite his room was the one which he said was to be the chapel, and out of this room rose the turret-stairs. This part of the house is only two stories high, but the turret itself is high enough to see over the roofs of the upright part of the L, as those rooms, although there are three stories of them, are much lower than these others.

"Very well, then... I heard Mr. Baxter go across and go into the chapel-room. Then I heard his footsteps stop; he was looking, he told us afterwards, at the place where the altar would have stood, and so on.

"When I had changed my things I thought I would go out and see how he was getting on. It was very nearly dark by now, so I took one of my candles and went across. The door of the chapel-room was open and I went in."

Father Maddox paused once more. I could see that a climax was coming, and I must confess that I felt oddly excited. He seemed such a common-sense man, too.

"Now, those of you who have ever shot over dogs know what happens when a dog points; how he stiffens all over and is all strung up tight. Well, that is what Mr. Baxter was doing. He was standing, rather crouching, with his hands out on either side, palms down, staring sideways up the little staircase that led to the turret. This staircase, I must tell you, ran diagonally up across the further end of the room, like a loft staircase. There were no open bannisters; it was masked by panelling, and was generally closed by a door in the panelling; but this was open now, and, as I said, he had twisted his head sideways so that his eyes looked up it—up to the right.

"Well, at first I thought he was calculating something, but he did not move as I came in; he was like a statue. I said something, but he paid no attention. I went right up to him.

"'Mr. Baxter,' I said, 'I have come to see—'

"Then a sort of horrid moan came from him, and he suddenly jumped back and seized me by the arm so that the candle dropped and we were almost in the dark; but I caught a sight of his face.

"'He is coming down, he is coming down, Father,' he whispered. 'Oh! for God's sake!' Then he gave a great wrench at my arm, still moaning; and somehow we were out of the room, across the landing, and half tumbling downstairs together. Mr. Hudson ran out at the noise, and somehow we got him into the study and in a deep chair, and he went off into a swoon."

The old man paused, and looked round with rather a tremulous smile; and, I must confess, the silence in the room was very much marked.

"Well, half-an-hour later Mr. Baxter seemed himself again. He was able to tell us what had happened. It seemed that he had gone into the room, and, as I had thought, had stopped a moment or two there, trying to imagine the old arrangements that he had invented—*invented*, Reverend Fathers; remember that: there was no tradition about the house at all. Neither then nor afterwards. Then he had gone to the staircase to go up to the turret.

"Now, this is what he said he saw—he told us all this gradually, of course. He saw a man in a cassock and cap standing on the top step of the little stairs, looking out through the tiny window that is in the wall opposite. At first he thought it was I. It was very dark; there was only a little dim light from the turret-room behind the figure, and his face, as I said, was pressed against the darkening window, exactly as if he were watching for somebody. He had called out, and the figure had turned, and he had seen it to be a young man, under thirty, with very large dark eyes, thin lips, and a little round chin. He had seen that absolutely plainly in the light from the window. He also saw, as he looked, that the face was exactly that of the priest whom he had imagined in his story, and who, as he had told us at lunch, was completely vivid to his brain. Well, he had simply stared and stared. He said that fear was not the word at all: it was a kind of paralysis. He could not move or take his eyes away; and what was odd too was that this other man seemed paralysed too. He said that the lips moved, and that the eyes were wide and dilated, but that he said nothing. Mr. Baxter had heard me come in, and at the sound the figure at the top of the stairs had winced and clasped its hands, and that then, with some sort of hopeless gesture, it had begun to come down. Then I had spoken, and Mr. Baxter had turned and seized my arm.

"Well, there was no doing anything with Mr. Baxter. He lay still, starting at every sound, telling us this little by little. Then he asked that his things might be packed. He must go away at once, he said.

"We told him what nonsense it all was, and how he had been worked up; and Mr. Hudson talked about the artistic temperament and all the rest. But it was no good; he must go; and Mr. Hudson rang the bell to give the order. As Mr. Baxter stood up at last, still all white and trembling, he saw his manuscript on the table, and before I could say a word he had seized it and tossed it into the fire: there would be thirty or forty pages, I should think.

"We went to the door to see him off—he had entirely refused to go upstairs again; even his boots were brought down—and he hardly said anything more after he had told us his story; he said he would write in a day or two. Then we went back to the parlour and talked it all over.

"Of course we said what we thought. It seemed to us plain enough that he had worked himself up to a most frightful pitch of nerves, and—well, all the rest of it. The whole thing, we said, was sheer imagination; you see, it was not that there was any story about the house.

"Just as Mr. Hudson was going to dress, the butler came in."

Father Maddox stopped again.

"Now, Reverend Fathers, this is the point of the story, and you may draw your own conclusions. The butler came in, looking rather puzzled, and asked how many there would be for dinner. Mr. Hudson told him two: Mr. Baxter was not coming back.

"'I beg your pardon, sir,' said the man; 'but what of the other gentleman?'

"'Why, here he is,' said my friend. 'One and one makes two, Manthorpe.'

"'But the gentleman upstairs, sir, and his servant?'

"You may imagine we jumped rather at that; and he told us then.

"One of the maids going across the landing ten minutes before had seen two persons—one of them a young gentleman, she said, in a long cloak, and the other an old man, his servant, she thought, for he was carrying a great bag—come out of Mr. Baxter's room and go into the turret-room. *The young gentleman was limping*, she said. 'She had particularly noticed that.'"

Father Maddox stopped, and there was a sudden chorus of questions.

"No," he said, "there was no explanation at all. The maid had not been at all frightened; she had supposed it was another visitor come by the same train as that by which Mr. Baxter had come the night before. She had not followed them; she had just gone and told Manthorpe, and asked where the gentleman was to sleep. We went everywhere—into the turret-room, up the stairs—everywhere. There was nothing; there never was anything; none at all.

"Now you see the difficulty, Reverend Fathers," ended the old man, smiling again. "The question is, did Mr. Baxter's imagination in a kind of way create those things so strongly that not only he saw them, but the maid as well—a kind of violent thought transference? Or was it that there was truth in the story—that something of the sort had happened in the house, and that this was the reason why, firstly, the idea had come so vividly to Mr. Baxter's mind, and secondly that he and the maid had actually seen—well, what they did see?"

He took out his snuff-box.

1912

THE DUST-CLOUD

E. F. Benson

Edward Frederic Benson (1867–1940), known to his family and close acquaintances as Fred, was born in 1867 in Berkshire, where his father Edward White Benson was at the time headmaster of the recently established Wellington College. Despite being the second youngest of the six siblings, he was to be the last of the family left standing—surviving his brother Arthur by 15 years.

The popularity of the writings of E. F. Benson has also outlived those of his brothers. He achieved instant sensation in 1893 with his first book, *Dodo*, a novel that satirised the frivolities of upper-class society, and whose title character was a woman based on Margot Tennant, the future wife of Prime Minister Herbert Asquith. After *Dodo*, the other big success in E. F. Benson's prolific career came between the wars with the *Mapp and Lucia* books, the works for which he is now best remembered. They feature two snobbish, well-to-do women and their comedic social rivalry.

E. F. Benson's first anthology of supernatural stories, *The Room in the Tower*, was published in 1912, with his last dedicated ghostly collection, *More Spook Stories*, appearing in 1934. Physical repugnance is a feature of many of E. F. Benson's tales, leading M. R. James—although an admirer—to note of his long-time acquaintance that "to my mind he sins occasionally by stepping over the line of legitimate horridness".

Away from his house at Rye in East Sussex, E. F. Benson enjoyed numerous holidays to the north Norfolk coast; there he came upon the isolated Halfway House on Blakeney Point, the setting for "A Tale of an Empty House" (the Point was also surely the inspiration for another tale in this collection: R. H. Malden's "Stivinghoe Bank"). Other East Anglian-set stories by E. F. Benson to check out include "The Dance", "Outside the Door", "The Corner House" and "The Face". Here, though, I've included "The Dust-Cloud", an interesting early tale of a haunted motor vehicle. (Note that there is a real parish called Bircham, comprising of three villages, 15 miles north-east of King's Lynn.)

The big French windows were open on to the lawn, and, dinner being over, two or three of the party who were staying for the week at the end of August with the Combe-Martins had strolled out on to the terrace to look at the sea, over which the moon, large and low, was just rising and tracing a path of pale gold from horizon to shore, while others, less lunar of inclination, had gone in search of bridge or billiards. Coffee had come round immediately after dessert, and the end of dinner, according to the delectable custom of the house, was as informal as the end of breakfast. Every one, that is to say, remained or went away, smoked, drank port or abstained, according to his personal tastes. Thus, on this particular evening it so happened that Harry Combe-Martin and I were very soon left alone in the dining-room, because we were talking unmitigated motor "shop," and the rest of the party (small wonder) were bored with it, and had left us. The shop was home-shop, so to speak, for it was almost entirely concerned with the manifold perfections of the new six-cylinder Napier which my host in a moment of extravagance, which he did not in the least regret, had just purchased; in which, too, he proposed to take me over to lunch at a friend's house near Hunstanton on the following day. He observed with legitimate pride that an early start would not be necessary as the distance was only eighty miles and there were no police traps.

"Queer things these big motors are," he said, relapsing into generalities as we rose to go. "Often I can scarcely believe that my new car is merely a machine. It seems to me to possess an independent life of its own. It is really much more like a thoroughbred with a wonderfully fine mouth."

"And the moods of a thoroughbred?" I asked.

"No; it's got an excellent temper, I'm glad to say. It doesn't mind being checked, or even stopped, when it's going its best. Some of these big cars can't stand that. They get sulky—I assure you it is literally true—if they are checked too often."

He paused on his way to ring the bell. "Guy Elphinstone's car, for instance," he said: "it was a bad-tempered brute, a violent, vicious beast of a car."

"What make?" I asked.

"Twenty-five horse-power Amédée. They are a fretful strain of car; too thin, not enough bone—and bone is very good for the nerves. The brute liked running over a chicken or a rabbit, though perhaps it was less the car's ill-temper than Guy's, poor chap. Well, he paid for it—he paid to the uttermost farthing. Did you know him?"

"No; but surely I have heard the name. Ah, yes, he ran over a child, did he not?"

"Yes," said Harry, "and then smashed up against his own park gates."

"Killed, wasn't he?"

"Oh yes, killed instantly, and the car just a heap of splinters. There's an odd story about it, I'm told, in the village: rather in your line."

"Ghosts?" I asked.

"Yes, the ghost of his motor-car. Seems almost too up-to-date, doesn't it?"

"And what's the story?" I demanded.

"Why, just this. His place was outside the village of Bircham, ten miles out from Norwich; and there's a long straight bit of road there— that's where he ran over the child—and a couple of hundred yards farther on, a rather awkward turn into the park gates. Well, a month or two ago, soon after the accident, one old gaffer in the village swore he had seen a motor there coming full tilt along the road, but without a sound, and it disappeared at the lodge gates of the park, which were shut. Soon after another said he had heard a motor whirl by him at the same place, followed by a hideous scream, but he saw nothing."

"The scream is rather horrible," said I.

"Ah, I see what you mean! I only thought of his syren. Guy had a syren on his exhaust, same as I have. His had a dreadful frightened sort of wail, and always made me feel creepy."

"And is that all the story?" I asked: "that one old man thought he saw a noiseless motor, and another thought he heard an invisible one?"

Harry flicked the ash off his cigarette into the grate. "Oh dear no!" he said. "Half a dozen of them have seen something or heard something. It is quite a heavily authenticated yarn."

"Yes, and talked over and edited in the public-house," I said.

"Well, not a man of them will go there after dark. Also the lodge-keeper gave notice a week or two after the accident. He said he was always hearing a motor stop and hoot outside the lodge, and he was kept running out at all hours of the night to see what it was."

"And what was it?"

"It wasn't anything. Simply nothing there. He thought it rather uncanny, anyhow, and threw up a good post. Besides, his wife was always hearing a child scream, and while her man toddled out to the gate she would go and see whether the kids were all right. And the kids themselves—"

"Ah, what of them?" I asked.

"They kept coming to their mother, asking who the little girl was who walked up and down the road and would not speak to them or play with them."

"It's a many-sided story," I said. "All the witnesses seem to have heard and seen different things."

"Yes, that is just what to my mind makes the yarn so good," he said. "Personally I don't take much stock in spooks at all. But given that there are such things as spooks, and given that the death of the child and the death of Guy have caused spooks to play about there, it seems to me a very good point that different people should be aware of different phenomena. One hears the car, another sees it, one hears the child scream, another sees the child. How does that strike you?"

This, I am bound to say, was a new view to me, and the more I thought of it the more reasonable it appeared. For the vast majority of mankind have all those occult senses by which is perceived the spiritual world (which, I hold, is thick and populous around us), sealed up, as it were; in other words, the majority of mankind never hear or see a ghost at all. Is it not, then, very probable that of the remainder—those, in fact, to whom occult experiences have happened or can happen—few should have every sense unsealed, but that some should have the unsealed ear, others the unsealed eye—that some should be clairaudient, others clairvoyant?

"Yes, it strikes me as reasonable," I said. "Can't you take me over there?"

"Certainly! If you will stop till Friday I'll take you over on Thursday. The others all go that day, so that we can get there after dark."

I shook my head. "I can't stop till Friday, I'm afraid," I said. "I must leave on Thursday. But how about tomorrow? Can't we take it on the way to or from Hunstanton?"

"No; it's thirty miles out of our way. Besides, to be at Bircham after dark means that we shouldn't get back here till midnight. And as host to my guests—"

"Ah! things are only heard and seen after dark, are they?" I asked.

"That makes it so much less interesting. It is like a séance where all lights are put out."

"Well, the accident happened at night," he said. "I don't know the rules, but that may have some bearing on it, I should think."

I had one question more in the back of my mind, but I did not like to ask it. At least, I wanted information on this subject without appearing to ask for it.

"Neither do I know the rules of motors," I said; "and I don't understand you when you say that Guy Elphinstone's machine was an irritable, cross-grained brute, that liked running over chickens and rabbits. But I think you subsequently said that the irritability may have been the irritability of its owner. Did he mind being checked?"

"It made him blind-mad if it happened often," said Harry. "I shall never forget a drive I had with him once: there were hay-carts and perambulators every hundred yards. It was perfectly ghastly; it was like being with a madman. And when we got inside his gate, his dog came running out to meet him. He did not go an inch out of his course: it was worse than that—he went for it, just grinding his teeth with rage. I never drove with him again."

He stopped a moment, guessing what might be in my mind. "I say, you mustn't think—you mustn't think—" he began.

"No, of course not," said I.

Harry Combe-Martin's house stood close to the weather-eaten, sandy cliffs of the Suffolk shore, which are being incessantly gnawed away by the hunger of the insatiable sea. Fathoms deep below it, and now many hundred yards out, lies what was once the second port in England; but now of the ancient town of Dunwich, and of its seven great churches, nothing remains but one, and that ruinous and already half destroyed by the falling cliff and the encroachments of the sea. Foot by foot, it too is disappearing, and of the graveyard which surrounded it more than half is gone, so that from the face of the sandy cliff on which it stands there stick out like straws in glass, as Dante says, the bones of those who were once committed there to the kindly and stable earth.

Whether it was the remembrance of this rather grim spectacle as I had seen it that afternoon, or whether Harry's story had caused some trouble in my brain, or whether it was merely that the keen bracing air of this place, to one who had just come from the sleepy languor of the Norfolk Broads, kept me sleepless, I do not know; but, anyhow, the moment I put out my light that night and got into bed, I felt that all the footlights and gas-jets in the internal theatre of my mind sprang into flame, and that I was very vividly and alertly awake. It was in vain that I counted a hundred forwards and a hundred backwards, that I pictured to myself a flock of visionary sheep coming singly through a gap in an imaginary hedge, and tried to number their monotonous and uniform countenances, that I played noughts and crosses with myself, that I marked out scores of double lawn-tennis courts,—for with each repetition of these supposedly soporific exercises I only became more intensely wakeful. It was not in remote hope of sleep that I continued to repeat these weary performances long after their inefficacy was proved to the hilt, but because I was strangely unwilling in this timeless hour of the night to think about those protruding relics of humanity; also I quite distinctly did not desire to think about that subject with regard to which I had, a few hours ago, promised Harry that I would not make it the subject of reflection. For these reasons I continued during the black hours to practise these narcotic exercises of the mind, knowing well that if I paused on the tedious treadmill my thoughts, like some released spring, would fly back to rather gruesome subjects. I kept my mind, in fact, talking loud to itself, so that it should not hear what other voices were saying.

Then by degrees these absurd mental occupations became impossible; my mind simply refused to occupy itself with them any longer; and next moment I was thinking intently and eagerly, not about the bones protruding from the gnawed section of sand-cliff, but about the subject I had said I would not dwell upon. And like a flash it came upon me why Harry had bidden me not think about it. Surely in order that I should not come to the same conclusion as he had come to.

Now the whole question of "haunt"—haunted spots, haunted houses, and so forth—has always seemed to me to be utterly unsolved, and to be neither proved nor disproved to a satisfactory degree. From the earliest times, certainly from the earliest known Egyptian records, there has been a belief that the scene of a crime is often revisited, sometimes by the spirit of him who has committed it—seeking rest, we must suppose, and finding none; sometimes, and more inexplicably, by the spirit of his victim, crying perhaps, like the blood of Abel, for vengeance. And though the stories of these village gossips in the alehouse about noiseless visions and invisible noises were all as yet unsifted and unreliable, yet I could not help wondering if they (such as they were) pointed to something authentic and to be classed under this head of appearances. But more striking than the yarns of the gaffers seemed to me the questions of the lodge-keeper's children. How should children have imagined the figure of a child that would not speak to them or play with them? Perhaps it was a real child, a sulky child. Yes—perhaps. But perhaps not. Then after this preliminary skirmish I found myself settling down to the question that I had said I would not think about; in other words, the possible origin of these phenomena interested me more than the phenomena themselves. For what exactly had Guy Elphinstone, that savage driver, done? Had or had not the death of the child been entirely an accident, a thing (given he drove a motor at all) outside his own control? Or had he, irritated beyond endurance at the checks and delays of the day, not pulled up when it was just possible he might have, but had run over the child as he would have run over a rabbit or a hen, or even his own dog? And what, in any case, poor wretched brute, must have been his thoughts in that terrible instant that intervened between the child's death and his own, when a moment later he smashed into the closed gates of his own lodge? Was remorse his—bitter, despairing contrition? That could hardly have been so; or else surely, knowing only for certain that he had knocked a child down, he would have stopped; he would have done his best, whatever that might be, to repair the irreparable harm. But he had not stopped: he had gone on, it seemed, at full speed, for on the collision the car had been smashed into matchwood and steel shavings. Again, with double force, had this dreadful thing been a complete accident, he would have stopped. So then—most terrible question of all—had he, after making murder, rushed on to what proved to be his own death, filled with some hellish glee at what he had done? Indeed, as in the churchyard on the cliff, bones of the buried stuck starkly out into the night.

The pale tired light of earliest morning had turned the window-blinds into glimmering squares before I slept; and when I woke, the servant who called me was already rattling them briskly up on their rollers, and letting the calm serenity of the August day stream into the room. Through the open windows poured in sunlight and sea-wind, the scent of flowers and the song of birds; and each and all were wonderfully reassuring, banishing the hooded forms that had haunted the night, and I thought of the disquietude of the dark hours as a traveller may think of the billows and tempests of the ocean over which he has safely journeyed, unable, now that they belong to the limbo of the past, to recall his qualms and tossings with any vivid uneasiness. Not without a feeling of relief, too, did I dwell on the knowledge that I was definitely not going to visit this equivocal spot. Our drive today, as Harry had said, would not take us within thirty miles of it, and tomorrow I but went to the station and away. Though a thorough-paced seeker after truth might, no doubt, have regretted that the laws of time and space did not permit him to visit Bircham after the sinister dark had fallen, and test whether for him there was visible or audible truth in the tales of the village gossips, I was conscious of no such regret. Bircham and its fables had given me a very bad night, and I was perfectly aware that I did not in the least want to go near it, though yesterday I had quite truthfully said I should like to do so. In this brightness, too, of sun and sea-wind I felt none of the *malaise* at my waking moments which a sleepless night usually gives me; I felt particularly well, particularly pleased to be alive, and also, as I have said, particularly content not to be going to Bircham. I was quite satisfied to leave my curiosity unsatisfied.

The motor came round about eleven, and we started at once, Harry and Mrs. Morrison, a cousin of his, sitting behind in the big back seat, large enough to hold a comfortable three, and I on the left of the driver, in a sort of trance—I am not ashamed to confess it—of expectancy and delight. For this was in the early days of motors, when there was still the sense of romance and adventure round them. I did not want to drive, any more than Harry wanted to; for driving, so I hold, is too absorbing; it takes the attention in too firm a grip: the mania of the true motorist is not consciously enjoyed. For the passion for motors is a taste—I had almost said a gift—as distinct and as keenly individual as the passion for music or mathematics. Those who use motors most (merely as a means of getting rapidly from one place to another) are often entirely without it, while those whom adverse circumstances (over which they have no control) compel to use them least may have it to a supreme degree. To those who have it, analysis of their passion is perhaps superfluous; to those who have it not, explanation is almost unintelligible. Pace, however, and the control of pace, and above all the sensuous consciousness of pace, is at the root of it; and pleasure in pace is common to most people, whether it be in the form of a galloping horse, or the pace of the skate hissing over smooth ice, or the pace of a free-wheel bicycle humming down-hill, or, more impersonally, the pace of the smashed ball at lawn-tennis, the driven ball at golf, or the low boundary hit at cricket. But the sensuous consciousness of pace, as I have said, is needful: one might experience it seated in front of the engine of an express train, though not in a wadded, shut-windowed carriage, where the wind of movement is not felt. Then add to this rapture of the rush through riven air the knowledge that huge relentless force is controlled by a little lever, and directed by a little wheel on which the hands of the driver seem to lie so negligently. A great untamed devil has there his bridle, and he answers to it, as Harry had said, like a horse with a fine mouth. He has hunger and thirst, too, unslakeable, and greedily he laps of his soup of petrol which turns to fire in his mouth: electricity, the force that rends clouds asunder, and causes towers to totter, is the spoon with which he feeds himself; and as he eats he races onward, and the road opens like torn linen in front of him. Yet how obedient, how amenable is he!—for with a touch on his snaffle his speed is redoubled, or melts into thin air, so that before you know you have touched the rein he has exchanged his swallow-flight for a mere saunter through the lanes. But he ever loves to run; and knowing this, you will bid him lift up his voice and tell those who are in his path that he is coming, so that he will not need the touch that checks. Hoarse and jovial is his voice, hooting to the wayfarer; and if his hooting be not heard he has a great guttural falsetto scream that leaps from octave to octave, and echoes from the hedges that are passing in blurred lines of hanging green. And, as you go, the romantic isolation of divers in deep seas is yours; masked and hooded companions may be near you also, in their driving-dress for this plunge through the swift tides of air; but you, like them, are alone and isolated, conscious only of the ripped riband of road, the two great lantern-eyes of the wonderful monster that look through drooped eyelids by day, but gleam with fire by night, the two ear-laps of splash-boards, and the long lean bonnet in front which is the skull and brain-case of that swift, untiring energy that feeds on fire, and whirls its two tons of weight up hill and down dale, as if some new law as everlasting as gravity, and like gravity making it go ever swifter, was its sole control.

For the first hour the essence of these joys, any description of which compared to the real thing is but as a stagnant pond compared to the bright rushing of a mountain stream, was mine. A straight switchback road lay in front of us, and the monster plunged silently down hill, and said below his breath, "Ha-ha—ha-ha—ha-ha," as, without diminution of speed, he breasted the opposing slope. In my control were his great vocal chords (for in those days hooter and syren were on the driver's left, and lay convenient, to the hand of him who occupied the box-seat), and it rejoiced me to let him hoot to a pony-cart, three hundred yards ahead, with a hand on his falsetto scream if his ordinary tones of conversation were unheard or disregarded. Then came a road crossing ours at right angles, and the dear monster seemed to say, "Yes, yes,—see how obedient and careful I am. I stroll with my hands in my pockets." Then again a puppy from a farmhouse staggered warlike into the road, and the monster said, "Poor little chap! get home to your mother, or I'll talk to you in earnest." The poor little chap did not take the hint, so the monster slackened speed and just said, "Whoof!" Then it chuckled to itself as the puppy scuttled into the hedge, seriously alarmed; and next moment our self-made wind screeched and whistled round us again.

Napoleon, I believe, said that the power of an army lay in its feet: that is true also of the monster. There was a loud bang, and in thirty seconds we were at a standstill. The monster's off fore-foot troubled it, and the chauffeur said, "Yes, sir,—burst."

So the burst boot was taken off and a new one put on, a boot that had never been on foot before. The foot in question was held up on a jack during this operation, and the new boot laced up with a pump. This took exactly twenty-five minutes. Then the monster got his spoon going again, and said, "Let me run: oh, let me run!" And for fifteen miles on a straight and empty road it ran. I timed the miles, but shall not produce their chronology for the benefit of a forsworn constabulary.

But there were no more dithyrambics that morning. We should have reached Hunstanton in time for lunch. Instead, we waited to repair our fourth puncture at 1.45 P.M., twenty-five miles short of our destination. This fourth puncture was caused by a spicule of flint three-quarters of an inch long—sharp, it is true, but weighing perhaps two pennyweights, while we weighed two tons. It seemed an impertinence. So we lunched at a wayside inn, and during lunch the pundits held a consultation, of which the upshot was this:

We had no more boots for our monster, for his off fore-foot had burst once, and punctured once (thus necessitating two socks and one boot). Similarly, but more so, his off hind-foot had burst twice (thus necessitating two boots and two socks). Now, there was no certain shoemaker's shop at Hunstanton, as far as we knew, but there was a regular universal store at King's Lynn, which was about equidistant.

And, so said the chauffeur, there was something wrong with the monster's spoon (ignition), and he didn't rightly know what, and therefore it seemed the prudent part not to go to Hunstanton (lunch, a thing of the preterite, having been the object), but to the well-supplied King's Lynn. And we all breathed a pious hope that we might get there.

Whizz: hoot: purr! The last boot held, the spoon went busily to the monster's mouth, and we just flowed into King's Lynn. The return journey, so I vaguely gathered, would be made by other roads; but personally, intoxicated with air and movement, I neither asked nor desired to know what those roads would be. This one small but rather salient fact is necessary to record here, that as we waited at King's Lynn, and as we buzzed homewards afterwards, no thought of Bircham entered my head at all. The subsequent hallucination, if hallucination it was, was not, as far as I know, self-suggested. That we had gone out of our way for the sake of the garage, I knew, and that was all. Harry also told me that he did not know where our road would take us.

The rest that follows is the baldest possible narrative of what actually occurred. But it seems to me, a humble student of the occult, to be curious.

While we waited we had tea in a hotel looking on to a big empty square of houses, and after tea we waited a very long time for our monster to pick us up. Then the telephone from the garage inquired for "the gentleman on the motor," and since Harry had strolled out to get a local evening paper with news of the last Test Match, I applied ear and mouth to that elusive instrument. What I heard was not encouraging: the ignition had gone very wrong indeed, and "perhaps" in an hour we should be able to start. It was then about half-past six, and we were just seventy-eight miles from Dunwich.

Harry came back soon after this, and I told him what the message from the garage had been. What he said was this: "Then we shan't get back till long after dinner. We might just as well have camped out to see your ghost."

As I have already said, no notion of Bircham was in my mind, and I mention this as evidence that, even if it had been, Harry's remark would have implied that we were not going through Bircham.

The hour lengthened itself into an hour and a half. Then the monster, quite well again, came hooting round the corner, and we got in.

"Whack her up, Jack," said Harry to the chauffeur. "The roads will be empty. You had better light up at once."

The monster, with its eyes agleam, was whacked up, and never in my life have I been carried so cautiously and yet so swiftly. Jack never took a risk or the possibility of a risk, but when the road was clear and open he let the monster run just as fast as it was able. Its eyes made day of the road fifty yards ahead, and the romance of night was fairyland round us. Hares started from the roadside, and raced in front of us for a hundred yards, then just wheeled in time to avoid the ear-flaps of the great triumphant brute that carried us. Moths flitted across, struck sometimes by the lenses of its eyes, and the miles peeled over our shoulders. When It occurred we were going top-speed. And this was It—quite unsensational, but to us quite inexplicable unless my midnight imaginings happened to be true.

As I have said, I was in command of the hooter and of the syren. We were flying along on a straight down-grade, as fast as ever we could go, for the engines were working, though the decline was considerable. Then quite suddenly I saw in front of us a thick cloud of dust, and knew instinctively and on the instant, without thought or reasoning, what that must mean. Evidently something going very fast (or else so large a cloud could not have been raised) was in front of us, and going in the same direction as ourselves. Had it been something on the road coming to meet us, we should of course have seen the vehicle first and run into the dust-cloud afterwards. Had it, again, been something of low speed—a horse and dogcart, for instance—no such dust could have been raised. But, as it was, I knew at once that there was a motor travelling swiftly just ahead of us, also that it was not going as fast as we were, or we should have run into its dust much more gradually. But we went into it as into a suddenly lowered curtain.

Then I shouted to Jack. "Slow down, and put on the brake," I shrieked. "There's something just ahead of us."

As I spoke I wrought a wild concerto on the hooter, and with my right hand groped for the syren, but did not find it. Simultaneously I heard a wild, frightened shriek, just as if I had sounded the syren myself. Jack had felt for it too, and our hands fingered each other. Then we entered the dust-cloud.

We slowed down with extraordinary rapidity, and still peering ahead we went dead-slow through it. I had not put on my goggles after leaving King's Lynn, and the dust stung and smarted in my eyes. It was not, therefore, a belt of fog, but real road-dust. And at the moment we crept through it I felt Harry's hands on my shoulder.

"There's something just ahead," he said. "Look! don't you see the tail light?"

As a matter of fact, I did not; and, still going very slow, we came out of that dust-cloud. The broad empty road stretched in front of us; a hedge was on each side, and there was no turning either to right or left. Only, on the right, was a lodge, and gates which were closed. The lodge had no lights in any window.

Then we came to a standstill; the air was dead-calm, not a leaf in the hedgerow trees was moving, not a grain of dust was lifted from the road. But, behind, the dust-cloud still hung in the air, and stopped dead-short at the closed lodge-gates. We had moved very slowly for the last hundred yards: it was difficult to suppose that it was of our making. Then Jack spoke, with a curious crack in his voice.

"It must have been a motor, sir," he said. "But where is it?"

I had no reply to this, and from behind another voice, Harry's voice, spoke. For the moment I did not recognise it, for it was strained and faltering.

"Did you open the syren?" he asked. "It didn't sound like our syren. It sounded like, like—"

"I didn't open the syren," said I.

Then we went on again. Soon we came to scattered lights in houses by the wayside.

"What's this place?" I asked Jack.

"Bircham, sir," said he.

1912

THE MAN WITH THE ROLLER

E. G. Swain

Edmund Gill Swain (1861–1938) was born in Stockport and, after attending Manchester Grammar School, carried on the tradition of the authors so far in this anthology in going to Cambridge University (Emmanuel College, where he studied Natural Sciences). He was ordained a Deacon in the Church of England after graduating, returning to Cambridge in 1892, when he took up the role of Chaplain at King's College. While there, he was to become a friend and colleague of M. R. James and was present at many of the Christmas Eve social gatherings in the College where Monty James and others would delight their guests with the reading of a ghost story.

In 1905 Swain left King's to become vicar of the Parish of Stanground (now a suburb of Peterborough), where he wrote his excellent, solitary collection of supernatural stories, *The Stoneground Ghost Tales* (1912). Told from the recollections of the very endearing Reverend Roland Batchel (a fictionalised version of Swain), they're rather milder in their horrors than those that permeate James's stories, but are beautifully written and bear repeated reading. The book is dedicated from the Rev. Batchel to his friend M. R. James, and the latter's influence can be seen here in "The Man with the Roller", which would seem to draw its inspiration from "The Mezzotint". Here, though, the introduction of photography into the proceedings is a novel touch.

Swain died in January 1938, eighteen months after his friend and ghost-story mentor. He's buried in the grounds of Peterborough Cathedral, where there's also a memorial plaque to him on the door to the tower.

On the edge of that vast tract of East Anglia, which retains its ancient name of the Fens, there may be found, by those who know where to seek it, a certain village called Stoneground. It was once a picturesque village. Today it is not to be called either a village, or picturesque. Man dwells not in one "house of clay," but in two, and the material of the second is drawn from the earth upon which this and the neighbouring villages stood. The unlovely signs of the industry have changed the place alike in aspect and in population. Many who have seen the fossil skeletons of great saurians brought out of the clay in which they have lain from pre-historic times, have thought that the inhabitants of the place have not since changed for the better. The chief habitations, however, have their foundations not upon clay, but upon a bed of gravel which anciently gave to the place its name, and upon the highest part of this gravel stands, and has stood for many centuries, the Parish Church, dominating the landscape for miles around.

Stoneground, however, is no longer the inaccessible village, which in the middle ages stood out above a waste of waters. Occasional floods serve to indicate what was once its ordinary outlook, but in more recent times the construction of roads and railways, and the drainage of the Fens, have given it freedom of communication with the world from which it was formerly isolated.

The Vicarage of Stoneground stands hard by the Church, and is renowned for its spacious garden, part of which, and that (as might be expected) the part nearest the house, is of ancient date. To the original plot successive Vicars have added adjacent lands, so that the garden has gradually acquired the state in which it now appears.

The Vicars have been many in number. Since Henry de Greville was instituted in the year 1140 there have been 30, all of whom have lived, and most of whom have died, in successive vicarage houses upon the present site.

The present incumbent, Mr. Batchel, is a solitary man of somewhat studious habits, but is not too much enamoured of his solitude to receive visits, from time to time, from schoolboys and such. In the summer of the year 1906 he entertained two, who are the occasion of this narrative, though still unconscious of their part in it, for one of the two, celebrating his 15th birthday during his visit to Stoneground, was presented by Mr. Batchel with a new camera, with which he proceeded to photograph, with considerable skill, the surroundings of the house.

One of these photographs Mr. Batchel thought particularly pleasing. It was a view of the house with the lawn in the foreground. A few small copies, such as the boy's camera was capable of producing, were sent to him by his young friend, some weeks after the visit, and again Mr. Batchel was so much pleased with the picture, that he begged for the negative, with the intention of having the view enlarged.

The boy met the request with what seemed a needlessly modest plea. There were two negatives, he replied, but each of them had, in the same part of the picture, a small blur for which there was no accounting otherwise than by carelessness. His desire, therefore, was to discard these films, and to produce something more worthy of enlargement, upon a subsequent visit.

Mr. Batchel, however, persisted in his request, and upon receipt of the negative, examined it with a lens. He was just able to detect the blur alluded to; an examination under a powerful glass, in fact revealed something more than he had at first detected. The blur was like the nucleus of a comet as one sees it represented in pictures, and seemed to be connected with a faint streak which extended across the negative. It was, however, so inconsiderable a defect that Mr. Batchel resolved to disregard it. He had a neighbour whose favourite pastime was photography, one who was notably skilled in everything that pertained to the art, and to him he sent the negative, with the request for an enlargement, reminding him of a long-standing promise to do any such service, when as had now happened, his friend might see fit to ask it.

This neighbour who had acquired such skill in photography was one Mr. Groves, a young clergyman, residing in the Precincts of the Minster near at hand, which was visible from Mr. Batchel's garden. He lodged with a Mrs. Rumney, a superannuated servant of the Palace, and a strong-minded vigorous woman still, exactly such a one as Mr. Groves needed to have about him. For he was a constant trial to Mrs. Rumney, and but for the wholesome fear she begot in him, would have converted his rooms into a mere den. Her carpets and tablecloths were continually bespattered with chemicals; her chimney-piece ornaments had been unceremoniously stowed away and replaced by labelled bottles; even the bed of Mr. Groves was, by day, strewn with drying films and mounts, and her old and favourite cat had a bald patch on his flank, the result of a mishap with the pyrogallic acid.

Mrs. Rumney's lodger, however, was a great favourite with her, as such helpless men are apt to be with motherly women, and she took no small pride in his work. A life-size portrait of herself, originally a peace-offering, hung in her parlour, and had long excited the envy of every friend who took tea with her.

"Mr. Groves," she was wont to say, "is a nice gentleman, AND a gentleman; and chemical though he may be, I'd rather wait on him for nothing than what I would on anyone else for twice the money."

Every new piece of photographic work was of interest to Mrs. Rumney, and she expected to be allowed both to admire and to criticise. The view of Stoneground Vicarage, therefore, was shown to her upon its arrival. "Well may it want enlarging," she remarked, "and it no bigger than a postage stamp; it looks more like a doll's house than a vicarage," and with this she went about her work, whilst Mr. Groves retired to his dark room with the film, to see what he could make of the task assigned to him.

Two days later, after repeated visits to his dark room, he had made something considerable; and when Mrs. Rumney brought him his chop for luncheon, she was lost in admiration. A large but unfinished print stood upon his easel, and such a picture of Stoneground Vicarage was in the making as was calculated to delight both the young photographer and the Vicar.

Mr. Groves spent only his mornings, as a rule, in photography. His afternoons he gave to pastoral work, and the work upon this enlargement was over for the day. It required little more than "touching up," but it was this "touching up" which made the difference between the enlargements of Mr. Groves and those of other men. The print, therefore, was to be left upon the easel until the morrow, when it was to be finished. Mrs. Rumney and he, together, gave it an admiring inspection as she was carrying away the tray, and what they agreed in admiring most particularly was the smooth and open stretch of lawn, which made so excellent a foreground for the picture. "It looks," said Mrs. Rumney, who had once been young, "as if it was waiting for someone to come and dance on it."

Mr. Groves left his lodgings—we must now be particular about the hours—at half-past two, with the intention of returning, as usual, at five. "As reg'lar as a clock," Mrs. Rumney was wont to say, "and a sight more reg'lar than some clocks I knows of."

Upon this day he was, nevertheless, somewhat late, some visit had detained him unexpectedly, and it was a quarter-past five when he inserted his latch-key in Mrs. Rumney's door.

Hardly had he entered, when his landlady, obviously awaiting him, appeared in the passage: her face, usually florid, was of the colour of parchment, and, breathing hurriedly and shortly, she pointed at the door of Mr. Groves' room.

In some alarm at her condition, Mr. Groves hastily questioned her; all she could say was: "The photograph! the photograph!" Mr. Groves could only suppose that his enlargement had met with some mishap for which Mrs. Rumney was responsible. Perhaps she had allowed it to flutter into the fire. He turned towards his room in order to discover the worst, but at this Mrs. Rumney laid a trembling hand upon his arm, and held him back. "Don't go in," she said, "have your tea in the parlour."

"Nonsense," said Mr. Groves, "if that is gone we can easily do another."

"Gone," said his landlady, "I wish to Heaven it was."

The ensuing conversation shall not detain us. It will suffice to say that after a considerable time Mr. Groves succeeded in quieting his landlady, so much so that she consented, still trembling violently, to enter the room with him. To speak truth, she was as much concerned for him as for herself, and she was not by nature a timid woman.

The room, so far from disclosing to Mr. Groves any cause for excitement, appeared wholly unchanged. In its usual place stood every article of his stained and ill-used furniture, on the easel stood the photograph, precisely where he had left it; and except that his tea was not upon the table, everything was in its usual state and place.

But Mrs. Rumney again became excited and tremulous, "It's there," she cried. "Look at the lawn."

THE MAN WITH THE ROLLER

Mr. Groves stepped quickly forward and looked at the photograph. Then he turned as pale as Mrs. Rumney herself.

There was a man, a man with an indescribably horrible suffering face, rolling the lawn with a large roller.

Mr. Groves retreated in amazement to where Mrs. Rumney had remained standing. "Has anyone been in here?" he asked.

"Not a soul," was the reply, "I came in to make up the fire, and turned to have another look at the picture, when I saw that dead-alive face at the edge. It gave me the creeps," she said, "particularly from not having noticed it before. If that's anyone in Stoneground, I said to myself, I wonder the Vicar has him in the garden with that awful face. It took that hold of me I thought I must come and look at it again, and at five o'clock I brought your tea in. And then I saw him moved along right in front, with a roller dragging behind him, like you see."

Mr. Groves was greatly puzzled. Mrs. Rumney's story, of course, was incredible, but this strange evil-faced man had appeared in the photograph somehow. That he had not been there when the print was made was quite certain.

The problem soon ceased to alarm Mr. Groves; in his mind it was investing itself with a scientific interest. He began to think of suspended chemical action, and other possible avenues of investigation. At Mrs. Rumney's urgent entreaty, however, he turned the photograph upon the easel, and with only its white back presented to the room, he sat down and ordered tea to be brought in.

He did not look again at the picture. The face of the man had about it something unnaturally painful: he could remember, and still see, as it were, the drawn features, and the look of the man had unaccountably distressed him.

He finished his slight meal, and having lit a pipe, began to brood over the scientific possibilities of the problem. Had any other photograph upon the original film become involved in the one he had enlarged? Had the image of any other face, distorted by the enlarging lens, become a part of this picture? For the space of two hours he debated this possibility, and that, only to reject them all. His optical knowledge told him that no conceivable accident could have brought into his picture a man with a roller. No negative of his had ever contained such a man; if it had, no natural causes would suffice to leave him, as it were, hovering about the apparatus.

His repugnance to the actual thing had by this time lost its freshness, and he determined to end his scientific musings with another inspection of the object. So he approached the easel and turned the photograph round again. His horror returned, and with good cause. The man with the roller had now advanced to the middle of the lawn. The face was stricken still with the same indescribable look of suffering. The man seemed to be appealing to the spectator for some kind of help. Almost, he spoke.

Mr. Groves was naturally reduced to a condition of extreme nervous excitement. Although not by nature what is called a nervous man, he trembled from head to foot. With a sudden effort, he turned away his head, took hold of the picture with his outstretched hand, and opening a drawer in his sideboard thrust the thing underneath a folded tablecloth which was lying there. Then he closed the drawer and took up an entertaining book to distract his thoughts from the whole matter.

In this he succeeded very ill. Yet somehow the rest of the evening passed, and as it wore away, he lost something of his alarm. At ten o'clock, Mrs. Rumney, knocking and receiving answer twice, lest by any chance she should find herself alone in the room, brought in the cocoa usually taken by her lodger at that hour. A hasty glance at the easel showed her that it stood empty, and her face betrayed her relief. She made no comment, and Mr. Groves invited none.

The latter, however, could not make up his mind to go to bed. The face he had seen was taking firm hold upon his imagination, and seemed to fascinate him and repel him at the same time. Before long, he found himself wholly unable to resist the impulse to look at it once more. He took it again, with some indecision, from the drawer and laid it under the lamp.

The man with the roller had now passed completely over the lawn, and was near the left of the picture.

The shock to Mr. Groves was again considerable. He stood facing the fire, trembling with excitement which refused to be suppressed. In this state his eye lighted upon the calendar hanging before him, and it furnished him with some distraction. The next day was his mother's birthday. Never did he omit to write a letter which should lie upon her breakfast-table, and the pre-occupation of this evening had made him wholly forgetful of the matter. There was a collection of letters, however, from the pillar-box near at hand, at a quarter before midnight, so he turned to his desk, wrote a letter which would at least serve to convey his affectionate greetings, and having written it, went out into the night and posted it.

The clocks were striking midnight as he returned to his room. We may be sure that he did not resist the desire to glance at the photograph he had left on his table. But the results of that glance, he, at any rate, had not anticipated. The man with the roller had disappeared. The lawn lay as smooth and clear as at first, "looking," as Mrs. Rumney had said, "as if it was waiting for someone to come and dance on it."

The photograph, after this, remained a photograph and nothing more. Mr. Groves would have liked to persuade himself that it had never undergone these changes which he had witnessed, and which we have endeavoured to describe, but his sense of their reality was too insistent. He kept the print lying for a week upon his easel. Mrs. Rumney, although she had ceased to dread it, was obviously relieved at its disappearance, when it was carried to Stoneground to be delivered to Mr. Batchel. Mr. Groves said nothing of the man with the roller, but gave the enlargement, without comment, into his friend's hands. The work of enlargement had been skilfully done, and was deservedly praised.

Mr. Groves, making some modest disclaimer, observed that the view, with its spacious foreground of lawn, was such as could not have failed to enlarge well. And this lawn, he added, as they sat looking out of the Vicar's study, looks as well from within your house as from without. It must give you a sense of responsibility, he added, reflectively, to be sitting where your predecessors have sat for so many centuries and to be continuing their peaceful work. The mere presence before your window, of the turf upon which good men have walked, is an inspiration.

The Vicar made no reply to these somewhat sententious remarks. For a moment he seemed as if he would speak some words of conventional assent. Then he abruptly left the room, to return in a few minutes with a parchment book.

"Your remark, Groves," he said as he seated himself again, "recalled to me a curious bit of history: I went up to the old library to get the book. This is the journal of William Longue who was Vicar here up to the year 1602. What you said about the lawn will give you an interest in a certain portion of the journal. I will read it."

> Aug. 1, 1600.—I am now returned in haste from a journey to Brightelmstone whither I had gone with full intention to remain about the space of two months. Master Josiah Wilburton, of my dear College of Emmanuel, having consented to assume the charge of my parish of Stoneground in the meantime. But I had intelligence, after 12 days' absence, by a messenger from

the Churchwardens, that Master Wilburton had disappeared last Monday sennight, and had been no more seen. So here I am again in my study to the entire frustration of my plans, and can do nothing in my perplexity but sit and look out from my window, before which Andrew Birch rolleth the grass with much persistence. Andrew passeth so many times over the same place with his roller that I have just now stepped without to demand why he so wasteth his labour, and upon this he hath pointed out a place which is not levelled, and hath continued his rolling.

Aug. 2.—There is a change in Andrew Birch since my absence, who hath indeed the aspect of one in great depression, which is noteworthy of so chearful a man. He haply shares our common trouble in respect of Master Wilburton, of whom we remain without tidings. Having made part of a sermon upon the seventh Chapter of the former Epistle of St. Paul to the Corinthians and the 27th verse, I found Andrew again at his task, and bade him desist and saddle my horse, being minded to ride forth and take counsel with my good friend John Palmer at the Deanery, who bore Master Wilburton great affection.

Aug. 2 continued.—Dire news awaiteth me upon my return. The Sheriff's men have disinterred the body of poor Master W. from beneath the grass Andrew was rolling, and have arrested him on the charge of being his cause of death.

Aug. 10—Alas! Andrew Birch hath been hanged, the Justice having mercifully ordered that he should hang by the neck until he should be dead, and not sooner molested. May the Lord have mercy on his soul. He made full confession before me, that he had slain Master Wilburton in heat upon his threatening to make me privy to certain peculation of which I should not have suspected so old a servant. The poor man bemoaned his evil temper in great contrition, and beat his breast, saying that he knew himself doomed for ever to roll the grass in the place where he had tried to conceal his wicked fact.

"Thank you," said Mr. Groves. "Has that little negative got the date upon it?" "Yes," replied Mr. Batchel, as he examined it with his glass. The boy has marked it August 10. The Vicar seemed not to remark the coincidence with the date of Birch's execution. Needless to say that it did not escape Mr. Groves. But he kept silence about the man with the roller, who has been no more seen to this day.

Doubtless there is more in our photography than we yet know of. The camera sees more than the eye, and chemicals in a freshly prepared and active state, have a power which they afterwards lose. Our units of time, adopted for the convenience of persons dealing with the ordinary movements of material objects, are of course conventional. Those who turn the instruments of science upon nature will always be in danger of seeing more than they looked for. There is such a disaster as that of knowing too much, and at some time or another it may overtake each of us. May we then be as wise as Mr. Groves in our reticence, if our turn should come.

1919

THE TRUE HISTORY OF ANTHONY FFRYAR

Ingulphus

Ingulphus is the pseudonym of Arthur Gray (1852–1940). He was born in York and schooled at Blackheath in London, before going on to become an eminent scholar of Shakespeare. In 1912 Gray became the Master of—where else!—Jesus College, Cambridge, where he had earlier studied and been a Fellow. There he contributed ten antiquarian ghost stories to three Cambridge periodicals, the majority appearing in the *Cambridge Review*. Nine of these were collected together in the 1919 volume *Tedious Brief Tales of Granta and Gramarye*, at which point their author's identity was finally revealed, solving a long-standing local mystery. Eight of the nine stories, including "The True History of Anthony Ffryar" (about a sixteenth-century alchemist) which is reprinted here, tell of various purported events in the annals of Jesus College; the other, "The Palladium", ventures slightly further afield to Ramsey and Soham in the Fens. ("Suggestion", a later effort from 1925 that came too late to be included in his book, has for its setting the imaginary Bishop's College.)

Away from his Shakespeare scholarship and esoteric stories, Gray was also a keen and respected local historian whose books on Cambridge paint a more reliable picture of the past than those given to us by his pseudonym in *Tedious Brief Tales of Granta and Gramarye*. Ingulphus was the name of a real historical figure of the Fens—an early

Abbot of Crowland in south Lincolnshire; Gray chose knowingly, as the chronicle of the Abbey attributed to him (the *Historia Monasterii Croylandensis*) is notoriously untrustworthy and most likely a later fake.

Arthur Gray died in the Master's Lodge at Jesus in 1940, at the grand age of 87.

The world, it is said, knows nothing of its greatest men. In our Cambridge microcosm it may be doubted whether we are better informed concerning some of the departed great ones who once walked the confines of our Colleges. Which of us has heard of Anthony Ffryar of Jesus? History is dumb respecting him. Yet but for the unhappy event recorded in this unadorned chronicle his fame might have stood with that of Bacon of Trinity, or Harvey of Caius. *They* lived to be old men: Ffryar died before he was thirty—his work unfinished, his fame unknown even to his contemporaries.

So meagre is the record of his life's work that it is contained in a few bare notices in the College Bursar's Books, in the Grace Books which date his matriculation and degrees, and in the entry of his burial in the register of All Saints' Parish. These simple annals I have ventured to supplement with details of a more or less hypothetical character which will serve to show what humanity lost by his early death. Readers will be able to judge for themselves the degree of care which I have taken not to import into the story anything which may savour of the improbable or romantic.

Anthony Ffryar matriculated in the year 1541–2, his age being then probably 15 or 16. He took his B.A. degree in 1545, his M.A. in 1548. He became a Fellow about the end of 1547, and died in the summer of 1551. Such are the documentary facts relating to him. Dr. Reston was Master of the College during the whole of his tenure of a Fellowship and died in the same year as Ffryar. The chamber which Ffryar occupied as a Fellow was on the first floor of the staircase at the west end of the Chapel. The staircase has since been absorbed in the Master's Lodge, but the doorway through which it was approached from the cloister may still be seen. At the time when Ffryar lived there the nave of the Chapel was used as a parish church, and his windows overlooked the graveyard, then called "Jesus churchyard," which is now a part of the Master's garden.

Ffryar was of course a priest, as were nearly all the Fellows in his day. But I do not gather that he was a theologian, or complied more than formally with the obligation of his orders. He came to Cambridge when the Six Articles and the suppression of the monasteries were of fresh and burning import: he became a Fellow in the harsh Protestant days of Protector Somerset: and in all his time the Master and the Fellows were in scarcely disavowed sympathy with the rites and beliefs of the Old Religion. Yet in the battle of creeds I imagine that he took no part and no interest. I should suppose that he was a somewhat solitary man, an insatiable student of Nature, and that his sympathies with humanity were starved by his absorption in the New Science which dawned on Cambridge at the Reformation.

When I say that he was an alchemist do not suppose that in the middle of the sixteenth century the name of alchemy carried with it any associations with credulity or imposture. It was a real science and a subject of University study then, as its god-children, Physics and Chemistry, are now. If the aims of its professors were transcendental its methods were genuinely based on research. Ffryar was no visionary, but a man of sense, hard and practical. To the study of alchemy he was drawn by no hopes of gain, not even of fame, and still less by any desire to benefit mankind. He was actuated solely by an unquenchable passion for enquiry, a passion sterilising to all other feeling. To the somnambulisms of the less scientific disciples of his school, such as the philosopher's stone and the elixir of life, he showed himself a chill agnostic. All his thought and energies were concentrated on the discovery of the *magisterium*, the master-cure of all human ailments.

For four years in his laboratory in the cloister he had toiled at this pursuit. More than once, when it had seemed most near, it had eluded his grasp; more than once he had been tempted to abandon it as a mystery insoluble. In the summer of 1551 the discovery waited at his door. He was sure, certain of success, which only experiment could prove. And with the certainty arose a new passion in his heart—to make the name of Ffryar glorious in the healing profession as that of Galen or Hippocrates. In a few days, even within a few hours, the fame of his discovery would go out into all the world.

The summer of 1551 was a sad time in Cambridge. It was marked by a more than usually fatal outbreak of the epidemic called "the sweat," when, as Fuller says, "patients ended or mended in twenty-four hours." It had smouldered some time in the town before it appeared with sudden and dreadful violence in Jesus College. The first to go was little Gregory Graunge, schoolboy and chorister, who was lodged in the College school in the outer court. He was barely thirteen years old, and known by sight to Anthony Ffryar. He died on July 31, and was buried the same day in Jesus churchyard. The service for his burial was held in the Chapel and at night, as was customary in those days. Funerals in College were no uncommon events in the sixteenth century. But in the death of the poor child, among strangers, there was something to move even the cold heart of Ffryar. And not the pity of it only impressed him. The dim Chapel, the Master and Fellows obscurely ranged in their stalls and shrouded in their hoods, the long-drawn miserable chanting and the childish trebles of the boys who had been Gregory's fellows struck a chill into him which was not to be shaken off.

Three days passed and another chorister died. The College gates were barred and guarded, and, except by a selected messenger, communication with the town was cut off. The precaution was unavailing, and the boys' usher, Mr. Stevenson, died on August 5. One of the junior Fellows, sir Stayner—"sir" being the equivalent of B.A.—followed on August 7. The Master, Dr. Reston, died the next day. A gaunt, severe man was Dr. Reston, whom his Fellows feared. The death of a Master of Arts on August 9 for a time completed the melancholy list.

Before this the frightened Fellows had taken action. The scholars were dismissed to their homes on August 6. Some of the Fellows abandoned the College at the same time. The rest—a terrified conclave—met on August 8 and decreed that the College should be closed until the pestilence should have abated. Until that time it was to be occupied by a certain Robert Laycock, who was a College servant, and his only communication with the outside world was to be through his son, who lived in Jesus Lane. The decree was perhaps the result of the Master's death, for he was not present at the meeting.

Goodman Laycock, as he was commonly called, might have been the sole tenant of the College but for the unalterable decision of Ffryar to remain there. At all hazards his research, now on the eve of realisation, must proceed; without the aid of his laboratory in College it would miserably hang fire. Besides, he had an absolute assurance of his own immunity if the experiment answered his confident expectations, and his fancy was elated with the thought of standing, like another Aaron, between the living and the dead, and staying the pestilence with the potent *magisterium*. Until then he would bar his door even against Laycock, and his supplies of food should be left on the staircase landing. Solitude for him was neither unfamiliar nor terrible.

So for three days Ffryar and Laycock inhabited the cloister, solitary and separate. For three days, in the absorption of his research, Ffryar forgot fear, forgot the pestilence-stricken world beyond the gate, almost forgot to consume the daily dole of food laid outside his door. August 12 was the day, so fateful to humanity, when his labours were to be crowned with victory: before midnight the secret of the *magisterium* would be solved.

Evening began to close in before he could begin the experiment which was to be his last. It must of necessity be a labour of some hours, and, before it began, he bethought him that he had not tasted food since early morning. He unbarred his door and looked for the expected portion. It was not there. Vexed at the remissness of Laycock he waited for a while and listened for his approaching footsteps. At last he took courage and descended to the cloister. He called for Laycock, but heard no response. He resolved to go as far as the Buttery door and knock. Laycock lived and slept in the Buttery.

At the Buttery door he beat and cried on Laycock; but in answer he heard only the sound of scurrying rats. He went to the window, by the hatch, where he knew that the old man's bed lay, and called to him again. Still there was silence. At last he resolved to force himself through the unglazed window and take what food he could find. In the deep gloom within he stumbled and almost fell over a low object, which he made out to be a truckle-bed. There was light enough from the window to distinguish, stretched upon it, the form of Goodman Laycock, stark and dead.

Sickened and alarmed Ffryar hurried back to his chamber. More than ever he must hasten the great experiment. When it was ended his danger would be past, and he could go out into the town to call the buryers for the old man. With trembling hands he lit the brazier which he used for his experiments, laid it on his hearth and placed thereon the alembic which was to distil the *magisterium*.

Then he sat down to wait. Gradually the darkness thickened and the sole illuminant of the chamber was the wavering flame of the brazier.

He felt feverish and possessed with a nameless uneasiness which, for all his assurance, he was glad to construe as fear: better that than sickness. In the college and the town without was a deathly silence, stirred only by the sweltering of the distilment, and, as the hours struck, by the beating of the Chapel clock, last wound by Laycock. It was as though the dead man spoke. But the repetition of the hours told him that the time of his emancipation was drawing close.

Whether he slept I do not know. He was aroused to vivid consciousness by the clock sounding *one*. The time when his experiment should have ended was ten, and he started up with a horrible fear that it had been ruined by his neglect. But it was not so. The fire burnt, the liquid simmered quietly, and so far all was well.

Again the College bell boomed a solitary stroke: then a pause and another. He opened, or seemed to open, his door and listened. Again the knell was repeated. His mind went back to the night when he had attended the obsequies of the boy-chorister. This must be a funeral tolling. For whom? He thought with a shudder of the dead man in the Buttery.

He groped his way cautiously down the stairs. It was a still, windless night, and the cloister was dark as death. Arrived at the further side of the court he turned towards the Chapel. Its panes were faintly lighted from within. The door stood open and he entered.

In the place familiar to him at the chancel door one candle flickered on a bracket. Close to it—his face cast in deep shade by the light from behind—stood the ringer, in a gown of black, silent and absorbed in his melancholy task. Fear had almost given way to wonder in the heart of Ffryar, and, as he passed the sombre figure on his way to the chancel door, he looked him resolutely in the face. The ringer was Goodman Laycock.

Ffryar passed into the choir and quietly made his way to his accustomed stall. Four candles burnt in the central walk about a figure laid on trestles and draped in a pall of black. Two choristers—one on either side—stood by it. In the dimness he could distinguish four figures, erect in the stalls on either side of the Chapel. Their faces were concealed by their hoods, but in the tall form which occupied the Master's seat it was not difficult to recognise Dr. Reston.

The bell ceased and the service began. With some faint wonder Ffryar noted that it was the proscribed Roman Mass for the Dead. The solemn introit was uttered in the tones of Reston, and in the deep responses of the nearest cowled figure he recognised the voice of Stevenson, the usher. None of the mourners seemed to notice Ffryar's presence.

The dreary ceremony drew to a close. The four occupants of the stalls descended and gathered round the palled figure in the aisle. With a mechanical impulse, devoid of fear or curiosity, and with a half-prescience of what he should see, Anthony Ffryar drew near and uncovered the dead man's face. He saw—himself.

At the same moment the last wailing notes of the office for the dead broke from the band of mourners, and, one by one, the choristers extinguished the four tapers.

"Requiem aeternam dona ei, Domine," chanted the hooded four: and one candle went out.

"Et lux perpetua luceat ei," was the shrill response of the two choristers: and a second was extinguished.

"Cum sanctis tuis in aeternum," answered the four: and one taper only remained.

The Master threw back his hood, and turned his dreadful eyes straight upon the living Anthony Ffryar: he threw his hand across the bier and held him tight. "Cras tu eris mecum,"[1] he muttered, as if in antiphonal reply to the dirge-chanters.

---

1 Samuel xxvii. 19.

With a hiss and a sputter the last candle expired.

The hiss and the sputter and a sudden sense of gloom recalled Ffryar to the waking world. Alas for labouring science, alas for the fame of Ffryar, alas for humanity, dying and doomed to die! The vessel containing the wonderful brew which should have redeemed the world had fallen over and dislodged its contents on the fire below. An accident reparable, surely, within a few hours; but not by Anthony Ffryar. How the night passed with him no mortal can tell. All that is known further of him is written in the register of All Saints' parish. If you can discover the ancient volume containing the records of the year 1551—and I am not positive that it now exists—you will find it written:

"Die Augusti xiii
　　Buryalls in Jhesus churchyarde
　　　　Goodman Laycock ⎫
　　　　Anthony Ffryar"　⎭ of ye sicknesse

Whether he really died of "the sweat" I cannot say. But that the living man was sung to his grave by the dead, who were his sole companions in Jesus College, on the night of August 12, 1551, is as certain and indisputable as any other of the facts which are here set forth in the history of Anthony Ffryar.

1923

DEARTH'S FARM

Gerald Bullett

Writer and broadcaster Gerald William Bullett (1893–1958) grew up in suburban north London, leaving school at the age of 16 to become a bank clerk. While serving in the Royal Flying Corps in France during the Great War, he had his debut novel, *The Progress of Kay* (1916), published. Bullett was able to attend Jesus College, Cambridge as an ex-serviceman, graduating with first-class honours in English in 1921. He then happily married, moved to the Sussex countryside and began his career as a man of letters, authoring some forty books during his lifetime. These included poetry, a biography of George Eliot, a study of the English Mystics, and several popular novels including *Mr. Godly Beside Himself* (1924), a humorous work of fantasy. He also wrote short stories—which brings us to the weird fiction collection *The Street of the Eye* (1923), where "Dearth's Farm" first appeared. It's an unusual and unsettling tale, with an extremely atmospheric setting, though I still can't quite place whether the farm's topography of that shallow basin a few miles inland from the North Sea shoreline corresponds with any real locale. The wind, however, often does seem preternaturally strong when you're standing on the top of the ridge of land that forms the coastal Norfolk hinterland, so it feels—at least to me—an eminently authentic backdrop…

A conversation between the narrator of "Dearth's Farm" and his friend Saunders that takes place in the title story at the beginning of

The Street of the Eye—the pair are discussing the nature of supernatural fiction—is also worth bearing in mind as you read the tale:

"As for your friend's [Bailey's] experiences at the farm, I think, frankly, that there was sheer devilry in it, black magic. But it isn't always so."

I

It is really not far: our fast train does it in eighty minutes. But so sequestered is the little valley in which I have made my solitary home that I never go to town without the delicious sensation of poising my hand over a lucky-bag full of old memories. In the train I amuse myself by summoning up some of those ghosts of the past, a past not distant but sufficiently remote in atmosphere from my present to be invested with a certain sentimental glamour. "Perhaps I shall meet you—or you." But never yet have I succeeded in guessing what London held up her sleeve for me. She has that happiest of tricks—without which paradise will be dull indeed—the trick of surprise. In London, if in no other place, it is the unexpected that happens. For me Fleet Street is the scene *par excellence* of these adventurous encounters, and it was in Fleet Street, three months ago, that I ran across Bailey, of Queens', whom I hadn't seen for five years. Bailey is not his name, nor Queens' his college, but these names will serve to reveal what is germane to my purpose and to conceal the rest.

His recognition of me was instant; mine of him more slow. He told me his name twice; we stared at each other, and I struggled to disguise the blankness of my memory. The situation became awkward. I was the more embarrassed because I feared lest he should too odiously misinterpret my non-recognition of him, for the man was shabby and unshaven enough to be suspicious of an intentional slight. Bailey, Bailey... now who the devil was Bailey? And then, when he had already made a gesture of moving on, memory stirred to activity.

"Of course, I remember. Bailey. Theosophy. You used to talk to me about theosophy, didn't you? I remember perfectly now." I glanced at my watch. "If you're not busy let's go and have tea somewhere."

He smiled, with a hint of irony in his eyes, as he answered: "I'm not busy." I received the uncomfortable impression that he was hungry and with no ordinary hunger, and the idea kept me silent, like an awkward schoolboy, while we walked together to a tea-shop that I knew.

Seated on opposite sides of the tea-table we took stock of each other. He was thin, and his hair greying; his complexion had a soiled unhealthy appearance; the cheeks had sunk in a little, throwing into prominence the high cheekbones above which his sensitive eyes glittered with a new light, a light not of heaven. Compared with the Bailey I now remembered so well, a rather sleek young man with an almost feline love of luxury blossoming like a tropical plant in the exotic atmosphere of his Cambridge rooms, compared with that man this was but a pale wraith. In those days he had been a flaming personality, suited well—too well, for my plain taste—to the highly-coloured orientalism that he affected in his mural decorations. And co-existent in him with this lust for soft cushions and chromatic orgies, which repelled me, there was an imagination that attracted me: an imagination delighting in highly-coloured metaphysical theories of the universe. These theories, which were as fantastic as *The Arabian Nights* and perhaps as unreal, proved his academic undoing: he came down badly in his Tripos, and had to leave without a degree. Many a man has done that and yet prospered, but Bailey, it was apparent, hadn't prospered. I made the conventional inquiries, adding, "It must be six or seven years since we met last."

"More than that," said Bailey morosely, and lapsed into silence. "Look here," he burst out suddenly, "I'm going to behave like a cad.

I'm going to ask you to lend me a pound note. And don't expect it back in a hurry."

We both winced a little as the note changed hands. "You've had bad luck," I remarked, without, I hope, a hint of pity in my voice. "What's wrong?"

He eyed me over the rim of his teacup. "I look a lot older to you, I expect?"

"You don't look very fit," I conceded.

"No, I don't." His cup came down with a nervous slam upon the saucer. "Going grey, too, aren't I?" I was forced to nod agreement. "Yet, do you know, a month ago there wasn't a grey hair in my head. You write stories, don't you? I saw your name somewhere. I wonder if you could write my story. You may get your money back after all... By God, that would be funny, wouldn't it!"

I couldn't see the joke, but I was curious about his story. And after we had lit our cigarettes he told it to me, to the accompaniment of a driving storm of rain that tapped like a thousand idiot fingers upon the plate-glass windows of the shop.

2

A few weeks ago, said Bailey, I was staying at the house of a cousin of mine. I never liked the woman, but I wanted free board and lodging, and hunger soon blunts the edge of one's delicacy. She's at least ten years my senior, and all I could remember of her was that she had bullied me when I was a child into learning to read. Ten years ago she married a man named Dearth—James Dearth, the resident owner of a smallish farm in Norfolk, not far from the coast. All her relatives opposed the marriage. Relatives always do. If people waited for the approval of relatives before marrying, the world would be depopulated in a generation. This time it was religion. My cousin's people were primitive and methodical in their religion, as the name of their sect confessed; whereas Dearth professed a universal toleration that they thought could only be a cloak for indifference. I have my own opinion about that, but it doesn't matter now. When I met the man I forgot all about religion: I was simply repelled by the notion of any woman marrying so odd a being. Rather small in build, he possessed the longest and narrowest face I have ever seen on a man of his size. His eyes were set exceptionally wide apart, and the nose, culminating in large nostrils, made so slight an angle with the rest of the face that seen in profile it was scarcely human. Perhaps I exaggerate a little, but I know no other way of explaining the peculiar revulsion he inspired in me. He met me at the station in his dogcart, and wheezed a greeting at me. "You're Mr. Bailey, aren't you? I hope you've had an agreeable journey. Monica will be delighted." This seemed friendly enough, and my host's conversation during that eight-mile drive did much to make me forget my first distaste of his person. He was evidently a man of wide reading, and he had a habit of polite deference that was extremely flattering, especially to me who had had more than my share of the other thing. I was cashiered during the war, you know. Never mind why. Whenever he laughed, which was not seldom, he exhibited a mouthful of very large regular teeth.

Dearth's Farm, to give it the local name, is a place with a personality of its own. Perhaps every place has that. Sometimes I fancy that the earth itself is a personality, or a community of souls locked fast in a dream from which at any moment they may awake, like volcanos, into violent action. Anyhow Dearth's Farm struck me as being peculiarly personal, because I found it impossible not to regard its climatic changes as changes of mood. You remember my theory that chemical action is only psychical action seen from without? Well, I'm inclined to think in just the same way of every manifestation of natural energy. But you don't want to hear about my fancies. The farmhouse, which is approached by a narrow winding lane from the main road, stands high up in a kind of shallow basin of land, a few acres ploughed but mostly grass. The countryside has a gentle prettiness more characteristic of the southeastern counties. On three sides wooded hills slope gradually to the horizon; on the fourth side grassland rises a little for twenty yards and then curves abruptly down. To look through the windows that give out upon this fourth side is to have the sensation of being on the edge of a steep cliff, or at the end of the world. On a still day, when the sun is shining, the place has a languid beauty, an afternoon atmosphere. You remember Tennyson's Lotus Isles, "in which it seemed always afternoon": Dearth's Farm has something of that flavour on a still day. But such days are rare; the two or three I experienced shine like jewels in the memory. Most often that stretch of fifty or sixty acres is a gathering-ground for all the bleak winds of the earth. They seem to come simultaneously from the land and from the sea, which is six miles away, and they swirl round in that shallow basin of earth, as I have called it, like maddened devils seeking escape from a trap. When the storms were at their worst I used to feel as though I were perched insecurely on a gigantic saucer held a hundred miles above the earth. But I am not a courageous person. Monica, my cousin, found no fault with the winds. She had other fears, and I had not been with her three days before she began to confide them to me. Her overtures were as surprising as they were unwelcome, for that she was not a confiding person by nature I was certain. Her manners were reserved to the point of diffidence, and we had nothing in common save a detestation of the family from which we had both sprung. I suppose you will want to know something of her looks. She was a tall, full-figured woman, handsome for her years, with jet black hair, a sensitive face, and a complexion almost Southern in its dark colouring. I love beauty and I found pleasure in her mere presence, which did something to lighten for me the gloom that pervaded the house; but my pleasure was innocent enough, and Dearth's watchdog airs only amused me. Monica's eyes—unfathomable pools—seemed troubled whenever they rested on me: whether by fear or by some other emotion I didn't at first know.

She chose her moment well, coming to me when Dearth was out of the house, looking after his men, and I, pleading a headache, had refused to accompany him. The malady was purely fictitious, but I was bored with the fellow's company, and sick of being dragged at his heels like a dog for no better reason than his too evident jealousy afforded.

"I want to ask a kindness of you," she said. "Will you promise to answer me quite frankly?" I wondered what the deuce was coming, but I promised, seeing no way out of it. "I want you to tell me," she went on, "whether you see anything queer about me, about my behaviour? Do I say or do anything that seems to you odd?"

Her perturbation was so great that I smiled to hide my perception of it. I answered jocularly: "Nothing at all odd, my dear Monica, except this question of yours. What makes you ask it?"

But she was not to be shaken so easily out of her fears, whatever they were. "And do you find nothing strange about this household either?"

"Nothing strange at all," I assured her. "Your marriage is an unhappy one, but so are thousands of others. Nothing strange about that."

"What about him?" she said. And her eyes seemed to probe for an answer.

I shrugged my shoulders. "Are you asking for my opinion of your husband? A delicate thing to discuss."

"We're speaking in confidence, aren't we!" She spoke impatiently, waving my politeness away.

"Well, since you ask, I don't like him. I don't like his face: it's a parody on mankind. And I can't understand why you threw yourself away on him."

She was eager to explain. "He wasn't always like this. He was a gifted man, with brains and an imagination. He still is, for all I know. You spoke of his face—now how would you describe his face, in one word?"

I couldn't help being tickled by the comedy of the situation: a man and a woman sitting in solemn conclave seeking a word by which to describe another man's face, and that man her husband. But her air of tragedy, though I thought it ridiculous, sobered me. I pondered her question for a while, recalling to my mind's eye the long narrow physiognomy and the large teeth of Dearth.

At last I ventured the word I had tried to avoid. "Equine," I suggested.

"Ah!" There was a world of relief in her voice. "You've seen it too."

She told me a queer tale. Dearth, it appears, had a love and understanding of horses that was quite unparalleled. His wife too had loved horses and it had once pleased her to see her husband's astonishing power over the creatures, a power which he exercised always for their good. But his benefactions to the equine race were made at a hideous cost to himself of which he was utterly unaware. Monica's theory was too fantastic even for me to swallow, and I, as you know, have a good stomach for fantasy. You will have already guessed what it was. Dearth was growing, by a process too gradual and subtle for perception, into the likeness of the horses with whom he had so complete sympathy. This was Mrs. Dearth's notion of what was happening to her husband. And she pointed out something significant that had escaped my notice. She pointed out that the difference between him and the next man was not altogether, or even mainly, a physical difference. In effect she said: "If you scrutinise the features more carefully, you will find them to be far less extraordinary than you now suppose. The poison is not in his features. It is in the psychical atmosphere he carries about with him: something which infects you with the idea of horse and makes you impose that idea on his appearance, magnifying his facial peculiarities." Just now I mentioned that in the early days of her marriage Monica had shared this love of horses. Later, of course, she came to detest them only one degree less than she detested her husband. That is saying much. Only a few months before my visit matters had come to a crisis between the two. Without giving any definite reason, she had confessed, under pressure, that he was unspeakably offensive to her; and since then they had met only at meals and always reluctantly. She shuddered to recall that interview, and I shuddered to imagine it. I was no longer surprised that she had begun to entertain doubts of her own sanity.

But this wasn't the worst. The worst was Dandy, the white horse. I found it difficult to understand why a white horse should alarm her, and I began to suspect that the nervous strain she had undergone was making her inclined to magnify trifles. "It's his favourite horse," she said. "That's as much as saying that he dotes on it to a degree that is unhuman. It never does any work. It just roams the fields by day, and at night sleeps in the stable." Even this didn't, to my mind, seem a very terrible indictment. If the man were mad on horses, what more natural than this petting of a particular favourite?—a fine animal, too, as Monica herself admitted. "Roams the fields," cried my poor cousin urgently. "Or did until these last few weeks. Lately it has been kept in its stable, day in, day out, eating its head off and working up energy enough to kill us all." This sounded to me like the language of hysteria, but I waited for what was to follow. "The day you came, did you notice how pale I looked? I had had a fright. As I was crossing the yard with a pail of separated milk for the calves, that beast broke loose from the stable and sprang at me. Yes, Dandy. He was in a fury. His eyes burned with ferocity. I dodged him by a miracle, dropped the pail, and ran back to the house shrieking for help. When I entered the living-room my husband feigned to be waking out of sleep. He didn't seem interested in my story, and I'm convinced that he had planned the whole thing." It was past my understanding how Dearth could have made his horse spring out of his stable and make a murderous attack upon a particular woman, and I said so. "You don't know him yet," retorted Monica. "And you don't know Dandy. Go and look at the beast. Go now, while James is out."

The farmyard, with its pool of water covered in green slime, its manure and sodden straw, and its smell of pigs, was a place that seldom failed to offend me. But on this occasion I picked my way across the cobblestones thinking of nothing at all but the homicidal horse that I was about to spy upon. I have said before that I'm not a courageous man, and you'll understand that I stepped warily as I neared the stable. I saw that the lower of the two doors was made fast and with the more confidence unlatched the other.

I peered in. The great horse stood, bolt upright but apparently in a profound sleep. It was indeed a fine creature, with no spot or shadow, as far as I could discern, to mar its glossy whiteness. I stood there staring and brooding for several minutes, wondering if both Monica and I were the victims of some astounding hallucination. I had no fear at all of Dandy, after having seen him; and it didn't alarm me when, presently, his frame quivered, his eyes opened, and he turned to look at me. But as I looked into his eyes an indefinable fear possessed me. The horse stared dumbly for a moment, and his nostrils dilated. Although I half-expected him to tear his head out of the halter and prance round upon me, I could not move. I stared, and as I stared, the horse's lips moved back from the teeth in a grin, unmistakably a grin, of malign intelligence. The gesture vividly recalled Dearth to my mind. I had described him as equine, and if proof of the word's aptness were needed, Dandy had supplied that proof.

"He's come back," Monica murmured to me, on my return to the house. "Ill, I think. He's gone to lie down. Have you seen Dandy?"

"Yes. And I hope not to see him again."

But I was to see him again, twice again. The first time was that same night, from my bedroom window. Both my bedroom and my cousin's looked out upon that grassy hill of which I spoke. It rose from a few yards until almost level with the second storey of the house and then abruptly curved away. Somewhere about midnight, feeling restless and troubled by my thoughts, I got out of bed and went to the window to take an airing.

I was not the only restless creature that night. Standing not twenty yards away, with the sky for background, was a great horse. The moonlight made its white flank gleam like silver, and lit up the eyes that stared fixedly at my window.

3

For sixteen days and nights we lived, Monica and I, in the presence of this fear, a fear none the less real for being non-susceptible to definition. The climax came suddenly, without any sort of warning, unless Dearth's idiotic hostility towards myself could be regarded as a warning. The utterly unfounded idea that I was making love to his wife had taken root in the man's mind, and every day his manner to me became more openly vindictive. This was the cue for my departure, with warm thanks for my delightful holiday; but I didn't choose to take it. I wasn't exactly in love with Monica, but she was my comrade in danger and I was reluctant to leave her to face her nightmare terrors alone.

The most cheerful room in that house was the kitchen, with its red-tiled floor, its oak rafters, and its great open fireplace. And when in the evenings the lamp was lit and we sat there, listening in comfort to the everlasting gale that raged round the house, I could almost have imagined myself happy, had it not been for the presence of my reluctant host. He was a skeleton at a feast, if you like! By God, we were a genial party. From seven o'clock to ten we would sit there, the three of us, fencing off silence with the most pitiful of small talk. On this particular night I had been chaffing him gently, though with intention, about his fancy for keeping a loaded rifle hanging over the kitchen mantelpiece; but at last I sickened of the pastime, and the conversation, which had been sustained only by my efforts, lapsed. I stared at the red embers in the grate, stealing a glance now and again at Monica to see how she was enduring the discomfort of such a silence. The cheap alarum clock ticked loudly, in the way that cheap alarum clocks have. When I looked again at Dearth he appeared to have fallen asleep. I say "appeared," for I instantly suspected him of shamming sleep in order to catch us out. I knew that he believed us to be in love with each other, and his total lack of evidence must have occasioned him hours of useless fury. I suspected him of the most melodramatic intentions: of hoping to see a caress pass between us that would justify him in making a scene. In that scene, as I figured it, the gun over the mantelpiece might play an important part. I don't like loaded guns.

The sight of his closed lids exasperated me into a bitter speech designed for him to overhear. "Monica, your husband is asleep. He is asleep only in order that he may wake at the chosen moment and pour out the contents of his vulgar little mind upon our heads."

This tirade astonished her, as well it might. She glanced up, first at me, then at her husband; and upon him her eyes remained fixed. "He's not asleep," she said, rising slowly out of her chair.

"I know he's not," I replied.

By now she was at his side, bending over him. "No," she remarked coolly. "He's dead."

At those words the wind outside redoubled its fury, and it seemed as though all the anguish of the world was in its wail. The spirit of Dearth's Farm was crying aloud in a frenzy that shook the house, making all the windows rattle. I shuddered to my feet. And in the moment of my rising the wail died away, and in the lull I heard outside the window a sudden sound of feet, of pawing, horse's feet. My horror found vent in a sort of desperate mirth.

"No, not dead. James Dearth doesn't die so easily."

Shocked by my levity, she pointed mutely to the body in the chair. But a wild idea possessed me, and I knew that my wild idea was the truth. "Yes," I said, "that may be dead as mutton. But James Dearth is outside, come to spy on you and me. Can't you hear him?"

I stretched out my hand to the blind cord. The blind ran up with a rattle, and, pressed against the window, looking in upon us, was the face of the white horse, its teeth bared in a malevolent grin. Without losing sight of the thing for a moment, I backed towards the fire. Monica, divining my intention, took down the gun from its hook and yielded it to my desirous fingers. I took deliberate aim, and shot.

And then, with the crisis over, as I thought, my nerves went to rags. I sat down limply, Monica huddled at my feet; and I knew with a hideous certitude that the soul of James Dearth, violently expelled from the corpse that lay outside the window, was in the room with me, seeking to re-enter that human body in the chair. There was a long moment of agony during which I trembled on the verge of madness, and then a flush came back into the dead pallid cheeks, the body breathed, the eyes opened... I had just enough strength left to drag myself out of my seat. I saw Monica's eyes raised to mine; I can never for a moment cease to see them. Three hours later I stumbled into the arms of the station-master, who put me in the London train under the impression that I was drunk. Yes, I left alone. I told you I wasn't a courageous man...

4

Bailey's voice abruptly ceased. The tension in my listening mind snapped, and I came back with a jerk, as though released by a spring, to my seat in the tea-shop. Bailey's queer eyes glittered across at me for a moment, and then, their light dying suddenly out, they became infinitely weary of me and of all the sorry business of living. A rationalist in grain, I find it impossible to accept the story quite as it stands. Substantially true it may be, probably is, but that it has been distorted by the prism of Bailey's singular personality I can hardly doubt. But the angle of that distortion must remain a matter for conjecture.

No such dull reflections came then to mar my appreciation of the quality of the strange hush that followed his last words. Neither of us spoke. An agitated waitress made us aware that the shop was closing, and we went into the street without a word. The rain was unremitting. I shrank back into the shelter of the porch while I fastened the collar of my mackintosh, and when I stepped out upon the pavement again, Bailey had vanished into the darkness.

I have never ceased to be vexed at losing him, and never ceased to fear that he may have thought the loss not unwelcome to me. My only hope is that he may read this and get into touch with me again, so that I may discharge my debt to him. It is a debt that lies heavily on my conscience—the price of this story, less one pound.

1928

THE SEVENTEENTH HOLE AT DUNCASTER

H. R. Wakefield

Herbert Russell Wakefield (1888–1964) was, like M. R. James, born in Kent, the son of an Anglican vicar (though his father, Henry Wakefield, went on to become the Bishop of Birmingham). Unlike James and every writer so far to appear in this anthology, Wakefield did not go up to Cambridge, instead moving from private school at Marlborough to University College, Oxford, where he read Modern History. Before the outbreak of the First World War Wakefield served as secretary to the press baron Lord Northcliffe, before becoming a captain in the Royal Scots Fusiliers during the hostilities.

After the conflict, Wakefield worked for a time as secretary to his father and, while accompanying him on a trip to the USA in 1920, met his first wife, a wealthy American. Back in England the couple settled in London, where Wakefield returned to the world of literature at the publisher William Collins. His own debut books came out in 1928: *Gallimaufry*, a novel, and the well-regarded volume of ghost stories, *They Return at Evening*. Several spooky collections followed, the most notable of which is *Old Man's Beard* from the following year.

"The Seventeenth Hole at Duncaster" comes from Wakefield's first collection, and its action takes place on the Norfolk links among the "superb sand-dune country bordering the North Sea" (Wakefield was himself reputedly a keen golfer). The name of the course and the geographical hints in the text nod firmly in the direction of Brancaster and the Royal West Norfolk Golf Club (founded in 1892) as being the inspiration for the story's setting.

Brancaster's current 17th hole is a 393-yard par four, though I couldn't say whether any more troublesome hazards beyond the usual bunkers and heavy rough lie in wait off its tee...

Mr. Baxter sauntered out of his office in the Dormy House at Duncaster Golf Club, just as the sun was setting one perfect evening late in September, 192—, meagre labours finished for the day. He gazed idly around him over one of the finest stretches of golfing in the world. Duncaster is a remote hamlet on the Norfolk coast and, being twelve miles from a railway station, would have remained delicately secluded if some roaming enthusiast in the late nineties had not felt his heart seized by so fair, so promising, so royal and ancient a prospect, and rallied his golfing acquaintance to found the Duncaster Golf Club, with a small and select membership, and small and select it had remained. Almost deserted for most of the year, it was thickly sprinkled in August, and there was always a pleasant gathering of old friends at the spring and autumn meetings. Mr. Baxter, the popular and efficient secretary, was a portly little person, kindly, considerate, but very happy. He let his eye roam placidly just over the superb sand-dune country bordering the North Sea, where gleaming alleyways of perfect turf burrowed their way through the golden ramparts above them, sweet isolated pathways ending in the World's Finest Greens—so the members considered—where little red flags gleamed, waving gently in a dying evening breeze; then his eyes wandered inland and became for a moment sharply intent as they reached the seventeenth green, the new seventeenth placed on a plateau in the big wood, the long shadows cast by the sleepy sun peeping through the trees, playing across it.

Mr. Baxter was in a slightly depressed and introspective mood. Golf secretaries, he decided, were born and not made, and born under no felicitous star. There was he, a student and a philosopher by taste and temperament, condemned to oversee for a slender remuneration the tiny activities of a blasted golf club. He had drifted into this blind alley as he had always drifted; it was all due, he supposed, to the fact that one of his glands functioned inadequately. Yes, golf secretaries were only explicable on some such derogatory hypothesis. This seventeenth green, for example, because it was the only alteration made since the opening of the links, what a "Yes and No," what a discordant clamour of debate, what a fuss about almost nothing! Of course it was an improvement; by hacking a fairway through the wood and making the green on that ideal little plateau a bad two hundred and seventy-yarder had been changed into a very fine two-shotter—the best, though not the most pleasing hole, for the dunes made the real charm of the course. And yet—the student and philosopher rebelled.

He strolled across to the Pro's shop, whose tenant was standing in the doorway smoking a pipe, and gazing reflectively in front of him.

"Evening, Dakers," said Mr. Baxter, "I thought I saw someone on the seventeenth a little while ago. Is anyone still out?"

The Pro took his pipe out of his mouth. His face did not command a wide range of expression, but for a moment a look of a certain sharpness and subtlety flitted across it.

"No, sir, everyone's in Mr. and Mrs. Stannard finished a quarter of an hour ago; they were the last."

"That's funny," said Mr. Baxter, "I could have sworn I saw someone."

The Pro paused a moment, as if carefully choosing his reply. "I think, sir, it's shadows. I've fancied the same thing."

"Well, what do you think of it?" asked the secretary.

"I'm sure it's a very fine hole, sir, but it's too good for me. I've played it seven times now, and done five fives and two sixes. It's funny, too, because it's just my length—a drive and push iron with the ground as hard as this, yet I haven't found the green with my second shot once. The ball seems to leave the club all right, and then—well, it's something I've never known happen before."

"I hope it's going to be a success, for it's been enough bother and expense," said Mr. Baxter.

The Pro did not answer for a moment. He put his pipe back in his mouth and looked away over the subject of discussion. At length he asked, "Did they ever discover what the contractor's men died of, sir?"

"Not for certain," replied the secretary, "blood poisoning of some kind—a very unfortunate affair."

"The other chaps thought it had something to do with those skulls and bones they dug up. They got talking to the villagers, who put the wind up them a bit, I'm thinking."

"How was that?" asked Mr. Baxter.

"It's some sort of talk about the wood, it seems," replied Dakers.

Mr. Baxter was interested. "I should like to hear more about this," he said, "but I have no time now. I'll see you tomorrow."

The next day, the Saturday before the opening of the autumn meeting, Mr. Baxter played an afternoon round with Colonel Senlis. It was for both of them their first introduction to the new seventeenth. The colonel had taken up the game after he retired, and he served it with an even more fanatical devotion than he had served his King. He was a jolly old maniac with a handicap of sixteen and a style of his own. Mr. Baxter might have been a very fine player; he had balance, rhythm, and a beautiful pair of hands, but his heart had never been in it, and he was content to be a perfectly reliable two.

No incident of any moment occurred during the first sixteen holes. The Colonel collected much fine sand in various portions of his attire; Mr. Baxter played sound but listless golf. When they reached the seventeenth tee the wind, which had been wandering vaguely and gustily round the compass, suddenly settled down to blow half a gale from due east, and the seventeenth became a tiger indeed. Mr. Baxter, after a couple of nice blows dead into the wind, lay some twenty yards short of the wood, which was beginning to shout wildly in the gale. The Colonel was in the rough on the right, an alliterative position he usually occupied. He played his fourth—one of the few properly struck golf shots of his existence—dead on the pin. The secretary took his number three iron, and knew from the moment the ball left the club that he didn't want it back. It was ruled on the flag.

As the Colonel came up, a look of swelling pride on his rubicund visage, he remarked, "Did you see mine, Baxter? Never say again I can't play a spoon shot! You hit yours, too, didn't you?"

"Yes," answered the secretary, smiling. "I'm inside you by a yard or two, I fancy."

"I don't," said the Colonel. "You'll be playing the odd, stroke gone, all right."

They walked together along the avenue of lurching Scotch firs and larches, and climbed the bank of the plateau.

"My God!" cried the Colonel. "We're neither of us on! Where the Hades are they?"

An exasperating search followed, which ended when the Colonel found his Dunlop No. 1 dozing behind a tree; and Mr. Baxter detected his No. 2 in a rabbit hole. The Colonel made robust use of an expletive much favoured by the gallant men he had once had the honour of commanding. Mr. Baxter quietly picked up his errant globe and walked off to the last tee.

"Damn it, Baxter!" cried the Colonel, "that hole meant to fight me, I felt it all the time."

The secretary had played many holes with the Colonel on many different courses, but had never noticed any of them displaying any Locarno spirit toward or desire to fraternise with him, but all the same he had voiced his own thoughts. It *had* been a ludicrous incident, but its humour did not appeal to him particularly. Both those shots should have been by the pin. Just what the Pro had said. It was very curious. "I'm going to hate that hole," he thought.

"There's a damned funny mark on my ball," grumbled the Colonel. "I suppose it hit a tree, though I could swear it didn't. Looks more like a burn. Why, there's the same thing on yours!"

Mr. Baxter examined them. They were funny symmetrical little marks, and they were remarkably like burns. "The wind must have caught them and blown them into the trees," he said, unconvincingly. "It's rather a gloomy spot in there, and it's hard to follow the flight exactly."

After tea the secretary went round to see Dakers.

"Well," he said, "I've tried the new hole."

"I saw you out, sir," said the Pro, smiling. "Did you get your four?"

"I almost deserved it," said Mr. Baxter. "My third was played like a golfer, and lined on the pin. I found it in a rabbit hole underneath the left bank."

"That's what I told you, sir. It's that sort of hole. I shall be interested to see how the members like it next week. In this wind it's certainly *some* hole."

"You mentioned last night something about talk in the village," insinuated Mr. Baxter. "What kind of talk?"

"Well, sir, there's been quite a clack, still is, for that matter; they're a funny, old-fashioned lot, with funny ideas. Do you know, sir, they won't go into that wood after dusk!"

"Why on earth not?"

"They don't seem to think it's healthy somehow; they call it 'Blood Wood,' some old superstition or other. I think some of them were a bit ashamed of feeling that way till the contractor's men died; but that started them off again."

"It's a pretty vague sort of yarn," said the secretary musingly. "Do they go into detail at all?"

"No, sir, it's a village tradition of very old standing. I should say. They are scared of the wood. Old Jim the Cobbler's father was found dead, apparently murdered, in it, and there are other tales of the old times like that."

Sunday was a busy day for Mr. Baxter. The Dormy House filled up steadily, and by the evening the highly satisfactory total of forty-four, mostly hale, and slightly too hearty elderly gentlemen had assembled.

The autumn meeting opened in a full easterly gale, and it was a battered and weary collection of competitors who arrived back at the clubhouse.

Mr. Baxter, greeting them as they came in, found them on one subject unanimously eloquent. They one and all cherished loathing mingled with respect for the new seventeenth. The secretary examined their cards with curiosity. Only one five was recorded; the average was eight. When young Cyril Ward, the only scratch player in the club, came in, the secretary asked him how he had fared. "My ancient friend," he replied, "I accomplished seventeen holes in seventy-two strokes; good going in this wind; my total is eighty. I give you one guess as to the other hole."

"Oh, the seventeenth, I suppose."

"You've said it. Baxter, there's something funny about it. I hit two perfect shots and then took six more to hole out."

"I'm sure of it," said the secretary, "but I'm getting most remarkably sick of hearing about it."

After the second round of the thirty-six holes stroke competition Mr. Baxter found himself the centre of one of the fiercest indignation meetings in the history of the golf game. Everyone had something to say. Eventually he was forced to promise that, if at the end of the week they were still of the same opinion, he would have the old seventeenth restored. "But," said he, "all this chopping and changing will cost us a lot of money."

"More likely save us a bit," grumbled a protestant. "I lost three new balls there today. Have you noticed what a stench there was coming from the back of the green?"

Cyril Ward went for a stroll with Mr. Baxter when the debate was over. "I wish the old boys weren't so impatient," he said. "That hole has beaten me badly twice, but I'd like to have many more shots at it. I shall protest strongly if they decide to change back. Look at it now, the green's like a pool of blood!"

("A sinister but apt description," thought Mr. Baxter.)

The sun was setting in a wild and tortured sky, and its fiery dying rays certainly painted the seventeenth a sanguine hue.

"It's funny you should say that," he remarked. "It's called 'Blood Wood' by the locals."

"From what I heard of the expletives used by our worthy fellow foozlers, they certainly agree with them," laughed Ward.

That night Mr. Baxter had a short but disturbing dream. He seemed to hear a deep bell tolling sullenly, and then suddenly a voice cried, "Sacred to the memory of Cyril Ward, who screamed once in Blood Wood," and then came a discordant chorus of vile and bestial laughter, and he awoke feeling depressed and ill at ease.

"This absurd business is getting on my nerves," he thought, "I'm even dreaming about it," and he suddenly felt he wanted to leave

Duncaster, and the sooner the better. It was too lonely and idle a life, he decided.

The next day the gale continued, bringing torrents of rain with it, and there was no competition. The course was a melancholy and deserted waste. Mr. Baxter, as he worked in his office could hear the great breakers booming beyond the dunes. About six the rain dwindled to a light drizzle, and Cyril Ward came in to see him, a couple of clubs under his arm. "There's just enough light to let me defeat that blasted hole," he said; "the swine fascinates me!"

Mr. Baxter found himself rather vehemently trying to persuade him otherwise. "I shouldn't; it's still raining, and it will be almost dark in the wood."

"Oh, rot," said Ward, and presently the secretary saw him tee up and drive off. He watched him until he had almost reached the wood, and then someone called him to settle a point of bridge law. The windows of the smoking room were open, and the gale suddenly increased in fury.

Mr. Baxter had just given his decision when there came a long scream of agony shaking down the wind. He rushed to the door, the other occupants of the room hustling after him.

That terrible cry had come from the wood, and they began running toward it. Suddenly just visible in the gloom, a figure came staggering out from the wood, threw up its arms, and fell. Mr. Baxter dashed toward it as he had not run for twenty years, the others after him.

Cyril Ward was lying on his back, his eyes wide, staring, and horrible—obviously dead.

Amongst those who came up was the local doctor, who knelt down and made a short examination. "Must be heart. I believe he had a weakness there, poor Cyril!" Mr. Baxter helped to carry the body back to the Dormy House; his burden was Cyril's left leg, a disgusting dangling thing. The memory of his dream came back to him, and his nerves shook. He tried to find reassurance by telling himself that such premonitions were common enough, however inexplicable.

It was decided at an informal meeting that the links should be closed the next day out of respect for the dead, but that the foursomes should be held on the Thursday. "A very typically British compromise," thought Mr. Baxter.

"Will an inquest be necessary?" he asked the doctor.

"I think not; it's clearly a case of heart."

"Did you notice his eyes?" asked the secretary.

The doctor gave him a quick glance. "I did," he replied, "but these attacks are often very painful. But did *you* notice that appalling stink coming from the wood?"

"Yes," said the secretary shortly.

"Well, I should find out the cause; it can't be healthy."

"I will tomorrow," said Mr. Baxter.

The next day he spent in his office, and never before had a sense of the futility of his occupation so swept over him. This shifting of pieces of india rubber from one spot to another! Oh, that a man should have to spend his few and gloriously potential days fussing about such banality! Perhaps he was only pitying himself. He went back to his card-marking. He felt utterly weary when he went to bed, and fell immediately asleep. "Boom! Boom! Boom!" there came that terrible tolling. He *must* wake! He must not hear what was to come. "Sacred to the memory of Sybil Grant, who screamed twice in Blood Wood," and once again came that foul and wicked laughter.

He awoke sweating and unnerved. He got up and mixed himself the strongest whiskey and soda of his temperate existence. "Sybil Grant! Sybil Grant!" Thank God, he knew no one of that name! He tried to read, till light came.

He went down to the clubhouse after breakfast, and met the doctor. "Hullo," said the latter, "you're not looking very fit! What's the matter?"

"Oh, just a rotten night," said the secretary. "By the way, I sent the green-keeper to find out about that smell, but he couldn't discover any cause for it; and, as a matter of fact, says he couldn't smell anything."

"Well, he's a lucky man," said the doctor. "It was the most loathsome reek I've encountered, and I've met a few!"

After the foursomes had started, everyone desperately light-hearted and pathetically determined to allow no echo of the horror of a few hours before to disturb the atmosphere of laboured cheerfulness, Mr. Baxter felt he must be alone. He wandered off to the long no man's land between the dunes and the sea, a famous haunt of sea birds; the sand showed everywhere the delicate tracings of their soft little feet.

As he reached the darker strata just surrendered by the angry, fading tide, his eye was caught by a patch of scarlet moving down to the sea some distance to his left. "A girl going to bathe," he thought casually. "She must have warm blood in her to face such a sea on such a day. I hope she knows what she's about. It's none too safe a spot." Presently he saw a man run down to join her, and felt reassured and yet depressed. "To be a dingy old bachelor like myself is the one unanswerable indictment. Ten King's Councillors could not make it seem excusable."

Then his mind turned to the question of the new post he was determined to secure. He would go up to London as soon as the meeting was over and get an exchange if possible.

His work kept him busy all the afternoon, and he did not emerge from his office till dusk was falling. "Best figure in England," he heard the Colonel declaring, as he entered the smoking room. "I believe she's engaged to Bob Renton."

"Who's that?" asked the secretary.

"The Grant girl," said the Colonel. "Sybil Grant."

The secretary felt a tug of horror at his heart.

"Is she coming down here?" he asked sharply.

"She is here," replied the Colonel. "If you'd been here ten minutes ago you'd have seen her."

"Well, where is she now?" asked the secretary, seizing his arm. "Where is this girl?" he cried, his voice rising.

"Hullo, young feller, what's all the excitement? I imagine she's about at the seventeenth green; she's staying with the Bartletts at the Old Cottage, and is walking back that way."

At that moment a bell seemed to toll once shatteringly in the secretary's ears. He put his hands to his head, and without a word started running frantically down the seventeenth fairway. Suddenly there sprang down the wind a terrible cry of terror, followed by a desperate and prolonged scream. Mr. Baxter stopped dead and shuddered. He heard shouts behind him and the patter of others running. He tottered on. Somebody—several people—passed him; as he reeled into the wood he could see the firefly gleam of electric torches, and as he neared them he could see they were focused on some object on the ground. It was white, and someone was kneeling over it. When he saw what it was he was suddenly and violently sick. It was flung down the bank, it was naked, its head was lolling hideously. It was sprawling, one knee flung high, its face—but someone covered that face with his coat and told Mr. Baxter to go for the doctor. And that terrible death stench kept him company.

The inquest was fixed for the following Monday, and Mr. Baxter was told his testimony would be required.

The little village swarmed with police and reporters. There hadn't been a mystery of such possibilities for many moons, and the whole country was stirred. Murder so foul cried out for vengeance. But there was no arrest, "And there never will be," thought Mr. Baxter as he took his stand in the improvised witness-box in the village school. The coroner, a corpulent, hirsute, and pompous person, soon put to him the question he had anticipated. "I understand that you started to run toward the scene of the tragedy before these screams were heard: is that so?"

"Yes," replied the secretary.

"Why was that?"

And then Mr. Baxter uncontrollably laughed.

"I may be mistaken," said the coroner, "but this hardly seems a laughing matter."

"I must beg your pardon," said Mr. Baxter. "I laughed against my will, I laughed because I suddenly realised how absurd you would consider my explanation to be."

"That is quite possible," said the coroner, "but I must ask you to let me hear it."

"I had a premonition, a dream."

"Of what character?"

"Well, I dreamed that Miss Grant would be killed."

"Did you warn her?"

"I had never heard of her except in this dream. I did not know she was here till I was so informed a moment before these screams were heard."

"A curious story," replied the representative of law and order, who clearly regarded Mr. Baxter as a person of limited intelligence and dubious veracity.

"Murder by some person or persons unknown," was the verdict, and unknown he, she, or they remained.

*

The nine days ran their course, police and reporters departed, and Mr. Baxter went off to London, where he secured a job at a new course in Surrey. He was to have no successor at Duncaster. Resignations poured in, and it was decided at a final meeting of the committee that the links should be abandoned.

On arriving in London it occurred to Mr. Baxter to call upon a friend of his, a Mr. Markes. He very much wanted an expert confidant, and Mr. Markes, besides being very wealthy, was by some trick of temperament fascinated by all types of psychic phenomena, and had amassed the finest library on such matters in the world.

"Jim," asked the secretary, "is there any mention of Duncaster in your records?"

"When I read about your troubles there," replied Mr. Markes, "I thought they sounded rather in the tradition, and so I looked up the history of Duncaster and was unexpectedly fortunate; for it is mentioned in a work, which, for the most part, is deservedly forgotten. *The Memoirs of Simon Tylor*, a peculiarly dull dog. I have them here," he continued, walking over to a shelf and taking down a bulky volume.

"In the year 1839 Simon took a walking tour through Norfolk and arrived at Duncaster on September tenth. He liked the look of it, and decided to spend a couple of days there at the inn, 'The Sleeping Sentinel.'"

"It is there still," said Mr. Baxter.

"All this," went on Mr. Markes, "is described at vast and damnable length, but his adventure, which occurred on the second evening of his stay, is much more crisply done. I will read it to you:

"I spent a pleasing and invigorating morning wandering over the wild expanse of moor and 'dunes,' as they call the great sand mounds; and afterward dined, rested, and had some talk with my good host of the inn. Late in the afternoon I decided to make further exploration of the neighbourhood, and, noticing a fine wood of tall trees some distance away across the moor, I remarked to my host that I proposed to visit it. Greatly to my surprise he strongly opposed my doing so, but when I asked him for what reason, he returned me evasive replies—'No one wanders there after nightfall,' he said. 'It has a bad repute.'

"'On account of robbers?' I asked. And though he replied with a short laugh that that was so, I did not believe it was the thought in his mind. To satisfy him, I declared that I would but walk toward it, a promise I had better have kept.

"So I wandered out as the light was fading, and drew near to the wood. Then I put it to myself that such village gossip was in most cases but idle tradition inscribed in the long and sparsely furnished memories of country folk. And this decision prevailing, I entered the wood, following a rough pathway. And then I had reason to doubt my host's word, for instead of it being shunned by the local folk it seemed that the wood did house quite a company. The light being low and the trees growing close, I failed clearly to distinguish my companions, but only, as it were, out of the corner of my eye, I glimpsed them many times. 'Lovers,' thought I. After I had traversed some two hundred paces I noted some little way in front of me a low mound with a single fine tree at its back. I was just fancying that I would go so far and then return when a movement in the gloom caught my eye, and at the same instant I perceived a very vile and curious stench. Something seemed to be reclining on the mound, a beast of some sort, and slowly gaining its feet. And then I knew the beginning of fear. This thing seemed to rise and rise till it towered above the tree, and then it couched its head as for a spring. I have no wish to see its like again. Seized with a great loathing and horror, I ran back along the path, and as I ran it seemed that many were running beside me and closing in upon me. I felt the Thing was close beside me, but I dared not turn to look. Just as my breath was leaving me I found myself at the edge of the wood, and then something seemed to touch me, and I screamed and swooned.

"When I regained my senses I found I was prone on the ground and my host and some others were standing round me conversing in low tones. They helped me back to the Inn, no one saying a word. I left early the next morning, that stench still lingering in my nostrils and the host seeming to avoid talk with me. All this is the truth as I have set it down."

"And that's what happened to Simon," said Markes.

"A curious story," said Mr. Baxter.

"Far more curious than uncommon. I could find you a dozen almost identical experiences. Almost certainly the work of our friends the Druids, whoever they were! A mound and an oak—such places are death traps. Not all the time; the peril is periodic. Why, we don't know. But our friend Simon was very lucky to be able to leave 'early next morning,' though he didn't escape altogether. The rest of his book reads like a coda to this adventure. Bad dreams, depression and always that smell in his nose. He died within a year or two. And now tell me exactly what happened at Duncaster, for I gather it is still a disturbed area."

So Mr. Baxter told him the curious events connected with the new seventeenth.

1931

THE CROWN DERBY PLATE

Marjorie Bowen

Marjorie Bowen was the best-known pseudonym of Gabrielle Margaret Vere Campbell (1885–1952). She was born on Hayling Island, Hampshire, and raised by her mother—her alcoholic father having left when she was young. By all accounts she had a poor upbringing, turning her hand early to writing in order to support her mother and sister. Her first novel, set in fourteenth-century Italy and titled *The Viper of Milan*, was penned when she was 16 (though it wasn't published until 1906)—it was read by a 14-year-old Graham Greene, leading him to later say that: "I think it was Miss Bowen's apparent zest that made me want to write. One could not read her without believing that to write was to live and to enjoy." Historical fiction formed much of her prolific output, but in addition she produced work for children, true crime, mysteries and biographies—and a number of her books were adapted into films. Several of her novels deal with witchcraft and the occult, including *Black Magic* (1909) and the posthumous *The Man with the Scales* (1954). However, it is for her supernatural short stories (around forty-five in total) that she is probably best remembered today.

One of her most well-known tales, rightly, is "The Crown Derby Plate". It's atypical of the genre in its light, almost comedic tone, but for me still possesses a visceral, chilling quality that lingers long after you've finished reading—much like the indescribable smell that pervades Hartleys, the solitary house on those Essex marshes. That setting too—its dampness and bleakness—is evocative and beautifully described. And I can never now see a piece of Crown Derby china without thinking of Marjorie Bowen's wonderful tale.

Martha Pym said that she had never seen a ghost and that she would very much like to do so, "particularly at Christmas for you can laugh as you like, that is the correct time to see a ghost."

"I don't suppose you ever will," replied her cousin Mabel comfortably, while her cousin Clara shuddered and said that she hoped they would change the subject for she disliked even to think of such things.

The three elderly, cheerful women sat round a big fire, cosy and content after a day of pleasant activities; Martha was the guest of the other two, who owned the handsome, convenient country house; she always came to spend her Christmas with the Wyntons and found the leisurely country life delightful after the bustling round of London, for Martha managed an antique shop of the better sort and worked extremely hard. She was, however, still full of zest for work or pleasure, though sixty years old, and looked backwards and forwards to a succession of delightful days.

The other two, Mabel and Clara, led quieter but none the less agreeable lives; they had more money and fewer interests, but nevertheless enjoyed themselves very well.

"Talking of ghosts," said Mabel, "I wonder how that old woman at Hartleys is getting on, for Hartleys, you know, is supposed to be haunted."

"Yes, I know," smiled Miss Pym, "but all the years that we have known of the place we have never heard anything definite, have we?"

"No," put in Clara; "but there *is* that persistent rumour that the house is uncanny, and for myself, *nothing* would induce me to live there!"

"It is certainly very lonely and dreary down there on the marshes," conceded Mabel. "But as for the ghost—you never hear *what* it is supposed to be even."

"Who has taken it?" asked Miss Pym, remembering Hartleys as very desolate indeed, and long shut up.

"A Miss Lefain, an eccentric old creature—I think you met her here once, two years ago—"

"I believe that I did, but I don't recall her at all."

"We have not seen her since, Hartleys is so un-get-at-able and she didn't seem to want visitors. She collects china, Martha, so really you ought to go and see her and talk 'shop.'"

With the word "china" some curious associations came into the mind of Martha Pym; she was silent while she strove to put them together, and after a second or two they all fitted together into a very clear picture.

She remembered that thirty years ago—yes, it must be thirty years ago, when, as a young woman, she had put all her capital into the antique business, and had been staying with her cousins (her aunt had then been alive) that she had driven across the marsh to Hartleys, where there was an auction sale; all the details of this she had completely forgotten, but she could recall quite clearly purchasing a set of gorgeous china which was still one of her proud delights, a perfect set of Crown Derby save that one plate was missing.

"How odd," she remarked, "that this Miss Lefain should collect china too, for it was at Hartleys that I purchased my dear old Derby service—I've never been able to match that plate—".

"A plate was missing? I seem to remember," said Clara. "Didn't they say that it must be in the house somewhere and that it should be looked for?"

"I believe they did, but of course I never heard any more and that missing plate has annoyed me ever since. Who had Hartleys?"

"An old connoisseur, Sir James Sewell; I believe he was some relation to Miss Lefain, but I don't know—"

"I wonder if she has found the plate," mused Miss Pym. "I expect she has turned out and ransacked the whole place—"

"Why not trot over and ask?" suggested Mabel. "It's not much use to her, if she has found it, one odd plate."

"Don't be silly," said Clara. "Fancy going over the marshes, this weather, to ask about a plate missed all those years ago. I'm sure Martha wouldn't think of it—"

But Martha did think of it; she was rather fascinated by the idea; how queer and pleasant it would be if, after all these years, nearly a lifetime, she should find the Crown Derby plate, the loss of which had always irked her! And this hope did not seem so altogether fantastical, it was quite likely that old Miss Lefain, poking about in the ancient house, had found the missing piece.

And, of course, if she had, being a fellow-collector, she would be quite willing to part with it to complete the set.

Her cousin endeavoured to dissuade her; Miss Lefain, she declared, was a recluse, an odd creature who might greatly resent such a visit and such a request.

"Well, if she does I can but come away again," smiled Miss Pym. "I suppose she can't bite my head off, and I rather like meeting these curious types—we've got a love for old china in common, anyhow."

"It seems so silly to think of it—after all these years—a plate!"

"A Crown Derby plate," corrected Miss Pym. "It is certainly strange that I didn't think of it before, but now that I have got it in my head I can't get it out. Besides," she added hopefully, "I might see the ghost."

So full, however, were the days with pleasant local engagements that Miss Pym had no immediate chance of putting her scheme into practice; but she did not relinquish it, and she asked several different people what they knew about Hartleys and Miss Lefain.

And no one knew anything save that the house was supposed to be haunted and the owner "cracky".

"Is there a story?" asked Miss Pym, who associated ghosts with neat tales into which they fitted as exactly as nuts into shells.

But she was always told—"Oh, no, there isn't a story, no one knows anything about the place, don't know how the idea got about; old Sewell was half-crazy, I believe, he was buried in the garden and that gives a house a nasty name—"

"Very unpleasant," said Martha Pym, undisturbed.

This ghost seemed too elusive for her to track down; she would have to be content if she could recover the Crown Derby plate; for that at least she was determined to make a try and also to satisfy that faint tingling of curiosity roused in her by this talk about "Hartleys" and the remembrance of that day, so long ago, when she had gone to the auction sale at the lonely old house.

So the first free afternoon, while Mabel and Clara were comfortably taking their afternoon repose, Martha Pym, who was of a more lively habit, got out her little governess cart and dashed away across the Essex flats.

She had taken minute directions with her, but she had soon lost her way.

Under the wintry sky, which looked as grey and hard as metal, the marshes stretched bleakly to the horizon, the olive-brown broken reeds were harsh as scars on the saffron-tinted bogs, where the sluggish waters that rose so high in winter were filmed over with the first stillness of a frost; the air was cold but not keen, everything was damp; faintest of mists blurred the black outlines of trees that rose stark from the ridges above the stagnant dykes; the flooded fields were haunted by black birds and white birds, gulls and crows, whining above the long ditch grass and wintry wastes.

Miss Pym stopped the little horse and surveyed this spectral scene, which had a certain relish about it to one sure to return to a homely village, a cheerful house and good company.

A withered and bleached old man, in colour like the dun landscape, came along the road between the sparse alders.

Miss Pym, buttoning up her coat, asked the way to "Hartley" as he passed her; he told her, straight on, and she proceeded, straight indeed across the road that went with undeviating length across the marshes.

"Of course," thought Miss Pym, "if you live in a place like this, you are bound to invent ghosts."

The house sprang up suddenly on a knoll ringed with rotting trees, encompassed by an old brick wall that the perpetual damp had overrun with lichen, blue, green, white colours of decay.

Hartleys, no doubt, there was no other residence of human being in sight in all the wide expanse; besides, she could remember it, surely, after all this time, the sharp rising out of the marsh, the colony of tall trees, but then fields and trees had been green and bright—there had been no water on the flats, it had been summer-time.

"She certainly," thought Miss Pym, "must be crazy to live here. And I rather doubt if I shall get my plate."

She fastened up the good little horse by the garden gate which stood negligently ajar and entered; the garden itself was so neglected that it was quite surprising to see a trim appearance in the house, curtains at the window and a polish on the brass door knocker, which must have been recently rubbed there, considering the taint in the sea damp which rusted and rotted everything.

It was a square-built, substantial house with "nothing wrong with it but the situation," Miss Pym decided, though it was not very attractive, being built of that drab plastered stone so popular a hundred years ago, with flat windows and door, while one side was gloomily shaded by a large evergreen tree of the cypress variety which gave a blackish tinge to that portion of the garden.

There was no pretence at flower-beds nor any manner of cultivation in this garden where a few rank weeds and straggling bushes matted together above the dead grass; on the enclosing wall, which appeared to have been built high as protection against the ceaseless winds that swung along the flats, were the remains of fruit trees; their crucified branches, rotting under the great nails that held them up, looked like the skeletons of those who had died in torment.

Miss Pym took in these noxious details as she knocked firmly at the door; they did not depress her; she merely felt extremely sorry for anyone who could live in such a place.

She noticed, at the far end of the garden, in the corner of the wall, a headstone showing above the sodden colourless grass, and remembered what she had been told about the old antiquary being buried there, in the grounds of Hartleys.

As the knock had no effect she stepped back and looked at the house; it was certainly inhabited—with those neat windows, white curtains and drab blinds all pulled to precisely the same level.

And when she brought her glance back to the door she saw that it had been opened and that someone, considerably obscured by the darkness of the passage, was looking at her intently.

"Good afternoon," said Miss Pym cheerfully. "I just thought that I would call to see Miss Lefain—it is Miss Lefain, isn't it?"

"It's my house," was the querulous reply.

Martha Pym had hardly expected to find any servants here, though the old lady must, she thought, work pretty hard to keep the house so clean and tidy as it appeared to be.

"Of course," she replied. "May I come in? I'm Martha Pym, staying with the Wyntons, I met you there—"

"Do come in," was the faint reply. "I get so few people to visit me, I'm really very lonely."

"I don't wonder," thought Miss Pym; but she had resolved to take no notice of any eccentricity on the part of her hostess, and so she entered the house with her usual agreeable candour and courtesy.

The passage was badly lit, but she was able to get a fair idea of Miss Lefain; her first impression was that this poor creature was most dreadfully old, older than any human being had the right to be, why, she felt young in comparison—so faded, feeble, and pallid was Miss Lefain.

She was also monstrously fat; her gross, flaccid figure was shapeless and she wore a badly cut, full dress of no colour at all, but stained with earth and damp where Miss Pym supposed she had been doing futile gardening; this gown was doubtless designed to disguise her stoutness, but had been so carelessly pulled about that it only added to it, being rucked and rolled "all over the place" as Miss Pym put it to herself.

Another ridiculous touch about the appearance of the poor old lady was her short hair; decrepit as she was, and lonely as she lived she had actually had her scanty relics of white hair cropped round her shaking head.

"Dear me, dear me," she said in her thin treble voice. "How very kind of you to come. I suppose you prefer the parlour? I generally sit in the garden."

"The garden? But not in this weather?"

"I get used to the weather. You've no idea how used one gets to the weather."

"I suppose so," conceded Miss Pym doubtfully. "You don't live here quite alone, do you?"

"Quite alone, lately. I had a little company, but she was taken away, I'm sure I don't know where. I haven't been able to find a trace of her anywhere," replied the old lady peevishly.

"Some wretched companion that couldn't stick it, I suppose," thought Miss Pym. "Well, I don't wonder—but someone ought to be here to look after her."

They went into the parlour, which, the visitor was dismayed to see, was without a fire but otherwise well kept.

And there, on dozens of shelves was a choice array of china at which Martha Pym's eyes glistened.

"Aha!" cried Miss Lefain. "I see you've noticed my treasures! Don't you envy me? Don't you wish that you had some of those pieces?"

Martha Pym certainly did and she looked eagerly and greedily round the walls, tables, and cabinets while the old woman followed her with little thin squeals of pleasure.

It was a beautiful little collection, most choicely and elegantly arranged, and Martha thought it marvellous that this feeble ancient creature should be able to keep it in such precise order as well as doing her own housework.

"Do you really do everything yourself here and live quite alone?" she asked, and she shivered even in her thick coat and wished that Miss Lefain's energy had risen to a fire, but then probably she lived in the kitchen, as these lonely eccentrics often did.

"There was someone," answered Miss Lefain cunningly, "but I had to send her away. I told you she's gone, I can't find her, and I am so glad. Of course," she added wistfully, "it leaves me very lonely, but then I couldn't stand her impertinence any longer. She used to say that it was her house and her collection of china! Would you believe it? She used to try to chase me away from looking at my own things!"

"How very disagreeable," said Miss Pym, wondering which of the two women had been crazy. "But hadn't you better get someone else."

"Oh, no," was the jealous answer. "I would rather be alone with my things, I daren't leave the house for fear someone takes them away—there was a dreadful time once when an auction sale was held here—"

"Were you here then?" asked Miss Pym; but indeed she looked old enough to have been anywhere.

"Yes, of course," Miss Lefain replied rather peevishly and Miss Pym decided that she must be a relation of old Sir James Sewell. Clara and Mabel had been very foggy about it all. "I was very busy hiding all the china—but one set they got—a Crown Derby tea service—"

"With one plate missing!" cried Martha Pym. "I bought it, and do you know, I was wondering if you'd found it—"

"I hid it," piped Miss Lefain.

"Oh, you did, did you? Well, that's rather funny behaviour. Why did you hide the stuff away instead of buying it?"

"How could I buy what was mine?"

"Old Sir James left it to you, then?" asked Martha Pym, feeling very muddled.

"She bought a lot more," squeaked Miss Lefain, but Martha Pym tried to keep her to the point.

"If you've got the plate," she insisted, "you might let me have it—I'll pay quite handsomely, it would be so pleasant to have it after all these years."

"Money is no use to me," said Miss Lefain mournfully. "Not a bit of use. I can't leave the house or the garden."

"Well, you have to live, I suppose," replied Martha Pym cheerfully. "And, do you know, I'm afraid you are getting rather morbid and dull, living here all alone—you really ought to have a fire—why, it's just on Christmas and very damp."

"I haven't felt the cold for a long time," replied the other; she seated herself with a sigh on one of the horsehair chairs and Miss Pym noticed with a start that her feet were covered only by a pair of white stockings; "one of those nasty health fiends," thought Miss Pym, "but she doesn't look too well for all that."

"So you don't think that you could let me have the plate?" she asked briskly, walking up and down, for the dark, neat, clean parlour was very cold indeed, and she thought that she couldn't stand this much longer; as there seemed no sign of tea or anything pleasant and comfortable she had really better go.

"I might let you have it," sighed Miss Lefain, "since you've been so kind as to pay me a visit. After all, one plate isn't much use, is it?"

"Of course not, I wonder you troubled to hide it—"

"I couldn't *bear*," wailed the other, "to see the things going out of the house!"

Martha Pym couldn't stop to go into all this; it was quite clear that the old lady was very eccentric indeed and that nothing very much could be done with her; no wonder that she had "dropped out" of everything and that no one ever saw her or knew anything about her, though Miss Pym felt that some effort ought really to be made to save her from herself.

"Wouldn't you like a run in my little governess cart?" she suggested. "We might go to tea with the Wyntons on the way back, they'd be delighted to see you, and I really think that you do want taking out of yourself."

"I was taken out of myself some time ago," replied Miss Lefain. "I really was, and I couldn't leave my things—though," she added with pathetic gratitude, "it is very, very kind of you—"

"Your things would be quite safe, I'm sure," said Martha Pym, humouring her. "Who ever would come up here, this hour of a winter's day?"

"They do, oh, they do! And *she* might come back, prying and nosing and saying that it was all hers, all my beautiful china, hers!"

Miss Lefain squealed in her agitation and rising up, ran round the wall fingering with flaccid yellow hands the brilliant glossy pieces on the shelves.

"Well, then, I'm afraid that I must go, they'll be expecting me, and it's quite a long ride; perhaps some other time you'll come and see us?"

"Oh, must you go?" quavered Miss Lefain dolefully. "I do like a little company now and then and I trusted you from the first—the others, when they do come, are always after my things and I have to frighten them away!"

"Frighten them away!" replied Martha Pym. "However do you do that?"

"It doesn't seem difficult, people are so easily frightened, aren't they?"

Miss Pym suddenly remembered that Hartleys had the reputation of being haunted—perhaps the queer old thing played on that; the lonely house with the grave in the garden was dreary enough around which to create a legend.

"I suppose you've never seen a ghost?" she asked pleasantly. "I'd rather like to see one, you know—"

"There is no one here but myself," said Miss Lefain.

"So you've never seen anything? I thought it must be all nonsense. Still, I do think it rather melancholy for you to live here all alone—"

Miss Lefain sighed:

"Yes, it's very lonely. Do stay and talk to me a little longer." Her whistling voice dropped cunningly. "And I'll give you the Crown Derby plate!"

"Are you sure you've really got it?" Miss Pym asked.

"I'll show you."

Fat and waddling as she was, she seemed to move very lightly as she slipped in front of Miss Pym and conducted her from the room, going slowly up the stairs—such a gross odd figure in that clumsy dress with the fringe of white hair hanging on to her shoulders.

The upstairs of the house was as neat as the parlour, everything well in its place; but there was no sign of occupancy; the beds were covered with dust sheets, there were no lamps or fires set ready. "I suppose," said Miss Pym to herself, "she doesn't care to show me where she really lives."

But as they passed from one room to another, she could not help saying:

"Where do *you* live, Miss Lefain?"

"Mostly in the garden," said the other.

Miss Pym thought of those horrible health huts that some people indulged in.

"Well, sooner you than I," she replied cheerfully.

In the most distant room of all, a dark, tiny closet, Miss Lefain opened a deep cupboard and brought out a Crown Derby plate which her guest received with a spasm of joy, for it was actually that missing from her cherished set.

"It's very good of you," she said in delight. "Won't you take something for it, or let me do something for you?"

"You might come and see me again," replied Miss Lefain wistfully.

"Oh, yes, of course I should like to come and see you again."

But now that she had got what she had really come for, the plate, Martha Pym wanted to be gone; it was really very dismal and depressing in the house and she began to notice a fearful smell—the place had been shut up too long, there was something damp rotting somewhere, in this horrid little dark closet no doubt.

"I really must be going," she said hurriedly.

Miss Lefain turned as if to cling to her, but Martha Pym moved quickly away.

"Dear me," wailed the old lady. "Why are you in such haste?"

"There's—a smell," murmured Miss Pym rather faintly.

She found herself hastening down the stairs, with Miss Lefain complaining behind her.

"How peculiar people are—*she* used to talk of a smell—"

"Well, you must notice it yourself."

Miss Pym was in the hall; the old woman had not followed her, but stood in the semi-darkness at the head of the stairs, a pale shapeless figure.

Martha Pym hated to be rude and ungrateful but she could not stay another moment; she hurried away and was in her cart in a moment—really—that smell—

"Good-bye!" she called out with false cheerfulness, "and thank you *so* much!"

There was no answer from the house.

Miss Pym drove on; she was rather upset and took another way than that by which she had come, a way that led past a little house raised above the marsh; she was glad to think that the poor old creature at Hartleys had such near neighbours, and she reined up the horse, dubious as to whether she should call someone and tell them that poor old Miss Lefain really wanted a little looking after, alone in a house like that, and plainly not quite right in her head.

A young woman, attracted by the sound of the governess cart, came to the door of the house and seeing Miss Pym called out, asking if she wanted the keys of the house?

"What house?" asked Miss Pym.

"Hartleys, mum, they don't put a board out, as no one is likely to pass, but it's to be sold. Miss Lefain wants to sell or let it—"

"I've just been up to see her—"

"Oh, no, mum—she's been away a year, abroad somewhere, couldn't stand the place, it's been empty since then, I just run in every day and keep things tidy—"

Loquacious and curious the young woman had come to the fence; Miss Pym had stopped her horse.

"Miss Lefain is there now," she said. "She must have just come back—"

"She wasn't there this morning, mum, 'tisn't likely she'd come, either—fair scared she was, mum, fair chased away, didn't dare move her china. Can't say I've noticed anything myself, but I never stay long—and there's a smell—"

"Yes," murmured Martha Pym faintly, "there's a smell. What—what—chased her away?"

The young woman, even in that lonely place, lowered her voice.

"Well, as you aren't thinking of taking the place, she got an idea in her head that old Sir James—well, he couldn't bear to leave Hartleys, mum, he's buried in the garden, and she thought he was after her, chasing round them bits of china—"

"Oh!" cried Miss Pym.

"Some of it used to be his, she found a lot stuffed away, he said they were to be left in Hartleys, but Miss Lefain would have the things sold, I believe—that's years ago—"

"Yes, yes," said Miss Pym with a sick look. "You don't know what he was like, do you?"

"No, mum—but I've heard tell he was very stout and very old—I wonder who it was you saw up at Hartleys?"

Miss Pym took a Crown Derby plate from her bag.

"You might take that back when you go," she whispered. "I shan't want it, after all—"

Before the astonished young woman could answer Miss Pym had darted off across the marsh; that short hair, that earth-stained robe, the white socks, "I generally live in the garden—"

Miss Pym drove away, breakneck speed, frantically resolving to mention to no one that she had paid a visit to Hartleys, nor lightly again to bring up the subject of ghosts.

She shook and shuddered in the damp, trying to get out of her clothes and her nostrils—that indescribable smell.

1935

MISS DE MANNERING OF ASHAM

F. M. Mayor

Flora Macdonald Mayor (1872–1932) was a novelist and short-story writer. Her clergyman father was a Classics professor at King's College, London, while her mother was a linguist and musician. She grew up in southwest London before, unusually for the time, attending Newnham College, Cambridge, where she studied History. Her fiancé died from typhoid in India in 1904 and this tragedy, along with severe asthma, curtailed a short acting career. Her first book, *Mrs. Hammond's Children*, was a collection of children's stories and was published under the pseudonym of Mary Strafford in 1901, and it was not until 1913 that her first adult book, the novel *The Third Miss Symons*—a powerful psychological study of its titular character—was published. Her second, and best-known novel, *The Rector's Daughter*, came in 1924, followed by a third, *The Squire's Daughter*, in 1929.

The Room Opposite: And Other Tales of Mystery and Imagination was issued posthumously in 1935, and it is here that we find the East Anglian-set "Miss de Mannering of Asham" as well as several other effective ghostly tales. M. R. James, no less, gave the following recommendation on the book's front flap: "The stories in this volume which introduce the supernatural commend themselves to me very strongly."

"OCT. 9.

"My dear Evelyn,

"As you say you really are interested in this experience of mine, I am doing what you asked, and writing you an account of it. You can accept it as a token of friendship for, to tell you the truth, I had been trying to forget it, whatever it was. I hope in the end to bring myself to the belief that I never had it, but at present my remembrance is more vivid than I care for.

"YOURS AFFECTIONATELY,
"MARGARET LATIMER."

*

You remember my friend, Kate Ware? She had been ill, and she asked me to stay in lodgings with her at an East Coast resort. "It is simply Brixton-by-the-Sea, with a dash of Kensington," Kate wrote, "but I ought to go, because my aunt lives there, and likes to see me. So come, if you can bear it."

"I think we might take a day off," said Kate one morning, after we had been there a week. "Too much front makes me think there really is no England but this. Let's have some sandwiches, and bicycle out as far away as we can."

We came to a wayside inn, so quiet, so undisturbed, so cheerful in its quietness, that we felt at last we had found the soothing and rest we were in need of. Yes, I suppose our nerves were a little unstrung; at any rate, being high school mistresses, we knew what nerves were. But hitherto I have felt capable of controlling mine, only, as Hamlet says, I have bad dreams. And Kate is rather strange by nature; I do not think her nerves make her any stranger.

"Now," said Kate, when we had finished our meal—she always settles everything—"I propose we borrow the pony here, and have a drive. I don't like desecrating these solitary lanes, which have existed for generations and generations before bicycles, with anything more modern than Tommy."

Kate generally wants to have a map, and know exactly where she is going, but today we agreed to take the first turn to the left, and see where it led to. It was a sleepy afternoon, and Tommy trotted so gently that we were all three dozing, before we had gone a mile or two. Then we came to what had been magnificent wrought iron gates with stone pillars on either side. The pillars were now ruined, and the wall beyond was falling down. Kate said, "Let's go in." I said it was private, but we did go in.

We came into an avenue of laurels, resembling the sepulchral shrubberies with which our fathers and our fathers' fathers loved to surround their residences, only those were generally more serpentine. It must have been there many years, and had had time to grow so high as to block out almost all the sky. It was very narrow, and the dankness, the closeness, the black ground that never gets dry, which have always oppressed me in such places, seemed almost intolerable here. I thought we should never get out to the small piece of white light we saw at the end of it. At the same time I dreaded what I expected to find there; one of those great, lugubrious, black mausoleums of a mansion, which so often are the complement of the shrubbery. But this avenue seemed to have been planted at haphazard, for it led only to another gate, and that opened on a neglected park. We saw before us an expanse of unfertile-looking grass, and then the horizon was completely hidden by ridges of very heavy greenish-black trees. There were other trees scattered about; they looked very old, and some had been struck by lightning. I felt sorry for their wounds; it seemed as if no one cared whether they lived or died.

There was a small church standing at the left-hand corner of the park, so small that it must have been a chapel for the private worship of the owners of the park; but we thought they could not have valued their church, for there was actually no path to it, nothing but grass, long, rank and damp.

I do not know when it was that I became so certain that I abhorred parks, but I remember it came over me very strongly all of a sudden. I was extremely anxious that Kate should not know what I felt. However, I said to her that grandeur was oppressive, and that after all I preferred small gardens.

"Yes," said Kate, "one might feel too much enclosed, if one lived in a park, as if one could never get out, and as if other things..."

Here Kate stopped. I asked her to go on, and she said that was all she had to say. I don't know if you want to hear these minute details, but nearly everything I have to tell you is merely a succession of minute details. I remember looking up at the sky, because I wanted to keep my eyes away from the distant trees. I did not like to see them—it seems a very poor reason for a woman of thirty-eight—because they were so black. When I was six years old, I was afraid of black, and also, though I loved the country, I used to feel a sense of fear and isolation, if the sun was not shining, and I was alone in a large field; but then a child's mind is open to every terror, or rather it creates a terror out of everything. I thought I had as much forgotten that condition as if I had never known it. I should have supposed the weight of my many grown-up years would have defended me, but I assure you that I felt all at once that I was—what after all we are—as much at the mercy of the universe as an insect.

I remember when I looked up at the sky I observed that it had changed. As we were coming it had had the ordinary pale no-colour aspect, which it bears for quite half the days in the year. Some people grumble at it, but it is very English, and if you do not like it, or more than like it, relish it, you cannot really relish England. The sky had now that strange appearance to which days in the north are liable; I do not think they know anything about it in Italy or the south of France. It is a fancy of mine that the sudden strangeness and wildness one finds in our literature is due to these days; it is something to compensate us for them.

If I said the day was dying, you would think of beautiful sunsets, and certainly the day could not be dying, for it was only three o'clock in the afternoon, but it looked ill; and the grey of the atmosphere was not that silvery grey, which I think the sweetest of all the skies in the year, but an unwholesome grey, which made the trees look blacker still. I should have felt it a relief if only it had begun to rain, then there would have been a noise; it was so utterly silent.

Just as I was wondering where I should turn my eyes next, Tommy came to a sudden stop, and nearly jerked us out of the cart. "Clever," said Kate, "you're letting Tommy stumble."

But it was simply that Tommy would not go on. He was such a mild little pony too, anxious, as Kate said, to do everything one asked, before one asked him.

"Tommy's frightened," said Kate. "He's all trembling and sweating."

Kate got out, and tried to soothe him, but for some time it was very little good.

"It's another snub for the men of science," said Kate. "Tommy sees an angel in the way. Animals are very odd you know. Haven't you noticed dogs scurrying past ghosts in the twilight? I am so glad we haven't got their faculties."

Then Tommy all at once surprised us by going on as quietly as before.

We drove a little further, and we came to the hall. It was built 150 years before the mausoleum period, but it could not well have been drearier, though it must formerly have been a noble Jacobean mansion. It was not that it looked out of repair; a house can be very cheerful, in fact rather more cheerful, if it is shabby. And here there was a terrace with greenhouse plants in stucco vases placed at intervals, and also a clean-shaven lawn, so that man must have been there recently; nevertheless it seemed as if it had been abandoned for years.

I cannot tell you how relieved I was when a respectable young man in shirt sleeves made his appearance. It is Kate generally who talks to strangers, but the moment he was in sight I felt I must cling to him, as a protection. I felt Tommy and Kate no protection.

I apologised for trespassing in private grounds.

"No trespassing at all, miss, I'm sure." He went on to say he wished it happened oftener, Colonel Winterton, the owner, being hardly ever there, only liking to keep the place up with servants, and "if there wasn't a number of us to make it lively, one room being shut up and all," he really did not know—

It did not seem right to encourage him on the subject of a shut-up room; we changed the conversation, and asked him about the church.

He said it was a very ancient church, and there was tombs and that, people came a wonderful way to see. Not that he cared much about them himself.

Kate, who is fond of sight-seeing, declared she would visit the church.

I would not go, though I should like to have seen the tombs. I said I must hold the pony. The young man said he was a groom, and would hold the pony for us. Then I said I was tired: Kate said she would go alone. She started.

"Don't go down there, miss," said the groom, "the grass is so wet. Round by the right it's better."

His way looked the same as her's to me, but Kate followed his advice.

I talked to the groom while Kate was away, and I was glad to hear that he liked the pictures in reason, and that his father was a saddler, living in the High Street of some small town. This was cheerful and distracting to my thoughts, and I had managed to become so much interested that it was the young man who said, "There's the lady coming back."

"Well," I said, "what was the church like?"

"It was locked," Kate answered, "however, it was nice outside."

"But Kate," I said, "how pale you are!"

"Of course I am," said Kate. "I always am."

The young man hastened to ask if he should get Kate a glass of water.

"Oh dear no, thank you," said Kate. "But I think we might be going now. Is there any other road out? I don't want to drive exactly the same way back."

There was, and we set off. As soon as we had said good-bye to the young man, Kate began: "About Grace Martin; what do you think of her chances for the Certificate?" and we talked about the Certificate until we got back to the inn. As to that oppressed feeling, I could hardly imagine now what it was. It had passed, and the world seemed its usual dear, safe self, irritating and comfortable. It was clearing up, and the trees and hedges looked as they generally look at the end of August. They were dusty and a little shabby, showing here and there a red leaf, occasional bits of toadflax, and all those little yellow flowers whose names one forgets, but to which one turns tenderly in recollection, when seeing the beauty of foreign lands. My thoughts broke away from our conversation now and then to wonder what I could possibly have been afraid of.

They gave us tea at Tommy's home, and the innkeeper's wife was glad to have some conversation.

"Yes the poor old Hall, it seems a pity the Colonel coming down so seldom. He only bought it seven years ago, and he seems tired of it already and then only bringing gentlemen. Gentlemen spend more, but I always think there's more life with ladies. It's changed hands so often. Yes, there's a shut-up room. They say it was something about a housemaid many years ago and a baby, if you'll excuse my mentioning it, but I'm sure I couldn't say. If you listen to all the tales in a village like this, in a little place you know, one says one thing and one another. I come from Norwich myself."

"The church looks rather dismal," said Kate. "The churchyard is so overgrown."

"Yes, poor Mr. Fuller, he's a nice gentleman, though he is so high. First when he come there was great goings on, services and antics. He says to me, 'Tell me, Mrs. Gage, is that why the people don't come?' 'Oh,' I says, 'well, of course, I've been about, and seen life, so whether it's high or low, I just take no notice.' I said that to put him off, poor gentleman, because it wasn't that. They won't come at all hardly after dark, particularly November; December it's better again; and for his communion service, what he sets his heart on so, we have such a small party, sometimes hardly more than two or three, and then he gets so downhearted. He seems to have lost all his spirit now."

"But why is it better in December?"

"I'm sure I couldn't tell you, miss, but they always say those things is worse in November. I always heard my grandfather say that."

I had rather expected that what I had forgotten in the day would come back at night, and about two, when I was reading *Framley Parsonage* with all possible resolution, I heard a knock at the door, and Kate came in.

"I saw your light," said she. "I can't sleep either. I think you felt uncomfortable in the park too, didn't you? Your face betrays you rather easily, you know. Going to the church, at least not going first of all, but as I got near the church, and the churchyard—ugh! However, I am *not* going to be conquered by a thought, and I mean to go there tomorrow. Still, I think, if you don't very much mind, I should like to sleep in here."

I asked her to get into my bed.

"Thank you, I will," said she. "It's very good of you, Margaret, for I'm sure you loathe sharing somebody's bed as much as I do, but things being as they are—"

The next morning Kate was studying the guidebook at breakfast.

"Here we are," said she. "'Asham Hall is a fine Jacobean mansion. The church, which is situated in the park, was originally the private chapel of the de Mannerings. Many members of the family are buried there, and their tombs are well worth a visit. The inscriptions in Norman French are of particular interest. The keys can be obtained from the sexton.' Nothing about the shut-up room; I suppose we could hardly hope for it. We must see the tombs, don't you think so?"

Kate was one who very rarely showed her feelings, and I knew better than to refer to last night.

We bicycled to the Hall. It was a very sweet, bright, windy morning, such a morning as would have pleased Wordsworth, I think, and may have brought forth many a poem from him.

"Now," said Kate, "when we get into the park, we'll walk our bicycles over the grass to the church."

I began: then exactly the same feeling came over me as before, only this time there could be nothing in calm, beautiful nature to have produced it. The trees, though dark, did not look at all sinister, but stately and benignant, as they often do in late August, and early September. Whatever it was, it was within me. I felt I could not go to the church.

"You go on alone," I said.

"You'd better come," said Kate. "I know just what you feel, but it will be worse here by yourself."

"I think perhaps I won't," I said.

"Very well," said Kate. "Bicycle on and meet me at the other gate."

I said I was a coward, and Kate said she did not think it mattered being a coward. I meant to start at once, but I found something wrong with the bicycle. It took quite half an hour to repair, but as I was repairing it all my oppression passed, and I felt light and at ease. By the time I was ready, Kate had visited the tombs, and was coming out of the church door. I looked at her going down the path, and saw there was another woman in the churchyard. She was walking rather slowly. She came up behind Kate, then passed quite close to Kate on her left side. I was too far off to see her face. I felt thankful Kate had someone with her. I mounted; when I looked again the woman was gone.

I met Kate outside the church. She always had odd eyes; now they had a glittering look, half scared and half excited, which made me very uncomfortable. I asked her if she had spoken to the woman about the church.

"What woman? Where?" said Kate.

"The one in the churchyard just now."

"I didn't see anyone."

"You must have. She passed quite close to you."

"Did she," said Kate. "She passed on my left side then?"

"Yes, she did. How did you know?"

"Oh, I don't know. We give the keys in here, and let's bicycle home fast, it's turned so cold."

I always think Kate rather manlike, and she was manlike in her extreme moodiness. If anything of any sort went wrong, she clothed herself in a mood, and became impenetrable. Such a mood came on her now.

"I don't know why I never will tell things at the time," said Kate next day. It was raining, and we were sitting over a nice little fire after tea. "It's a sign of great feebleness of mind, I think. However, if you like to hear about Asham Church, you shall. I saw the tombs, and they are all that they should be. I hope the de Mannerings were worthy of them. But the church; perhaps being a clergyman's daughter made me take it so much to heart, but there was a filthy old carpet rolled up on the altar, all the draperies are full of holes, the paint is coming off, part of the chancel rail is broken, and it seems an abode of insects. I did not know there were such forsaken churches in England. That rather spoilt the tombs for me, also an uncomfortable idea that I did not want to look behind me; I don't know what I thought I was going to see. However, I gave every tomb its due. Then, when I was in the churchyard, I had the same feeling as last time; I could not get it out of my head that something I did not like was going to happen the next minute. Then I had that sensation, which books call the blood running chill; that really means, I think, a catch in one's heart as if one cannot breathe; and at the same time I had such an acute consciousness of someone standing at my left side that I almost felt I was being pushed, no one being there at all, you understand. That lasted a second, I should think, but after that I felt as if I were an intruder in the churchyard, and had better go."

One afternoon a week later, the great-aunt of the smart townlike landlady at our lodgings came to clear away tea. First of all she was deferential and overwhelmed, but I have never known anyone have such a way with old ladies and gentlemen of the agricultural classes as Kate. In a few moments Mrs. Croucher was sitting on the sofa with Kate beside her.

"Asham Hall," said she. "Why, my dear mother was sewing maid there, when she was a girl. Oh dear me, yes, the times she's told me about it all. Oh, it's a beautiful place, and them lovely laurels in the avenue, where Miss de Mannering was so fond of walking. It was the old gentleman, Mr. de Mannering, he planted them; they was to have gone right up to the Hall, so they say. There was to be wonderful improvements, he was to have pulled down the old Hall and built something better, and then he hadn't the money. Yes, even then it was going down, for Mr. William, that was the only son, that lived abroad, he was so wild. Yes, my mother was there in the family's time, not with them things which hev a-took it since."

"You don't think much of Colonel Winterton, then?"

"Oh, I daresay he's a kind sort of gentleman, they say he's very free at Christmas with coals and that, but them new people they comes and goes, it stands to reason they can't be like the family. In the village we calls them jumped-up bit-of-a-things, but I'm sure I've nothing to say against Colonel Winterton."

"Are there any of the family still here?"

"Oh no, mum. They've all gone. Some says there's a Mr. de Mannering still in America, but he's never been near the place."

"It's very sad when the old families go," said Kate sympathetically.

"Oh, it is, mum. Poor old Mr. de Mannering; but the place wasn't sold till after his death. My mother, she did feel it."

"Was there a room shut up in your mother's time, Mrs. Croucher?"

"Not when she first went there, mum."

"It was a housemaid, wasn't it?"

"Not a housemaid," with a look of important mystery. "That's what they say, and it's better it *should* be said; I shouldn't tell it to everybody, but I don't mind telling a lady like you; it wasn't a housemaid at all."

"Not a housemaid?"

"No; my mother's often told me. Miss de Mannering, she was a very high lady, well, she was a lady that *was* a lady, if you catch my meaning, and she must have been six or seven and forty, when she was took with her last illness. And the night before she died, my mother she was sitting sewing in Mrs. Packe's room (she was the lady's maid, my mother was sewing maid, you know) and she heard Doctor Mason say, 'Don't take any notice of what Miss de Mannering says, Mrs. Packe. People get very odd fancies, when they're ill,' he says. And she says, 'No, sir, I won't,' and she comes straight to my mother, and she says, 'If you could hear the way she's a-going on. "Oh, my baby," she says, "if I could have seen him smile. Oh, if he had lived just one day, one hour, even one moment." I says to her, says Mrs. Packe to my mother, "Your baby, ma'am, whatever are you talking about?" It was such a peculiar thing for her to say,' says Mrs. Packe. 'Don't you think so, Bessie?' Bessie was my mother. 'I'm sure I don't know,' says my mother; she never liked Mrs. Packe. 'Miss de Mannering didn't take no notice,' Mrs. Packe went on, 'then she says, "If only I'd buried him in the churchyard." So I says to her, "But where did you bury him then, ma'am?" and fancy! she turns round, and looks at me, and she says, "I burnt him."' Well, that's the truth, that's what my mother told me, and she always said, my mother did, Mrs. Packe had no call to repeat such a thing."

"I think your mother was quite right," said Kate. "Burnt! Poor Miss de Mannering must have been delirious. It is such a frightful…"

"No, my mother didn't like carrying tales about the family," said Mrs. Croucher, engaged on quite a different line of thought. And whether it was that she had heard the story so often, or whether it was that they are still more inured to horrors in the country—I have observed far stranger things happen in the country than in the town—Mrs. Croucher did not seem to have any idea that she was relating what was terrible. On the contrary, I think she found it homely, recalling a happy part of her childhood.

"Then," went on Mrs. Croucher, "Mrs. Packe, she says to my mother, 'You come and hear her,' she says, and my mother says, 'I don't like to, whatever would she say?' 'Oh,' says Mrs. Packe, 'she don't take any notice of anything, you come and peep in at the door.' 'So I went,' my mother says, 'and I just peeped in, but I couldn't see anything, only just Miss de Mannering lying in bed, for there was no candle, only the firelight. Only I heard Miss de Mannering give a terrible sigh, and say very faint, but you could hear her quite plain, "Oh, if only I'd buried him in the churchyard." I wouldn't stay any longer,' says my mother, 'and Miss de Mannering died at seven in the evening next day.' Whenever my mother spoke of it to me, she always said, 'I only regretted going into her room once, and that was all my life. It was taking a liberty, which never should have been took.'"

"But," said Kate, framing the question with difficulty, "did anybody—? Had anybody had a suspicion that Miss de Mannering—?"

"No, mum. Miss de Mannering was always very reserved, she was not a lady that was at all free in her ways like some ladies; not like you are, if you'll excuse me, mum. Not that I mean she would have said anything to anyone of course, and she had no relations, no sisters, and they never had no company at the Hall, and the old gentleman, he'd married very late in life, so he was what you might call aged, and the servants was terrible afraid of him, his temper was so bad; even Miss de Mannering had a wonderful dread of him, they said.

"There was a deal of talk among the servants after what Mrs. Packe said, and there was a housemaid, she'd been in the family a long time, and she remembered one winter years before, I daresay eighteen or twenty years before, Miss de Mannering was ailing, and she sent away her maid, and then she didn't sleep in her own room, but in a room in another part of the house not near anyone, that's the room they shut up, mum. And they remembered once she was ill for months and months, and her nurse that lived at Selby, when she was very old, she got a-talking as sometimes old people will, she died years after Miss de Mannering, and she let out what she would have done better to keep to herself.

"It wasn't long after Miss de Mannering's death they began to say you could see her come out of that there room, walk down the stairs, out at the front door, down through the park, along the avenue, and back again to the house, and then across the park to the churchyard. And of course they say she's trying to find a place for her baby. Then there's some as says Mr. Northfield, what lived at Asham before Colonel Winterton came, he saw her. They say that's why he sold it. Mr. Fuller they say he's spoke to her; they say that's why he's turned so quiet.

"Then there's some say, Miss Jarvis—she kept The Blue Boar in the village, when I was a girl—she used to say, that Miss Emily Robinson, the daughter of Sir Thomas Robinson, who bought the place from Mr. Seaton, who bought it after Mr. de Mannering's death—he wasn't much of a 'Sir' to my mind, just kept a draper's shop in London, the saying was—she was took very sudden with the heart disease, and was found dead, flat on her face in the avenue. Of course the tale was, she met Miss de Mannering and she laid a hand on her. The footman that was attending Miss Robinson—she was regular pomped up with pride *she* was, and always would have a footman after her—he says he *see* a woman quite plain come up behind her, and then she fell. He told Mr. Jarvis. Poor Mrs. Dicey—they was at the Hall before the Northfields—she went off sudden too at the end, but she was always sickly, and I don't hold with all those tales myself.

"But people will believe anything. Why, not long ago, well, perhaps twenty years ago, in Northfield's time, there was a footman got one of the housemaids into trouble, and of course there's new people about in the village since the family went, and they say the room was shut up along of *her*. It's really ridickerlous."

"Did you ever see her, Mrs. Croucher?"

"Not to say see her, mum, but more than once as I've been walking in the park, I've *heard* her quite plain behind me. That was in November. November is the month, as you very well know, mum,"—I could see Kate was gratified that it was supposed she should know—"and you could hear the leaves a-rustling as she walked. There's no need to be frightened, if you don't take no notice, and just walk straight on. They won't never harm you; they only gives you a chill."

"Did your mother ever see her?"

"If she did, she never would say so. My mother wouldn't have any tales against Miss de Mannering. She said she never had any complaints to make. There was a young man treated my mother badly, and one day she was crying, and Miss de Mannering heard her, and she comes into the sewing-room, and she says, 'What is it?' and my mother told her, and Miss de Mannering spoke very feeling, and said, 'It's very sad, Bessie, but life is very sad.' In general Miss de Mannering never spoke to anybody.

"My mother bought a picture of Miss de Mannering, if you young ladies would like to see it. Everything was in great confusion when Mr. de Mannering died. Nothing had been touched for years, and there were all Miss de Mannering's dresses and her private things. No one had looked through them since her death. So what my mother could afford to buy she did, and she left them to me, and charged me to see they should never fall into hands that would not take care of them. There's a lot of writing I know, but I'm not much of a scholar myself, though my dear mother was, and I can't tell you what it's all about, not that my mother had read Miss de Mannering's papers, for she said that would never have been her place."

Mrs. Croucher went to her bedroom and brought us the papers and the portrait. It was a water-colour drawing dated Bath, 1805. The artist had done his best for Miss de Mannering with the blue sash to match the bit of blue sky, and the coral necklace to match her coral lips. The likeness presented to us was that of a young woman, dark, pale, thin, elegant, lady-like, long-nosed and plain. One gathers from pictures that such a type was not uncommon at that period. I should have been afraid of Miss de Mannering from her mouth and the turn of the head, they were so proud and aristocratic, but I loved her sad, timid eyes, which seemed appealing for kindness and protection.

Mrs. Croucher was anxious to give Kate the portrait, "for none of 'em don't care for my old things." Kate refused. "But after you are gone," she said, for she knows that all such as Mrs. Croucher are ready to discuss their deaths openly, "if your niece will send her to me, I should like to have Miss de Mannering; I shall prize her very much."

Then Mrs. Croucher withdrew, "for I shall be tiring you two young ladies with my talk." It is rather touching how poor people, however old and feeble, think that everything will tire "a lady," however young and robust.

We turned to Miss de Mannering's papers. It was strange to look at something, written over a century ago, so long put by and never read. I had a terrible sensation of intruding, but Kate said she thought, if we were going to be as fastidious as all that, life would never get on at all. So I have copied out the narrative for you. I am sure, if Mrs. Croucher knew you, she would feel you worthy to share the signal honour she conferred on us.

MISS DE MANNERING'S NARRATIVE

It is now twenty-two years since, yet the events of the year 1805 are engraved upon my memory with greater accuracy than those of any other in my life. It is to escape their pressing so heavily upon my brain that I commit them to paper, confiding to the pages of a book what may never be related to a human friend.

Had my lot been one more in accordance with that of other young women of my position, I might have been preserved from the calamity which befell me. But we are in the hands of a merciful Creator, who appoints to each his course. I sinned of my own free will, nor do I seek to mitigate my sin. My mother, Lady Jane de Mannering, daughter of the Earl of Poveril, died when I was five years old. She entrusted me to the care of a faithful governess and nurse, and owing to their affectionate solicitude in childhood and girlhood I hardly missed a mother's care. Of my father I saw but little. He was violent and moody. My brother, fourteen years older than I, was already causing him the greatest anxiety by his dissipation. Some words of my father's, and a chance remark, lightly spoken in my hearing, made an ineffaceable impression on me. In the unusual solitude of my existence I had ample, too ample, leisure to brood over recollections which had best be forgotten. Cheerful thoughts, natural to my age, should have left them no room in my heart. When I was thirteen years old, my father said to me one day, "I don't want you skulking here, you're too much of a Poveril. Everyone knows that a Poveril once, for all their pride, stooped to marry a French waiting-maid. That's why every man Jack of them is black and sallow, as you are." I fled from the room in terror.

Another day Miss Fanshawe was talking with the governess of a young lady who had come to spend the afternoon with me. They were walking behind us, and I heard their conversation.

"Is not Miss Maynard beautiful?" said Miss Adams. "I believe that golden hair and brilliant eye will make a sensation even in London. What a pity Miss de Mannering is so black! Fair beauties are all the rage they say, and her eyes are too small."

"Beauty is a very desirable possession for a young woman," said Miss Fanshawe, "but one which is perhaps too highly valued. Anyone may have beauty; a milkmaid may have beauty; but there is an air of rank and breeding which outlasts beauty, and is, I believe, more prized by a man of fastidious taste. Such an air is possessed by Miss de Mannering in a remarkable degree."

My kind, beloved Fan! but at fifteen how much rather would I have shared the gift possessed by milkmaids! From henceforth I was certain I should not please.

Miss Fanshawe, who never failed to give me the encouragement and confidence I lacked, died when I was seventeen and had reached the age which, above all others in a woman's life, requires the comfort and protection of a female friend. My father, more and more engrossed with money difficulties, made no arrangement for my introduction to the world. He had no relations, but my mother's sisters had several times invited me to visit them. My father, however, who was on bad terms with the family, would not permit me to go. The most rigid economy was necessary. He would allow no guests to be invited, and therefore no invitations to be accepted. The Hall was situated in a very solitary part of the country, and it was rare indeed for any visitor to find his way thither. My brother was forbidden the house. Months, nay years passed, and I saw no one.

Suddenly my father said to me one day, "You are twenty-five, so that cursed lawyer of the Poverils tells me; twenty-five, and not yet married. I have no money to leave you after my death. Write and tell your aunt at Bath that you will visit her, and she must find you a husband."

Secluded from society as I had been, the prospect of leaving the Hall and being plunged into the world of fashion filled me with the utmost apprehension. "I entreat you, sir, to excuse me," I cried. "Let me stay here. I ask nothing from you, but I cannot go to Bath."

I fell on my knees before him, but he would take no denial, and a few weeks after I found myself at Bath.

My aunt, Lady Theresa Lindsay, a widow, was one of the gayest in that gay city, and especially this season, for she was introducing her daughter Miss Leonora.

My father had given me ten pounds to buy myself clothes for my visit, but, entirely inexperienced as I was, I acquitted myself ill.

"My dear creature," said my cousin in a coaxing manner that could not wound. "Poor Nancy in the scullery would blush to see herself like you. You must hide yourself completely from the world for the next few days like the monks of La Trappe, and put yourself in Mamma's hands and mine. After that time I doubt not Miss Sophia de Mannering will rival the fashionable toast Lady Charlotte Harper."

My dear Leonora did all in her power to set me off to the best advantage, to praise and encourage me, and my formidable aunt was kind for my mother's sake. But my terror at the crowd of gentlemen, that filled my aunt's drawing-room, was not easily allayed.

"I tremble at their approach," I said to Leonora.

"Tremble at their approach?" said Leonora. "But it is their part to tremble at ours, my little cousin, to tremble with hopes that we shall be kind, or with fears that we shall not. I say my little cousin, because I am a giantess," she was very tall and exquisitely beautiful, "and also I am very old and experienced, and you are to look up to me in everything."

I wished to have remained retired at the assemblies, but Leonora always sought me out, and presented her partners to me. But my awkwardness and embarrassment soon wearied them, and after such attentions as courtesy required they left me for more congenial company. Certainly I could not blame them; it was what I had anticipated. Yet the mortification wounded me and I said to my cousin, "It is of no use, Leonora. I can never, never hope to please."

"Those who fish diligently," she replied, "shall not go unrewarded. A gentleman said to me this evening, 'Your cousin attracts me; she has so much countenance.' Captain Phillimore is accounted a connoisseur in our sex. That is a large fish, and I congratulate you with all my heart."

Captain Phillimore came constantly to my aunt's house. Once he entered into conversation with me. Afterwards he sought me out; at first I could not believe it possible, but again he sought me out, and yet again.

"Captain Phillimore is a connexion not to be despised by the ancient house of de Mannering," said my aunt. "There are tales of his extravagance it is true, and other matters; but the family is wealthy, and of what man of fashion are not such tales related? Marriage will steady him."

Weeks passed by. It was now April. My aunt was to leave Bath in a few days, and I was to return home; the season was drawing to its close. My aunt was giving a farewell reception to her friends. Captain Phillimore drew me into an anteroom adjoining one of the drawing-rooms. He told me that he loved me, that he had loved me from the moment he first saw me. He kissed me. Never, never can I forget the bliss of that moment. "There are," he said, "important reasons why our engagement must at present be known only to ourselves. As soon as it is possible I will apprise my father, and hasten to Asham to obtain Mr. de Mannering's consent. Till then not a word to your aunt. It will be safest not even to correspond." He told me that he had been summoned suddenly to join his regiment in Ireland and must leave Bath the following day. "I must therefore see you once more before I go. The night is as warm as summer. Have you the resolution to meet me in an hour's time in the garden? We must enjoy a few minutes' solitude away from the teasing crowd."

I, who was usually timid, had now no fears. I easily escaped unnoticed. The whole household was occupied with the reception. At the end of a long terrace there was an arbour. Here we met. He urged me to give myself entirely to him, using the wicked sophistries which had been circulated by the infidel philosophers of France; that marriage is a superstitious form with no value for the more enlightened of mankind. But alas, there was no need of sophistries. Whatever he had proposed, had he bidden me throw myself over a precipice, I should have obeyed. I loved him as no weak mortal should be loved. When his bright blue eye gazed into mine, and his hand caressed me, I sank before him as a worshipper before a shrine. With my eyes fully open I yielded to him.

I returned to the house. My absence had not been observed. My cousin came to my room, and said with her arch smile, "I ask no question, I am too proud to beg for confidences. But I know what I know. Kiss me, and receive my blessing."

I retired to rest, and could not sleep all night for feverish exaltation. It was not till the next day that I recognised my guilt. I hardly dared look my aunt and cousin in the face, but my demeanour passed unnoticed; for during the morning a Russian nobleman attached to the Imperial court, who had been paying Leonora great attentions, solicited her hand and was accepted. In the ensuing agitation I was forgotten, and my proposal that I should return to Asham a day or two earlier was welcomed. My aunt was anxious to go to London without delay to begin preparations for the wedding.

She made me a cordial farewell, engaging me to accompany her to Bath next year. "But, Mamma," said Leonora, "I think Captain Phillimore will have something to say to that. All I stipulate is that Captain and Mrs. Phillimore shall be my first visitors at St. Petersburgh."

Their kindness went through me like a knife, and I returned to Asham with a heavy heart.

"Where is your husband?" was my father's greeting.

"I have none, sir," said I.

"The more fool you," he answered, and asked no further particulars of my visit.

Time passed on. Every day I hoped for the appearance of Captain Phillimore. In vain; he came not. Certainty was succeeded by hope, hope by doubt, doubt by dread. I would not, I could not despair. Ere long it was evident that I was to become a mother. The horror of this discovery, with my total ignorance of Captain Phillimore's whereabouts, caused me the most miserable perturbation. I walked continually with the fever of madness along the laurel avenue and in the Park. I went to the Church, hoping that there I might find consolation, but the memorials of former de Mannerings reminded me too painfully that I alone of all the women of the family had brought dishonour on our name.

I longed to pour out my misery to some human ear, even though I exposed my disgrace. There was but one in my solitude whom I could trust; my old nurse, who lived at Selby three miles off. I walked thither one summer evening, and with many tears I told her all. She mingled her tears with mine. I was her nursling, she did not shrink from me. All in her power she would do for me. She knew a discreet woman in Ipswich, whither she might arrange for me to go as my time approached, who would later take charge of the infant. She suggested all that could be done to allay suspicion in the household and village.

At first my aunt and cousin wrote constantly, and even after Leonora's marriage I continued to hear from Russia. My letters were short and cold. When I knew that I was to be a mother, I could not bear to have further communication with them. My aunt wrote to me kindly and reproachfully. I did not answer, and gradually all correspondence ceased. Yet their affectionate letters were all I had to cheer the misery of those ensuing months. I shall never forget them. Although it was now summer, the weather was almost continuously gloomy and tempestuous. There were many thunder storms, which wrought havoc among our elm trees in the Park. The rushing of the wind at night through the heavy branches and the falling of the rain against my window gave me an indescribable feeling of apprehension, so that I hid my head under the bedclothes that I might hear nothing. Yet more terrible to me were the long days of August, when the leaden sky oppressed my spirit, and it seemed as if I and the world alike were dead. I struggled against the domination of such fancies, fancies perhaps not uncommon in my condition, and in general soothed by the tenderness of an indulgent husband. I could imagine such tenderness. Night and day Captain Phillimore was in my thoughts. No female pride came to my aid; I loved him more passionately than ever.

On the 20th of November some ladies visited us at the Hall. We had a common bond in two cousins of theirs I had met frequently in Bath. They talked of our mutual acquaintance. At length Captain Phillimore's name was mentioned. Shall I ever forget those words? "Have you heard the tale of Captain Phillimore, the all-conquering Captain Phillimore? Major Richardson, who was an intimate of his at Bath, told my brother that he said to him at the beginning of the season, 'What do you bet me that in one season I shall successfully assault the virtue of the three most innocent and immaculate maids, old or young, in Bath? Easy virtue has no charms for me, I prefer the difficult, but my passion is for the impregnable,' and Major Richardson assures my brother that Captain Phillimore won his bet. Mr. de Mannering, we are telling very shocking scandals; three ladies of strict virtue fallen in one season at Bath. What is the world coming to?"

My father had appeared to pay little heed to their chatter, but he now burst forth, "If any woman lets her virtue be assaulted by a rake, she's a rake herself. Should such a fate befall a daughter of mine, I should first horsewhip her, and then turn her from my doors."

During this conversation I felt a stab at the heart, so that I could neither speak nor breathe. How it was my companions noticed nothing I cannot say. I dared not move, I dared not leave my seat to get a glass of water to relieve me. Yet I believe I remained outwardly at ease, and as soon as speech returned, I forced myself to say with tolerable composure, "Major Richardson was paying great attention to Miss Burdett. Does your brother say anything of that affair?"

Shortly afterwards the ladies took their leave.

I retired to my room. I had moved to one in the most solitary part of the house, far from either my father or the servants. I tried in vain to calm myself, but each moment my fever became more uncontrollable. I dispatched a messenger to my nurse, begging her to come to me without delay. I longed to sob my sorrows out to her with her kind arms round me. The destruction of all my hopes was as nothing to the shattering of my idol. My love was dead, but though I might despise him, I could not, could not hate him.

Later in the day I was taken ill, and in the night my baby was born. My room was so isolated that I need have little fear of discovery. An unnatural strength seemed to be given me, so that I was able to do what was necessary for my little one. He opened his eyes; the look on his innocent face exactly recalled my mother. My joy who shall describe? I was comforted with the fancy that in my hour of trial my mother was with me. I lay with my sweet babe in my arms, and kissed him a hundred times. The little tender cries were the most melodious music to my ears. But short-lived was my joy; my precious treasure was granted me but three brief hours. It was long ere I could bring myself to believe he had ceased to breathe. What could I do with the lovely waxen body? The horror that my privacy would be invaded, that some intruder should find my baby, and desecrate the sweet lifeless frame by questions and reproaches, was unendurable. I would have carried him to the churchyard, and dug the little grave with my own hands. But the first snow of the winter had been falling for some hours; it would be useless to venture forth.

The fire was still burning; I piled wood and coal upon it. I wrapped him in a cashmere handkerchief of my mother's; I repeated what I could remember of the funeral service, comforting and tranquillising myself with its promises. I could not watch the flames destroy him. I fled to the other end of the room, and hid my face on the floor. Afterwards I remember a confused feeling that I myself was burning and must escape the flames. I knew no more, till I opened my eyes and found myself lying on my bed, with my nurse near me, and our attached old Brooks, the village apothecary, sitting by my side.

"How do you feel yourself, Miss de Mannering?" said he.

"Have I been ill?"

"Very ill for many weeks," said he, "but I think we shall do very well now."

My nurse told me that, as soon as my message had reached her, she had set out to walk to Asham, but the snow had impeded her progress, and she was forced to stop the night at an inn not far from Selby. She was up before dawn, and reached the Hall, as the servants were unbarring the shutters. She hastened to my room, and found me lying on the floor, overcome by a dangerous attack of fever. She tended me all the many weeks of my illness, and would allow none to come near me but the doctor, for throughout my delirium I spoke constantly of my child.

The doctor visited me daily. At first I was so weak that I hardly noticed him, but my strength increased, and with strength came remembrance. He said to me one morning, "You have been brought from the brink of the grave, Miss de Mannering. I did not think it possible that we should have saved you."

In the anguish of my spirit I could not refrain from crying out, "Would God that I had died."

"Nay," said he, "since your life has been spared, should you reject the gift from the hands of the Almighty?"

"Ah," I said in bitterness. "You do not know—"

"Yes, madam," said he, looking earnestly upon me, "I know all."

I turned from him trembling.

"Do not fear," he said. "That knowledge will never be revealed."

I remained with my face against the wall.

"My dear Madam," he said with the utmost kindness. "Do not turn from an old man, who has attended you since babyhood and your mother also. My father and my father before me doctored the de Mannerings, and I wish to do all in my power to serve you. A physician may sometimes give his humble aid to the soul as well as to the body. Let me recall to your suffering soul that all of us sinners are promised mercy through our Redeemer. I entreat you not to lose heart. Now for my proper domain, the body. You must not spend your period of convalescence in this inclement native county of ours. You must seek sun and warmth, and change of scene to cheer your mind."

His benevolence touched me, and my tears fell fast. Amid tears I answered him, "Alas, I am without friends; I have nowhere to go."

"Do not let that discourage us," he said with a smile, "we shall devise a plan. Let me sit by my own fireside with my own glass of whisky, and I shall certainly devise a plan."

By his generous exertions I went on a visit to his sister at Worthing. She watched over me with a mother's care, and I returned to Asham with my health restored. Peace came to my soul; I learnt to forgive him. The years passed in outward tranquillity, but in each succeeding November, or whenever the winds were high or the sky leaden, I would suffer, as I had suffered in the months preceding the birth of my child. My mind was filled with baseless fears, above all that I should not meet my baby in Heaven, because his body did not lie in consecrated ground. Nor were the assurances of my Reason and my Faith able to conjure the delusion: yet I had—

Here the writing stopped.

"Wait, though," said Kate, "there's a letter."

She read the following:

> "3 HEN AND CHICKEN COURT,
> "CLERKENWELL.
> "MARCH 7, 1810.

"Madam,

"I have been told that my days are numbered. Standing as I do on the confines of eternity, I venture to address you. Long have I desired to implore your forgiveness, but have not presumed so far. I entreat you not to spurn my letter. God knows you have cause to hate the name of him who betrayed you. Yes, Madam, my vows were false, but even at the time I faltered, as I encountered your trusting and affectionate gaze, and often during my subsequent career of debauchery has that vision appeared before me. Had I embraced the opportunity offered me by Destiny to link my happiness with one as innocent and confiding as yourself, I might have been spared the wretchedness which has been my portion.

"I AM MADAM, YOUR OBEDIENT SERVANT,

"FREDERIC PHILLIMORE."

I could not speak for a minute; I was so engrossed with thinking what Miss de Mannering must have felt when she got that letter.

Kate said, "I wonder what she wrote back to him. How often it has been folded and refolded, read and re-read, and do you see where words have got all smudged? I believe those are her tears, tears for that skunk!"

But I felt I could imagine better than Kate all that letter, with its stilted old-fashioned style, which makes it hard for us to believe the writer was in earnest, would have meant to Miss de Mannering.

"Tomorrow is our last afternoon," said Kate. "What do you think," coaxingly, "of making a farewell visit to Asham?"

But though Miss de Mannering is a gentle ghost, I do not like ghosts; besides, now I know her secret, I *could* not intrude upon her. So we did not go to Asham again. Now we are back at school, and that is the end of my story.

1936

THE HOUSE ON THE MARSH

Frederick Cowles

Frederick Ignatius Cowles (1900–1948) was born in Cambridge, where he began his working career as a librarian at Trinity College—an excellent environment for a fledgling author of ghost stories. He went on to write several books and articles on travel and folklore before having two dedicated collections of supernatural tales published during his lifetime: *The Horror of Abbot's Grange* (1936) and *The Night Wind Howls* (1938). Cowles's final collection, *Fear Walks the Night* remained unpublished until many years after his premature death, first appearing only in 1993. These later stories are far more assured and varied—and less dependent on derivative antiquarian plotlines. The earlier tales tend to feature reworkings of ideas by fellow writers, including E. F. Benson, Dennis Wheatley and Bram Stoker. And M. R. James, as you will see here. Although "The House on the Marsh" is influenced by James's "Lost Hearts", it is an atmospheric story in its own right and a more effective piece than "The Bell", another of Cowles's East-Anglian-set tales, which borrows heavily from the opening story of this collection.

I was in Italy when my Uncle Richard died, and no one was more surprised than I when I heard from his solicitor that he had left me a house in Norfolk and the sum of £3000 a year.

I hadn't seen my uncle since I was about nine years old, and could only vaguely remember him as a very young-looking man, with a pale face and intensely black eyes. Our last meeting had been at my father's house in Kent, and I recalled that I had been very frightened of him. There was something nasty about him, and he had an unpleasant way of fondling me on every possible occasion.

I think my father quarrelled with him very soon after this visit, for I never saw him again, nor was his name mentioned.

It was two months before I returned to England, and then I went at once to the chambers of my late uncle's solicitor in Gray's Inn. Mr. Priestley, of Priestley, Priestley, and Morton, turned out to be quite a charming little man, but he wasn't at all enthusiastic about the legacy.

"We attended to your uncle's business affairs," he said, "but, if you will excuse me for saying so, he was not a pleasant man. I only saw him about five times in twenty odd years, and there was always something uncanny about him. The most remarkable thing was the way he retained his youthful appearance—at least, I should say, he looked about twenty-five years old when I last saw him alive, although in death he was old and withered."

"How did he die?" I asked.

"Ah! That is a most shocking story. For years he had lived the life of a recluse in a dismal house on Brenton Marsh, about five miles from King's Lynn. He kept no servants, doing all his own shopping, and having a half-witted old woman in to tidy up about twice a week. The woman died about six months before your uncle, and he never replaced her.

"Just over two months ago I wanted your uncle's signature to a document, and sent one of my clerks down to Brenton to obtain it. The man knocked at the door of the house but could get no reply. All the windows were shuttered, and the place seemed deserted. Inquiries in the village revealed that Mr. Slade had not been seen about for some weeks.

"My clerk, a very sensible fellow, got hold of the local policeman, and together they went up to the place and forced an entrance. The house was in a filthy state, but there was no sign of your uncle in any of the ground-floor rooms or the bedrooms. At last they discovered him or what had been him, in a little attic under the roof. He had evidently been dead for over a week, and he had died by his own hand. A razor was at his side, and his throat was slashed across.

"My clerk told me that the most horrible part of the ghastly business was a swarm of horrible flies that were clinging to the wound.

"They wired for me at once, and I went down without delay. It was necessary for me to inspect the body, and, I can tell you, I got a shock. As I have already said, the last time I had seen your uncle alive he had the appearance of a young man. In death he was old and wizened. In fact I was only able to recognise him by his clothes and his watch and ring. Corruption had made the remains nauseating, and those loathsome flies were everywhere. As fast as we brushed them off his throat they returned again. The body was coffined that same night, and even then they swarmed on the top of the casket.

"An inquest had to be held, of course, and it was three days before we could bury him. I was the only mourner, and I shall never forget that funeral. The coffin was taken down to the church on a hand-bier, and all the way those flies buzzed about it. And then, in the middle of the service, the clergyman fainted. When he recovered all he would say was, 'Bury it! Bury it!' and so the service was never completed. It was a most ghastly business from beginning to end."

I was naturally shocked to hear such a horrible story, and had some thought of renouncing the legacy. But I am a poor man, and a house in Norfolk, together with £3000 a year, was a small fortune to me.

That afternoon I journeyed down to King's Lynn, and put up at a small hotel there. Next morning, accompanied by a house decorator, I went out to Brenton to inspect my property.

It turned out to be a rambling old house, standing alone in the marsh about a mile from the village. The garden must have been neglected for more than half a century, and a large pond, dark and weed-grown, was at the back.

The inside of the building was in an awful state. Filth was everywhere, the furniture was old and worn, and there were no coverings on the floor. Together we inspected the rooms, the decorator making his estimates. At last we climbed up to the attic.

It was a tiny place under the roof, and in the centre of the floor was what appeared to be a dark stain. Even as we looked at it the stain moved, and we saw that it was a swarm of beastly black flies. They made us both feel sick, and I instructed the man to have the door of the room securely fastened up.

As we passed through the garden gate on our way back to the village, I turned to look at the house again. I glanced up at the attic window, and there, pressed against the glass, was a white face. It was gone almost immediately, and I tried to convince myself that it had only been the reflection of a passing cloud.

Six weeks later I moved into the house on the marsh. My man, Jenkins, and a maidservant we had engaged in London, went down with me. The decorator had made a very good job of the place, and the rooms seemed almost homely and cheerful.

And yet I didn't like the house. My feelings were evidently shared by Jenkins, for, when he was serving dinner, he said: "I don't like this place, sir. There's something creepy about it, and that pond is awful."

"Nonsense!" I exclaimed. "You haven't been here long enough to form any opinion."

I spent the evening in the library looking through my uncle's books. He certainly had a queer taste in literature. Nearly all the volumes were about magic, witchcraft, and occultism, and many of them must have been very rare.

In one corner of the room was an old desk, and I found the drawers stuffed with letters, circulars, and miscellaneous papers. At the back of a pigeon-hole was a small calf-bound volume which seemed to be my late relative's diary. It was past eleven o'clock when I discovered it, so I deferred an inspection of its contents until another day.

As far as I was concerned the first night passed quietly enough. I slept well, although I did have one queer dream. It seemed that three young men came into my bedroom and stood over me. Their faces were very white, and each one had a ghastly wound in his breast.

In the morning there seemed to be a certain amount of tension in the atmosphere. After breakfast the maid came in to me and asked permission to leave at once.

"I can't stand this place, sir," she cried. "There is a tall man, with a white face, who peeps in at the windows."

Nothing would convince her of the folly of such a statement, and by midday she had left the house. Jenkins too seemed unnerved, but he had been with me for ten years and I could trust him not to leave.

In the afternoon I walked down to the village and called on the vicar. He was a quiet, studious type of man, an ex-Fellow of St. Chad's, from which college he held the living. I asked him point-blank what had caused him to faint at my uncle's funeral.

"I will tell you, Mr. Slade," he replied, "although I have never repeated this story to a living soul. I did not know your uncle, but he was a man with a most unsavoury reputation. All the villagers feared and hated him, although I have never been able to discover the reason for their antipathy.

"As I stood by the graveside, conducting the funeral service over his body, I noticed that hundreds of vile flies were clinging to the coffin. Into my mind came that verse from the 8th Chapter of Exodus, 'I will send swarms of flies upon thee.' Then, as I looked, it seemed that the insects formed themselves into the shape of a heart, and then the heart became red and bleeding. I saw gouts of blood drip from it, and I must have fainted. There was something unholy about your uncle, Mr. Slade, and no power on earth could induce me to finish the committal service. He was buried, but not with the full rites of the Church."

I thought over the parson's words as I crossed the marsh, and the more I thought of them the less I liked them. Jenkins was waiting for me at the gate, and I could see from his face that something had happened.

"For God's sake, sir," he blurted out, "let's get away from this place. The house is full of flies, there's a ghost in the library, and there's dead men in that pond."

With some difficulty I got a coherent story from him. It seems that, after I had left the house, Jenkins strolled out into the garden. He wandered down to the pond, and was gazing at the black water when he saw, or fancied he saw, three white faces looking up at him from the depths. For a moment he stood fascinated with horror, and then he fled back to the house. Then, as he was passing the library window, he swore that another white face looked out at him. For some time he dared not go in, and when he did overcome his fear he found the whole place swarming with flies.

I did my best to calm his fears, and we went inside together. It was just as he had said—the flies were everywhere. Black, hideous things of a species unknown to me.

Jenkins managed to dish up some sort of a dinner, and I made him sit at the table with me. He had risen to go over to the sideboard for the wine, and I was glancing at a newspaper, when he suddenly screamed. I looked up at once, and there, seated in the chair opposite—the chair just vacated by Jenkins—was my uncle Richard. He was dressed entirely in black, his face was deathly white, but his mouth was smeared with fresh red blood, and, buzzing around his head, were hundreds of those wretched flies. A more loathsome and terrifying sight I have never beheld. For a few moments I gazed spellbound at the apparition, and then it slowly faded away.

Neither Jenkins nor I could finish our meal. We got out of that awful room as quickly as possible, and went into the library. There we made ourselves as comfortable as the circumstances permitted, determining to spend the night in the room, and to leave the house first thing in the morning.

And then I remembered that little calf-bound volume, and thinking it might throw some light on the ghastly events, I fetched it from the desk. It wasn't exactly a diary: it was something far worse. The entries were few and were as follows.

"*March* 15, 1907. Today is my thirtieth birthday, and, if I am to test the theories of the ancients, I must soon make the experiment. I cannot bear the thought of this body of mine growing old with the years. Like the ancient philosophers I sought many years to discover the secret of eternal youth, and now success has crowned my efforts. Immortality is within my reach.

"Many of the occultists of the Middle Ages maintained that age could be conquered by those who had the courage to tear the heart from a living youth, and consume it while uttering certain mystic words. For five years I hunted the libraries of Europe for records of such an experiment, and last December I was fortunate enough to discover a fourteenth-century manuscript in a tiny library at Rhoenden, in Austria. The volume was the work of one Leo of Salzburg, and he claimed to have kept his youth for over a hundred years by repeating the experiment ten times. He recorded in detail the ritual to be observed, but stated that the actual formula to be uttered would be hidden in his coffin.

"On inquiring I found that this Leo had died at Rhoenden in 1454, and was buried in the ruined abbey of Sepeil, in the hills above the town. The grave was easy to discover. It was a stone vault, set in a side chapel of the abbey church. I determined to open it that very night. There was no danger of interruption, for the country people think the ruin is haunted and will not go near it after dusk.

"I secured the necessary tools and a lantern, and climbed up to the abbey about eight o'clock. The cover of the vault was difficult to raise, and I doubt if I should have managed it had it not been for a young man, who appeared suddenly from nowhere, and assisted me to lift the stone. I only caught a glimpse of his face, for, when I turned to thank him, he had gone. I was a little perturbed about this as I did not want any of the villagers to know of my activities.

"A flight of steps led down into the vault, and at the foot of them was the coffin standing on a stone slab. It was of lead and I had no difficulty in removing the lid. As I bent over the corpse a swarm of flies suddenly rose from it—so many of them that they seemed to fill the small chamber. How flies can have lived for centuries in a sealed coffin I cannot understand.

"The body seemed to be well preserved. It was wrapped in a black robe, and a square of linen covered the face. I removed this, and was horrified to find that the countenance beneath was that of the young man who had assisted me to raise the cover of the vault. My first inclination was to flee from the place, but, remembering that I must obtain possession of the formula at all costs, I mastered my fear. Under the head I found a small roll of vellum, and soon ascertained that this was the document I was in search of. As I was fitting the coffin lid on again, the flies came down and crept in through the edges. There was something ghastly about those flies living with the dead, and I was glad to get into the fresh air. It was easy to replace the stone.

"I left my implements under a buttress of the church, and, with the scroll safely in my pocket, returned to Rhoenden. I was possessed of the secret of eternal youth.

"*June* 30, 1907. Last night a young tramp called at the house to ask for food. I knew at once that he was the very person for my first experiment, and invited him to stay the night. A mild opiate in his beer ensured that he would sleep soundly, and, when I was certain that he was unconscious, I tied him firmly to the bed and gagged him. An hour or so later he awakened, and I was able to begin the ritual. After the solemn chant I braced my nerves, cut open his breast, tore out his living heart, and ate it. It was not unpleasant, and, when I had spoken the mystic words, I realised that new life was flowing through my veins.

"Fortunately I had had the forethought to put the young man in the attic, for he bled profusely. The body I have disposed of by placing it in a weighted sack and sinking it in the pond at the back of the house. One thing disturbs me. I have just been up to the attic to attempt to clean up the mess, and have found swarms of flies, similar in appearance to those that were in the coffin of Leo of Salzburg, feeding upon the blood.

"*June* 21, 1912. Five years have passed since my first experiment, and last night I was able to repeat my success. Yesterday, in Lynn, I fell in with a young foreign sailor, and invited him over to the house. He was friendless and alone, and came willingly enough. After drugging his beer I put him to sleep in the attic. Everything happened in the same manner as in my first attempt. He also is now at the bottom of the pond where he will find company awaiting him. But those awful flies are here again, gorging themselves on the blood.

"*June* 23, 1917. Again a victim has been found. This time I had to go to London before I could find a suitable subject for my experiment. I came across him in the East End—an unemployed youth who was glad to accept my offer of work. He did not take beer, but I was able to administer the drug in a cup of tea. In some manner he twisted the gag from his mouth, and screamed loudly when I was cutting him. I hope no one was crossing the marsh at the time. His body has joined those in the pond, and flies, thousands of them, are clearing up the blood on the floor.

"My experiments have certainly proved successful. Today I am just the same, in appearance and vitality, as I was fifteen years ago.

"*September* 2, 1922. I am in despair. The ritual must be repeated every five years if I am to retain my youth, and, for the past three months, I have sought a victim without success. The flies are all over the house. I have a horrible feeling that they will do me some hurt if I cannot supply them with the blood they require.

"*March* 20, 1923. Flies, flies, flies everywhere. They are sending me mad. Still I am unable to find a suitable person. Youth is slipping from me. I am growing old. I dare not face death, and yet I must die if I cannot perform the ritual.

"*May* 1, 1923. They buzz all around me. I must satisfy them before long. Only human blood will do. I have tried them with the blood of a dog, but it is of no use. Only human blood..."

Thus ended the terrible record of black and unnatural crime. How we got through that night I do not know. There we sat, huddled together, waiting for the dawn. At last it came, and, on opening the library door, we found the whole house to be full of those foul flies.

Jenkins packed our few personal effects, and removed the bags to the garden. Then we spread straw, soaked in paraffin, in all the ground-floor rooms and set light to it. Within a short time the old house was a blazing inferno, and in that holocaust perished, I hope, all the evil things that sheltered under its roof.

Last week the pond was drained, and, in the mud at the bottom, were found the bones of three young men. I have had them decently buried in the churchyard, and pray that I have destroyed for ever all memory of the filthy Satanic rites that made a haunted place of the house on the marsh.

1943

STIVINGHOE BANK

R. H. Malden

Richard Henry Malden (1879–1951) trod the same educational path as his mentor and friend, M. R. James, swapping Eton for King's College in 1895. After graduating from Cambridge he became a deacon in Manchester, eventually rising to the rank of the Dean of Wells in 1933, a role he served until just before his death. R. H. Malden published only one collection of supernatural tales, *Nine Ghosts* (1943), which was brought out during the Second World War by James's publisher Edward Arnold, who made grand claims on the dustjacket: "Dr. James has found his successor in the Dean of Wells." Malden's own introduction was more modest:

> It was my good fortune to know Dr. James for more than thirty years... Sufficient time has now elapsed since Dr. James's death to make some attempt to continue the tradition admissible or even welcome to his friends and readers. It is as such that these stories have been collected and revised now. They are in some sort a tribute to his memory, if not comparable to his work.

A couple of the stories from the collection, in particular, stand out to me. Perhaps because of it being set in the Fens landscape of my boyhood, I'm very fond of the atmospherically titled "Between Sunset and Moonrise". But, although it was a close call, here I've instead opted for a narrative inspired by north Norfolk: "Stivinghoe Bank". Its protagonist is visiting "Folkham House", where he hopes to peruse some antiquarian books in the library; the house fills in for the grand, real-life Holkham Hall that gazes north from the centre of the county's coastline. The narrator is staying in the nearby village of Stivinghoe, a place which bears a strong resemblance to Blakeney (also the inspiration for E. F. Benson's "A Tale of an Empty House"). Blakeney Point, the shingle spit that extends three miles out to the north-west in front of the village's harbour is one of the last vestiges of wildness remaining in East Anglia—and I can fully appreciate why these two master ghost-story writers found something otherworldly about its situation.

The coastline of Norfolk is one of those which have altered considerably in historic times. Along some stretches the sea has encroached. At low water traces of lost villages can still be seen, and in stormy weather pieces of wood from drowned forests are sometimes washed ashore. At Cromer a lighthouse which I remember has disappeared long since, though it was not very near the edge of the cliff when I knew it. A new one has been built at some distance inland.

Along other stretches the sea has receded and towns which were once thriving ports are separated from it by a wide expanse of marsh, where cattle graze and abundant mushrooms can be found in early autumn. These marshes are intersected by deep and muddy channels up which the tide creeps sluggishly. But even at high water nothing larger than an open boat can use them. The harbours whence the cloth was shipped in the great days of East Anglia, when Norwich was the third city in the kingdom and nearly wrested the second place from Bristol, are almost useless now. The towns which lived by them have dwindled to small villages. Here and there a fine old house may still be seen on the water-front. But for the most part the large and magnificent churches are all that remain of their former glories.

Melancholy as these villages are they have a beauty and dignity of their own. The wide horizon of marsh, beach and sea beyond gives a sense of spaciousness which can hardly be found elsewhere. Anyone who knows them will understand why a Norfolk nurserymaid when taken to Grasmere complained that she felt unable to breathe and that the mountains spoilt the view.

They have always been well known to sportsmen as the marshes teem with wildfowl in winter.

Of late years artists have begun to discover them. But I must admit that I hope they will never become popular resorts.

It was at one of them, which I will call Stivinghoe, that the experience (it hardly deserves to be called an adventure) which is set down here, befell me some years ago. If, when you have heard the story, you think it rather pointless, that is not my fault. I do not think that I should have admired Mr. Chadband[1] had I met him. But his insistence on what he called *The Terewth* always seemed to me worthy of imitation. And I could not make the story more exciting without departing from the standard set by that eloquent divine.

Stivinghoe differs from its neighbours in the possession of a bank; that is to say a causeway some eight feet high running across the marsh land and projecting beyond it into the sea. I suppose it is natural, as it is not easy to see why anyone should have taken the trouble to construct it. There is a rough track along the top. At the shoreward end the sides are clothed with coarse grass where sea-pinks and yellow horned poppies grow. The last half-mile is sand and shingle. At high water the sea comes up to it on both sides. When the tide is out it is flanked by a wide expanse of wet sand. At the far end there is a little hillock on which are the remains of a ruined chapel. It is as lonely and desolate a spot as can well be imagined. I suppose the chapel had escaped demolition because it had never been worth anyone's while to pull the walls down and cart the material away. It was a cell of the great house of Walsingham and had been established as a place where

---

[1] See *Bleak House*.

prayer might be offered continually for fishermen along the coast and all who got their living from the sea.

After the dissolution of the monasteries a large part of the lands of Walsingham had gone to the Earl of W., whose descendant is still one of the magnates of Norfolk. I had reason to believe that some books from the library had made their way to his great house at Folkham. There was no adequate catalogue of them and as I had known Lord W.'s son at Cambridge I ventured to write and ask whether I might come and look at them. His reply was very cordial. He regretted that he could not ask me to stay as the family was away and the house shut up. He had written to the housekeeper telling her to let me see anything I wanted, and added that while the only inn in the village was not to be recommended I should be sufficiently comfortable at the *Fishmongers' Arms* at Stivinghoe.

The map showed me that the distance from Stivinghoe to Folkham House was only about three miles. A bicycle would solve the question of transport. I had never slept at the *Fishmongers' Arms*, but had had tea there more than once when exploring the neighbourhood, and my recollection of it confirmed Lord W.'s opinion.

Accordingly I wrote engaging a bedroom (if possible with a table at which I could write) for a week and established myself there one fine afternoon in the middle of September.

The greater part of the next three days was spent in the library at Folkham. The result was, however, rather disappointing. The manuscripts were not many. Neither contents nor workmanship were of outstanding interest. I thought I had got to the end of them when I came upon a bundle of papers tied up with tape and docketed, in a modern hand, *Stivinghoe Chapel*.

The housekeeper had just come into the room with some tea and I noticed that she seemed to be disconcerted when she saw the bundle in my hand.

"Are these private papers, do you suppose?" I said. "They were on the same shelf as the other manuscripts. Is there any reason why I shouldn't read them? I see that somebody had them out not very long ago."

"Yes, Sir," she said. "That were his lordship's father, that were. The day before the great storm, not that that had anything to do with it, I do suppose. No, I don't see there'd be no harm—if so be as you're careful, Sir."

Of course I told her that I would take great care of them, that I was accustomed to handling old books and papers and so forth. But I couldn't help thinking that that was not quite what she meant.

It was too late to do any more that day. So I said I would come back and go through them tomorrow morning.

I mounted my bicycle at the front door expecting to enjoy the ride home as it was a beautiful evening. But somehow I did not. For some reason I felt uncomfortable and could not get rid of the idea that there was someone following me. Though after all why shouldn't there be on a public highroad? And what harm could he do me in broad daylight if he were evilly disposed? All the same so strong was the feeling that I looked behind me more than once. But I had the road to myself. All the same I rode faster than usual and was glad when I found myself at the *Fishmongers' Arms*.

After dinner I went into the bar-parlour as usual and got into conversation with its frequenters. The talk was of the usual description in such places. Interesting enough to anyone who, like myself, can find pleasure in listening to reminiscences of past harvests, speculations as to quality of the next one, the market prices of beasts and local affairs generally. But not worth attempting to set down here.

The company broke up early and I went early to bed. Contrary to my usual custom I did not sleep very well. I was troubled by a recurrent dream, the details of which eluded me, try as I would to recall them.

The general sense was that I was going somewhere where I expected to meet, or at least feared that I might meet, somebody whom I did not want to see. Just as I was on the point of coming face to face with him I always woke up. This performance was repeated with monotonous regularity four or five times between midnight (which I heard on the church clock) and dawn. As soon as it was light I gave up trying to go to sleep and read until it was time to get up.

After breakfast I bicycled to Folkham House as usual and got out the bundle of papers.

They proved more interesting than I had expected. They belonged to the years 1531–2 and appeared to relate to the incumbent of the chapel at the end of the bank. John of Costessey was his name.

The first document was brief. It was addressed to the Prior and Convent of Walsingham and was a request bearing about a dozen signatures, of which three seemed to be those of the rectors of Stivinghoe and two neighbouring villages, that John might be recalled to Walsingham and someone else despatched to take his place.

Presumably the Prior wrote, as he was bound to do, to ask the reason for this request, for the next letter was considerably longer. It appeared that John was suspected of having entered into a compact with the powers of evil. He was a man of violent and vindictive temper and it was noticeable that those who offended him were dogged by persistent and inexplicable misfortune. Next time they went to sea they met with no fish; or nets broke mysteriously as a catch was being brought on board. Unaccountable accidents, some fatal, occurred on board their boats. More than once a boat had been lost with all hands in a sudden and very violent storm, which had not been foreseen by the most weather-wise seamen along the coast.

More than once he had been seen from boats rounding the end of the bank close inshore to make the harbour, standing at the water's edge with an imp seated on his shoulder. The said imp had screamed and waved its arms [here followed an illegible word which I guessed to be meant for *devilishly*].

More than once at night-time the window of the Chapel had been seen to be brightly lighted, and bursts of song were heard proceeding from it. These melodies did not suggest the familiar offices of the Church and more than one voice seemed to be taking part.

Next came a letter from John himself, obviously in answer to a communication from the Prior. He protested that he could not be expected to reply in detail to such malicious and unfounded charges (*crimina tam perfida ac dolosa et omnino nugatoria*) and hinted that if his nocturnal vigils had been solaced by celestial company no fault could be found with him on that score (*quid in hoc improperii vel quae increpationis causa?*).

The Prior's answer to this may be inferred to have been a summons to repair to Walsingham forthwith. John's next letter was to the effect that his austerities, which it was his delight to practise, had made him too feeble to undertake the journey on foot, while the hard-heartedness and irreligion of the countryside, of which the Prior had had ample proof (*litteris supradictis satis probatum*), made it unlikely that any attempt to borrow so much as an ass would be successful.

The Prior could hardly be expected to put up with this, nor did he. He must have told John that he proposed to visit him in person, for the last letter was as follows:

> *Quamquam in rebus huius vitae delectari non fas, attamen cum hic viderim oculis meis sanctissimum Priorem una cum duobus fratribus dilectissimis libenter dicam Domine nunc dimittis servum tuum, etc.*

(Although we are forbidden to take pleasure in the things of this life, yet when I have seen here with my eyes the most holy Prior together with two of my dearly beloved brethren I shall gladly say, "Lord, now lettest thou Thy servant depart," etc.)

"Well," I said to myself, "he may have been an impudent rascal if nothing worse. But he seems to have had a sense of humour and to have been pretty sure of his ground. I wonder how the story ended?"

Next moment I gave a violent start, for I heard what sounded like a laugh close behind me. I whipped round in my chair. But there was no one there. The library was a large room and I was some distance from the door. Although the carpet was thick I did not think anyone could have come in without my knowledge. However, I got up, and went all round the room and even looked behind the window curtains. Of course I found nobody, and sat down again feeling rather ashamed of myself for being so fanciful.

There was only one more paper to be examined. Unfortunately the top had been torn off and the first words remaining were *nusquan inveniri potuit* (could not be found anywhere).

Then followed an inventory of the contents of the Chapel and cell. The only unusual item was *Duae cerae nigrae* (Two candles of black wax).

I concluded that the Prior had paid his visit, but that John's nerve had failed him at the last moment and he had disappeared. He could have made his way to Lynn without much difficulty and got on board a ship bound for the Low Countries.

No doubt the Prior was not sorry to be rid of him, and as the inventory was dated Festo S. Edithae MDXXXII (16 September 1532) the convent soon had other things to think about.

On my way home I speculated, not for the first time, upon the question whether there is or can be any foundation for any of the stories of compacts between human beings and evil spirits. In the abstract the possibility seems difficult to dispute. The belief is ancient and widely diffused. The real point seems to be whether the game could be worth the candle.

As I had finished all I meant to do at Folkham House I decided that I would spend tomorrow on a visit to the Chapel and perhaps sketch it. The day after I would return home.

When I imparted my plan to the landlord he naturally expressed a civil regret that my stay at Stivinghoe was coming to an end. He seemed doubtful whether the ruins (as I had learned the Chapel was called locally) were worth visiting, seeing as it were a dull trudge along the bank to get there. I thought from his manner that that was not his only reason for trying to discourage me. But he was summoned elsewhere before he had time to say more. While I was at dinner he looked in to see if I had everything I wanted. This was an unusual piece of condescension and I suspected an ulterior motive of some sort. I was not mistaken. After a moment or two he made an obvious effort.

"You'll excuse me, Sir. But the ruins is a queer place. Rare goings on there in those ancient times—by what I've heard."

This was interesting as it suggested that some reminiscence of John of Costessey lingered on the scene of his activities. But before I could ask for details he went on rapidly, "Not that I've any call to listen to the fishermen's talk—no more than what you 'ave."

After this there was obviously no more to be got out of him. But I thought I would try a cast among the company in the parlour later on. After some miscellaneous conversation I mentioned that I thought of spending my last day in walking out along the bank and making a sketch of the ruins. For some reason the company seemed to find this proposal disturbing. No one made any comment but there was an awkward pause. Then two ancients near the fireplace held a short muttered conversation. The only words I could catch sounded like "not lately, have he?"

Plainly they knew more than they meant to tell. Presently someone introduced some ordinary topic, and conversation flowed easily as before.

I went to bed about eleven and slept soundly.

Next morning I started soon after breakfast. I had ascertained that the tide would be low between 1 and 2 p.m. so that I should be able to find a position from which to make a sketch. I could hardly do this if I were confined to the bank itself. Also the day, though fine, was windy; windy enough, I thought, to make the top of the bank a wet place at high water.

I asked for some sandwiches to take with me and said that I should be back in time for dinner as usual, probably for tea. I thought the landlord looked at me rather reproachfully, but he said nothing. When I had gone a few steps on my way I found that I had not filled my tobacco pouch that morning. I turned back to make the omission good and my eye was caught by a horseshoe nailed over the front door. Nothing remarkable in that, you may say, but I wondered that I had not noticed it before, as it now seemed to be unusually conspicuous.

The walk along the bank was pleasant enough. I could see over miles of marsh on either hand. Inland there were groups of red-roofed cottages to be seen, with occasional windmills and church towers. In front of me lay the sea. At the moment no fishing-boats were visible, but the smoke of one or two large ships could be seen on the horizon.

Altogether an exhilarating prospect. But somehow or other I did not feel at all exhilarated. On the contrary I had to admit that I was nervous and depressed.

Certainly I had had some odd little experiences since I had touched the Stivinghoe papers. First there was the feeling that I was being followed on the way home. Then my uncomfortable and inconclusive dream. Then the laugh which I thought (no, *knew*) that I had heard in the library; and last of all the obvious conviction of the neighbourhood that the ruins were better left alone. What should I do if I saw a figure emerge from the Chapel and come along the bank to meet me? Should I enter into conversation or should I get down on to the sand and hope that he would pass me by? Or should I run for it? Or could I recall on the spur of the moment any form of exorcism which might prove effective? Fortunately I did not have to answer any of these questions.

The Chapel was a small building, roughly built of grey flint. It measured about twenty-two feet by ten and was lighted by a single lancet in the east wall. There was a door at the west end, I put its date at a little before 1350. Of course the roof was gone, but the walls looked fairly sound. The altar was still in place. But I noticed that the usual consecration crosses (one in the middle and one at each corner) had been deliberately obliterated. The chisel marks could be seen clearly. Such reforming zeal seemed to be almost excessive.

On the south (that is on the landward) side of the Chapel there were some small mounds which presumably indicated the site of the priest's dwelling. The superstructure had disappeared so completely that I wondered whether it had been of wood; also whether it could possibly be worth while to return with a spade.

I sat down on one of the mounds and ate my sandwiches. Then I thought it time to set about my sketch. I went down on to the sand and decided that the best position was a few yards to seaward. (In this part of Norfolk the coast runs east and west, so that the sea is to the north. The natives are fond of assuring visitors that there is nothing between them and the North Pole. No one who has been there in winter is likely to wish to dispute this statement.) The tide was still ebbing, so I should have plenty of time to do what I wanted.

I settled myself and my sketching materials, but somehow I did not make very good progress. I had an uncomfortable feeling, as if there was somebody behind me, and caught myself wondering what I should do if a hand (probably a large and bony one) were suddenly laid upon my shoulder. I said aloud "ridiculous" and as I did so a gull passed very close above my head and gave a derisive squawk, which seemed to indicate his complete concurrence.

The gulls were very many; which was not surprising. But they were so tame (or impudent, whichever you like to call it) that they were a positive nuisance. They flapped their wings almost in my face and one actually perched on my easel. I suppose they had never seen enough of men to be afraid of them. I had a sandwich or two left which I threw as far as I could towards the water's edge. This drew them off for a little, but they were soon as bad as ever. However, I got a sketch of some sort finished. I thought I would take one more look inside the Chapel before I started to walk home in case there were any detail of interest which I had missed. The floor was covered with coarse turf. Probably it had never been paved; if it had, the paving had been covered long since. But just in front of the altar I noticed a patch which somehow looked different from the rest. I had in my knife one of those curious implements said to be intended for taking stones out of horses' feet, and it seemed that at last I had a chance of using it. I scratched at the turf and very soon my hook grated upon a stone. A little scraping disclosed a small rectangular slab about twenty inches long by eight broad. A pentacle had been scratched upon it rather roughly. It was obviously the lid of something, if it were too small for any kind of coffin. A little more scraping of the earth round its edges and I got it up with less difficulty than I had expected. It was the lid of a coffin of sorts after all and in the coffin were some bones; clearly those of a small monkey. Its forepaws were crossed upon its breast and from some fragments of stuff which lay about I came to the conclusion that it had been buried in some sort of monastic habit.

This discovery explained the stories of the imp. Perhaps John had been really fond of his pet who must have been his only companion. Burial before the altar might perhaps be condoned. But the monastic habit looked like a profane jest. Or was it more than a jest? Taken in conjunction with the pentacle on the lid, the candles of black wax found by the Prior and the erasure of the consecration crosses (which I now began to think was John's handiwork and not the doing of any zealous follower of Dowsing) there was a definite suggestion of serious and sinister purpose. What unhallowed rites had been celebrated there, with what evil intent? And (I could not repress the further question) in what company?

However, there seemed to be nothing for me to do but to leave things as I had found them. Which I did. The afternoon was wearing on, so I started for home. The tide had probably turned but was still very low. At the seaward end the line of the bank was curved, so I saw that I could shorten my walk considerably if I took to the sands and struck the bank again in about a mile. When I had gone a little way I turned to take a final look at the Chapel. It was a sunny day with big white clouds driving before the wind. As I looked the shadow of one passed across the Chapel, and by some odd trick of light made it seem as if a dark figure had emerged from the door and dropped down the far side of the bank. For a moment I was really startled.

I turned and went on with my walk. I have never considered myself a fanciful person, but it was borne in upon me very forcibly that the sooner I was sitting down to tea at the *Fishmongers' Arms* the happier I should be.

Presently I reached the point at which I must take to the bank again. Just as I got to the edge of the sand I saw the print of a naked human foot, pointing towards the bank. It was very recent and could (apparently) only have been made by someone who had passed me quite close, having come across the sand as I had, and gone up the bank before me. This was frankly impossible. Had there been anyone else about I could not have failed to see him. The sand was too wet to hold impressions for long. Most of my own tracks had disappeared already. Yet there was the footprint, unmistakably. I stooped and looked at it (there was only one, which made it odder still) closely. It struck me as unusually bony, that is to say, the bones showed more plainly than I should have expected. I thought of the shadow which I had seen pass across the end of the Chapel. Had it, after all, emerged from the inside? If I went on, should I find someone waiting for me, and with what intent? However, there was nothing for it but to go on. I was within sight of the village now and there were people about who would see if any attack were made upon me, though what help they would be able to give was another matter. So on I went, and in a few minutes had reached my inn safely.

I turned on the doorstep to take a look over the marshes. Very lonely and solemn they were and very dark was the little Chapel. There was no one to be seen; I had not expected that there would be. By this time the wind had freshened and there was a hard brightness on the north-eastern horizon which foretold a full gale before morning. There was an old barometer just inside the front door which had fallen so low that I wondered whether it were trustworthy and hoped not. The landlord emerged and appeared ill at ease, and at the same time glad to see me—possibly by reason of the weather; possibly not. He murmured something to the effect of no harm done, as he returned to his occupations. I felt curiously tired, and when I had had tea, after a poor pretence of reading some book (I forget now what) dozed in an armchair by the fire.

I was roused by a clap of thunder and the storm broke with a roar like a train. The thunder was unusual, I thought, for the time of year, especially as the last few days had not been particularly hot. Also, the wind was off the sea, and I knew that there was a belief along the coast that when a thunderstorm comes up from the sea, that will be the beginning of the end of the world.

The *Fishmongers' Arms* was built to stand weather. But I doubt whether it ever had a worse buffeting than it got that night. There was no more thunder, but the rain came down in sheets and the wind tore at the house till I could almost imagine I felt it swaying to and fro. It was obvious that there would be no customers at the bar, so after dinner I invited the landlord to come to my sitting-room to smoke a cigar and drink a whisky and soda with me. I was really glad of his company, and he seemed to be of mine. We tried to talk of indifferent subjects, but could not do much save listen to the wind. We went to bed about eleven, though there was not much prospect of sleep. I wished that I had not remembered at that moment that Richard Kidder, Bishop of Bath and Wells, had been killed in his bed, together with his wife, by the fall of a chimney-stack through the roof of the palace during the terrible storm of 26–7 November, 1703.

Soon after midnight there was a screech (I can call it nothing else) like that of an animal in pain. I could hardly have believed that the wind could have made such a sound. This seemed to be its last effort, and the storm died away almost as quickly as it had arisen.

When I looked out next morning the Chapel was gone. The whole end of the bank had been washed away. The gale had coincided with a spring tide and I suspect that most of the marsh had been under water for some hours. Of course the tip of the bank had caught the full force of the sea.

I must confess that I felt relieved. At first I was glad that I had made a sketch of the Chapel. But after a little reflection I burned it. Somehow I felt safer as I saw it turn to ashes.

1955

RINGING THE CHANGES

Robert Aickman

Robert Aickman (1914–1981) was the grandson of the writer Richard Marsh whose 1897 novel *The Beetle* enjoyed similar success in its day to Bram Stoker's *Dracula*; when Aickman set up his own literary agency, around 1941, he named it after his grandfather. A fascinating figure, Aickman is certainly one of the twentieth century's greatest practitioners of what he referred to as "strange tales". Although married, Aickman began a complicated affair with the novelist Elizabeth Jane Howard in 1945; she left her husband, the conservationist Peter Scott, for Aickman two years later. The pair collaborated on a collection, *We Are for the Dark*, in 1951, each contributing three stories that form a template for the enigmatic "Aickman-esque" tale. The forty-eight short works he produced over the next thirty years can be as elusive as their author— much more mysterious and obtuse than the majority of supernatural stories that stem from the Victorian tradition. But they are also, on the whole, quite brilliant.

Robert Aickman's father was born in King's Lynn, Norfolk. And, via his work and travels with the Inland Waterways Association (the organisation he co-founded with L. T. C. Rolt, another writer of ghost stories), Aickman himself was familiar with much of East Anglia. Yet, only two of his stories have their setting in the region: his cautionary 1976 tale of a Suffolk marriage, "Wood"; and one of his most well-known pieces, "Ringing the Changes", another in which relationship difficulties between an older man and younger woman are at the forefront—it's perhaps no coincidence, as Howard left Aickman not long before the publication of *We Are for the Dark*.

According to his biographer Ray Russell, Aickman never suggested a specific model for Holihaven, the fictional east coast location of "Ringing the Changes". For me, it has elements of Suffolk's crumbling medieval port of Dunwich (with its legendary underwater church bells), or possibly the larger resort of Southwold. The name, though, might hint at Essex's Holland-on-Sea, with its nearby Holland Haven. Interestingly, the filming for the BBC's now-lost 1968 adaptation, *The Bells of Hell*, took place at another coastal Essex town, Wivenhoe.

He had never been among those many who deeply dislike church bells, but the ringing that evening at Holihaven changed his view. Bells could certainly get on one's nerves he felt, although he had only just arrived in the town.

He had been too well aware of the perils attendant upon marrying a girl twenty-four years younger than himself to add to them by a conventional honeymoon. The strange force of Phrynne's love had borne both of them away from their previous selves: in him a formerly haphazard and easy-going approach to life had been replaced by much deep planning to wall in happiness; and she, though once thought cold and choosy, would now agree to anything as long as she was with him. He had said that if they were to marry in June, it would be at the cost of not being able to honeymoon until October. Had they been courting longer, he had explained, gravely smiling, special arrangements could have been made; but, as it was, business claimed him. This, indeed, was true; because his business position was less influential than he had led Phrynne to believe. Finally, it would have been impossible for them to have courted longer, because they had courted from the day they met, which was less than six weeks before the day they married.

"'A village'," he had quoted as they entered the branch-line train at the junction (itself sufficiently remote), "'from which (it was said) persons of sufficient longevity might hope to reach Liverpool Street.'"

By now he was able to make jokes about age, although perhaps he did so rather too often.

"Who said that?"

"Bertrand Russell."

She had looked at him with her big eyes in her tiny face.

"Really." He had smiled confirmation.

"I'm not arguing." She had still been looking at him. The romantic gas light in the charming period compartment had left him uncertain whether she was smiling back or not. He had given himself the benefit of the doubt, and kissed her.

The guard had blown his whistle and they had rumbled out into the darkness. The branch line swung so sharply away from the main line that Phrynne had been almost toppled from her seat.

"Why do we go so slowly when it's so flat?"

"Because the engineer laid the line up and down the hills and valleys such as they are, instead of cutting through and embanking over them." He liked being able to inform her.

"How do you know? Gerald! You said you hadn't been to Holihaven before."

"It applies to most of the railways in East Anglia."

"So that even though it's flatter, it's slower?"

"Time matters less."

"I should have hated going to a place where time mattered or that you'd been to before. You'd have had nothing to remember me by."

He hadn't been quite sure that her words exactly expressed her thoughts, but the thought had lightened his heart.

Holihaven station could hardly have been built in the days of the town's magnificence, for they were in the Middle Ages; but it still implied grander functions than came its way now. The platforms were long enough for visiting London expresses, which had since gone elsewhere; and the architecture of the waiting rooms would have been not insufficient for occasional use by foreign royalty. Oil lamps on perches like those occupied by macaws lighted the uniformed staff, who numbered two and, together with every native of Holihaven, looked like storm-habituated mariners.

The station-master and porter, as Gerald took them to be, watched him approach down the platform, with a heavy suitcase in each hand and Phrynne walking deliciously by his side. He saw one of them address a remark to the other, but neither offered to help. Gerald had to put down the cases in order to give up their tickets. The other passengers had already disappeared.

"Where's the Bell?"

Gerald had found the hotel in a reference book. It was the only one allotted to Holihaven. But as Gerald spoke, and before the ticket collector could answer, the sudden deep note of an actual bell rang through the darkness. Phrynne caught hold of Gerald's sleeve.

Ignoring Gerald, the station-master, if such he was, turned to his colleague. "They're starting early."

"Every reason to be in good time," said the other man.

The station-master nodded, and put Gerald's tickets indifferently in his jacket pocket.

"Can you please tell me how I get to the Bell Hotel?"

The station-master's attention returned to him. "Have you a room booked?"

"Certainly."

"Tonight?" The station-master looked inappropriately suspicious.

"Of course."

Again the station-master looked at the other man.

"It's them Pascoes."

"Yes," said Gerald. "That's the name. Pascoe."

"We don't use the Bell," explained the station-master. "But you'll find it in Wrack Street." He gesticulated vaguely and unhelpfully. "Straight ahead. Down Station Road. Then down Wrack Street. You can't miss it."

"Thank you."

As soon as they entered the town, the big bell began to boom regularly.

"What narrow streets!" said Phrynne.

"They follow the lines of the medieval city. Before the river silted up, Holihaven was one of the most important seaports in Great Britain."

"Where's everybody got to?"

Although it was only six o'clock, the place certainly seemed deserted.

"Where's the hotel got to?" rejoined Gerald.

"Poor Gerald! Let me help." She laid her hand beside his on the handle of the suitcase nearest to her, but as she was about fifteen inches shorter than he, she could be of little assistance. They must already have gone more than a quarter of a mile. "Do you think we're in the right street?"

"Most unlikely, I should say. But there's no one to ask."

"Must be early-closing day."

The single deep notes of the bell were now coming more frequently.

"Why are they ringing that bell? Is it a funeral?"

"Bit late for a funeral."

She looked at him a little anxiously.

"Anyway it's not cold."

"Considering we're on the east coast it's quite astonishingly warm."

"Not that I care."

"I hope that bell isn't going to ring all night."

She pulled on the suitcase. His arms were in any case almost parting from his body. "Look! We've passed it."

They stopped, and he looked back. "How could we have done that?"

"Well, we have."

She was right. He could see a big ornamental bell hanging from a bracket attached to a house about a hundred yards behind them.

They retraced their steps and entered the hotel. A woman dressed in a navy-blue coat and skirt, with a good figure but dyed red hair and a face ridged with make-up, advanced upon them.

"Mr. and Mrs. Banstead? I'm Hilda Pascoe. Don, my husband, isn't very well."

Gerald felt full of doubts. His arrangements were not going as they should. Never rely on guidebook recommendations. The trouble lay partly in Phrynne's insistence that they go somewhere he did not know. "I'm sorry to hear that," he said.

"You know what men are like when they're ill?" Mrs. Pascoe spoke understandingly to Phrynne.

"Impossible," said Phrynne. "Or very difficult."

"Talk about 'Woman in our hours of ease'."

"Yes," said Phrynne. "What's the trouble?"

"It's always been the same trouble with Don," said Mrs. Pascoe; then checked herself. "It's his stomach," she said. "Ever since he was a kid, Don's had trouble with the lining of his stomach."

Gerald interrupted. "I wonder if we could see our rooms?"

"So sorry," said Mrs. Pascoe. "Will you register first?" She produced a battered volume bound in peeling imitation leather. "Just the name and address." She spoke as if Gerald might contribute a résumé of his life.

It was the first time he and Phrynne had ever registered in a hotel;

but his confidence in the place was not increased by the long period which had passed since the registration above.

"We're always quiet in October," remarked Mrs. Pascoe, her eyes upon him. Gerald noticed that her eyes were slightly bloodshot. "Except sometimes for the bars, of course."

"We wanted to come out of the season," said Phrynne soothingly.

"Quite," said Mrs. Pascoe.

"Are we alone in the house?" enquired Gerald. After all the woman was probably doing her best.

"Except for Commandant Shotcroft. You won't mind him, will you? He's a regular."

"I'm sure we shan't," said Phrynne.

"People say the house wouldn't be the same without Commandant Shotcroft."

"I see."

"What's that bell?" asked Gerald. Apart from anything else, it really was much too near.

Mrs. Pascoe looked away. He thought she looked shifty under her entrenched make-up. But she only said, "Practice."

"Do you mean there will be more of them later?"

She nodded. "But never mind," she said encouragingly. "Let me show you to your room. Sorry there's no porter."

Before they had reached the bedroom, the whole peal had commenced.

"Is this the quietest room you have?" enquired Gerald. "What about the other side of the house?"

"This *is* the other side of the house. Saint Guthlac's is over there." She pointed out through the bedroom door.

"Darling," said Phrynne, her hand on Gerald's arm, "they'll soon stop. They're only practising."

Mrs. Pascoe said nothing. Her expression indicated that she was one of those people whose friendliness has a precise and never-exceeded limit.

"If *you* don't mind," said Gerald to Phrynne, hesitating.

"They have ways of their own in Holihaven," said Mrs. Pascoe. Her undertone of militancy implied, among other things, that if Gerald and Phrynne chose to leave, they were at liberty to do so. Gerald did not care for that either: her attitude would have been different, he felt, had there been anywhere else for them to go. The bells were making him touchy and irritable.

"It's a very pretty room," said Phrynne. "I adore four-posters."

"Thank you," said Gerald to Mrs. Pascoe. "What time's dinner?"

"Seven-thirty. You've time for a drink in the bar first."

She went.

"We certainly have," said Gerald when the door was shut. "It's only just six."

"Actually," said Phrynne, who was standing by the window looking down into the street, "I *like* church bells."

"All very well," said Gerald, "but on one's honeymoon they distract the attention."

"Not mine," said Phrynne simply. Then she added, "There's still no one about."

"I expect they're all in the bar."

"I don't want a drink. I want to explore the town."

"As you wish. But hadn't you better unpack?"

"I ought to, but I'm not going to. Not until after I've seen the sea." Such small shows of independence in her enchanted Gerald.

Mrs. Pascoe was not about when they passed through the lounge, nor was there any sound of activity in the establishment.

Outside, the bells seemed to be booming and bounding immediately over their heads.

"It's like warriors fighting in the sky," shouted Phrynne. "Do you think the sea's down there?" She indicated the direction from which they had previously retraced their steps.

"I imagine so. The street seems to end in nothing. That would be the sea."

"Come on. Let's run." She was off, before he could even think about it. Then there was nothing to do but run after her. He hoped there were not eyes behind blinds.

She stopped, and held wide her arms to catch him. The top of her head hardly came up to his chin. He knew she was silently indicating that his failure to keep up with her was not a matter for self-consciousness.

"Isn't it beautiful?"

"The sea?" There was no moon; and little was discernible beyond the end of the street.

"Not only."

"Everything but the sea. The sea's invisible."

"You can smell it."

"I certainly can't hear it."

She slackened her embrace and cocked her head away from him.

"The bells echo so much, it's as if there were two churches."

"I'm sure there are more than that. There always are in old towns like this." Suddenly he was struck by the significance of his words in relation to what she had said. He shrank into himself, tautly listening.

"Yes," cried Phrynne delightedly. "It *is* another church."

"Impossible," said Gerald. "Two churches wouldn't have practice ringing on the same night."

"I'm quite sure. I can hear one lot of bells with my left ear, and another lot with my right."

They had still seen no one. The sparse gas lights fell on the furnishings of a stone quay, small but plainly in regular use.

"The whole population must be ringing the bells." His own remark discomfited Gerald.

"Good for them." She took his hand. "Let's go down on the beach and look for the sea."

They descended a flight of stone steps at which the sea had sucked and bitten. The beach was as stony as the steps, but lumpier.

"We'll just go straight on," said Phrynne. "Until we find it."

Left to himself, Gerald would have been less keen. The stones were very large and very slippery, and his eyes did not seem to be becoming accustomed to the dark.

"You're right, Phrynne, about the smell."

"Honest sea smell."

"Just as you say." He took it rather to be the smell of dense rotting weed; across which he supposed they must be slithering. It was not a smell he had previously encountered in such strength.

Energy could hardly be spared for thinking, and advancing hand in hand was impossible.

After various random remarks on both sides and the lapse of what seemed a very long time, Phrynne spoke again. "Gerald, where is it? What sort of seaport is it that has no sea?"

She continued onwards, but Gerald stopped and looked back. He had thought the distance they had gone overlong, but was startled to see how great it was. The darkness was doubtless deceitful, but the few lights on the quay appeared as on a distant horizon.

The far glimmering specks still in his eyes, he turned and looked after Phrynne. He could barely see her. Perhaps she was progressing faster without him.

"Phrynne! Darling!"

Unexpectedly she gave a sharp cry.

"Phrynne!"

She did not answer.

"Phrynne!"

Then she spoke more or less calmly. "Panic over. Sorry, darling. I stood on something."

He realised that a panic it had indeed been; at least in him.

"You're all right?"

"Think so."

He struggled up to her. "The smell's worse than ever." It was overpowering.

"I think it's coming from what I stepped on. My foot went right in, and then there was the smell."

"I've never known anything like it."

"Sorry darling," she said gently mocking him. "Let's go away."

"Let's go back. Don't you think?"

"Yes," said Phrynne. "But I must warn you I'm very disappointed. I think that seaside attractions should include the sea."

He noticed that as they retreated, she was scraping the sides of one shoe against the stones, as if trying to clean it.

"I think the whole place is a disappointment," he said. "I really must apologise. We'll go somewhere else."

"I like the bells," she replied, making a careful reservation.

Gerald said nothing.

"I don't want to go somewhere where you've been before."

The bells rang out over the desolate unattractive beach. Now the sound seemed to be coming from every point along the shore.

"I suppose all the churches practise on the same night in order to get it over with," said Gerald.

"They do it in order to see which can ring the loudest," said Phrynne.

"Take care you don't twist your ankle."

The din as they reached the rough little quay was such as to suggest that Phrynne's idea was literally true.

The Coffee Room was so low that Gerald had to dip beneath a sequence of thick beams.

"Why 'Coffee Room'?" asked Phrynne, looking at the words on the door. "I saw a notice that coffee will only be served in the lounge."

"It's the *lucus a non lucendo* principle."

"That explains everything. I wonder where we sit." A single electric lantern, mass-produced in an antique pattern, had been turned on. The bulb was of that limited wattage which is peculiar to hotels. It did little to penetrate the shadows.

"The *lucus a non lucendo* principle is the principle of calling white black."

"Not at all," said a voice from the darkness. "On the contrary. The word 'black' comes from an ancient root which means 'to bleach'."

They had thought themselves alone, but now saw a small man seated by himself at an unlighted corner table. In the darkness he looked like a monkey.

"I stand corrected," said Gerald.

They sat at the table under the lantern.

The man in the corner spoke again. "Why are you here at all?"

Phrynne looked frightened, but Gerald replied quietly. "We're on holiday. We prefer it out of the season. I presume you are Commandant Shotcroft?"

"No need to presume." Unexpectedly the Commandant switched on the antique lantern which was nearest to him. His table was littered with a finished meal. It struck Gerald that he must have switched off the light when he heard them approach the Coffee Room. "I'm going anyway."

"Are we late?" asked Phrynne, always the assuager of situations.

"No, you're not late," called the Commandant in a deep moody voice. "My meals are prepared half an hour before the time the rest come in. I don't like eating in company." He had risen to his feet. "So perhaps you'll excuse me."

Without troubling about an answer, he stepped quickly out of the Coffee Room. He had cropped white hair; tragic, heavy-lidded eyes; and a round face which was yellow and lined.

A second later his head reappeared round the door.

"Ring," he said; and again withdrew.

"Too many other people ringing," said Gerald. "But I don't see what else we can do."

The Coffee Room bell, however, made a noise like a fire alarm.

Mrs. Pascoe appeared. She looked considerably the worse for drink.

"Didn't see you in the bar."

"Must have missed us in the crowd," said Gerald amiably.

"Crowd?" enquired Mrs. Pascoe drunkenly. Then, after a difficult pause, she offered them a hand-written menu.

They ordered; and Mrs. Pascoe served them throughout. Gerald was apprehensive lest her indisposition increase during the course of the meal; but her insobriety, like her affability, seemed to have an exact and definite limit.

"All things considered, the food might be worse," remarked Gerald, towards the end. It was a relief that something was going reasonably well. "Not much of it, but at least the dishes are hot."

When Phrynne translated this into a compliment to the cook, Mrs. Pascoe said, "I cooked it all myself, although I shouldn't be the one to say so."

Gerald felt really surprised that she was in a condition to have accomplished this. Possibly, he reflected with alarm, she had had much practice under similar conditions.

"Coffee is served in the lounge," said Mrs. Pascoe.

They withdrew. In a corner of the lounge was a screen decorated with winning Elizabethan ladies in ruffs and hoops. From behind it projected a pair of small black boots. Phrynne nudged Gerald and pointed to them. Gerald nodded. They felt themselves constrained to talk about things which bored them.

The hotel was old and its walls thick. In the empty lounge the noise of the bells would not prevent conversation being overheard, but still came from all around, as if the hotel were a fortress beleaguered by surrounding artillery.

After their second cups of coffee, Gerald suddenly said he couldn't stand it.

"Darling, it's not doing us any harm. I think it's rather cosy." Phrynne subsided in the wooden chair with its sloping back and long mud-coloured mock-velvet cushions; and opened her pretty legs to the fire.

"Every church in the town must be ringing its bells. It's been going on for two and a half hours and they never seem to take the usual breathers."

"We wouldn't hear. Because of all the other bells ringing. I think it's nice of them to ring the bells for us."

Nothing further was said for several minutes. Gerald was beginning to realise that they had yet to evolve a holiday routine.

"I'll get you a drink. What shall it be?"

"Anything you like. Whatever *you* have." Phrynne was immersed in female enjoyment of the fire's radiance on her body.

Gerald missed this, and said, "I don't quite see why they have to keep the place like a hothouse. When I come back, we'll sit somewhere else."

"Men wear too many clothes, darling," said Phrynne drowsily.

Contrary to his assumption, Gerald found the lounge bar as empty as everywhere else in the hotel and the town. There was not even a person to dispense.

Somewhat irritably Gerald struck a brass bell which stood on the counter. It rang out sharply as a pistol shot.

Mrs. Pascoe appeared at a door among the shelves. She had taken off her jacket, and her make-up had begun to run.

"A cognac, please. Double. And a Kummel."

Mrs. Pascoe's hands were shaking so much that she could not get the cork out of the brandy bottle.

"Allow me." Gerald stretched his arm across the bar.

Mrs. Pascoe stared at him blearily. "Okay. But I must pour it."

Gerald extracted the cork and returned the bottle. Mrs. Pascoe slopped a far from precise dose into a balloon.

Catastrophe followed. Unable to return the bottle to the high shelf where it resided, Mrs. Pascoe placed it on a waist-level ledge. Reaching for the alembic of Kummel, she swept the three-quarters-full brandy bottle on to the tiled floor. The stuffy air became fogged with the fumes of brandy from behind the bar.

At the door from which Mrs. Pascoe had emerged appeared a man from the inner room. Though still youngish, he was puce and puffy, and in his braces, with no collar. Streaks of sandy hair laced his vast red scalp. Liquor oozed all over him, as if from a perished gourd. Gerald took it that this was Don.

The man was too drunk to articulate. He stood in the doorway, clinging with each red hand to the ledge, and savagely struggling to flay his wife with imprecations.

"How much?" said Gerald to Mrs. Pascoe. It seemed useless to try for the Kummel. The hotel must have another bar.

"Three and six," said Mrs. Pascoe, quite lucidly; but Gerald saw that she was about to weep.

He had the exact sum. She turned her back on him and flicked the cash register. As she returned from it, he heard the fragmentation of glass as she stepped on a piece of the broken bottle. Gerald looked at her husband out of the corner of his eye. The sagging, loose-mouthed figure made him shudder. Something moved him.

"I'm sorry about the accident," he said to Mrs. Pascoe. He held the balloon in one hand, and was just going.

Mrs. Pascoe looked at him. The slow tears of desperation were edging down her face, but she now seemed quite sober. "Mr. Banstead," she said in a flat, hurried voice. "May I come and sit with you and your wife in the lounge? Just for a few minutes."

"Of course." It was certainly not what he wanted, and he wondered what would become of the bar, but he felt unexpectedly sorry for her, and it was impossible to say no.

To reach the flap of the bar, she had to pass her husband. Gerald saw her hesitate for a second; then she advanced resolutely and steadily, and looking straight before her. If the man had let go with his hands, he would have fallen; but as she passed him, he released a great gob of spit. He was far too incapable to aim, and it fell on the side of his own trousers. Gerald lifted the flap for Mrs. Pascoe and stood back to let her precede him from the bar. As he followed her, he heard her husband maundering off into unintelligible inward searchings.

"The Kummel!" said Mrs. Pascoe, remembering in the doorway.

"Never mind," said Gerald. "Perhaps I could try one of the other bars?"

"Not tonight. They're shut. I'd better go back."

"No. We'll think of something else." It was not yet nine o'clock, and Gerald wondered about the licensing justices.

But in the lounge was another unexpected scene. Mrs. Pascoe stopped as soon as they entered, and Gerald, caught between two imitation-leather armchairs, looked over her shoulder.

Phrynne had fallen asleep. Her head was slightly on one side, but her mouth was shut, and her body no more than gracefully relaxed, so that she looked most beautiful, and, Gerald thought, a trifle unearthly, like a dead girl in an early picture by Millais.

The quality of her beauty seemed also to have impressed Commandant Shotcroft; for he was standing silently behind her and looking down at her, his sad face transfigured. Gerald noticed that a leaf of the pseudo-Elizabethan screen had been folded back, revealing a small cretonne-covered chair, with an open tome face downward in its seat.

"Won't you join us?" said Gerald boldly. There was that in the Commandant's face which boded no hurt. "Can I get you a drink?"

The Commandant did not turn his head, and for a moment seemed unable to speak. Then in a low voice he said, "For a moment only."

"Good," said Gerald. "Sit down. And you, Mrs. Pascoe." Mrs. Pascoe was dabbing at her face. Gerald addressed the Commandant. "What shall it be?"

"Nothing to drink," said the Commandant in the same low mutter. It occurred to Gerald that if Phrynne awoke, the Commandant would go.

"What about you?" Gerald looked at Mrs. Pascoe, earnestly hoping she would decline.

"No thanks." She was glancing at the Commandant. Clearly she had not expected him to be there.

Phrynne being asleep, Gerald sat down too. He sipped his brandy. It was impossible to romanticise the action with a toast.

The events in the bar had made him forget about the bells. Now, as they sat silently round the sleeping Phrynne, the tide of sound swept over him once more.

"You mustn't think," said Mrs. Pascoe, "that he's always like that." They all spoke in hushed voices. All of them seemed to have reason to do so. The Commandant was again gazing sombrely at Phrynne's beauty.

"Of course not." But it was hard to believe.

"The licensed business puts temptations in a man's way."

"It must be very difficult."

"We ought never to have come here. We were happy in South Norwood."

"You must do good business during the season."

"Two months," said Mrs. Pascoe bitterly, but still softly. "Two and a half at the very most. The people who come during the season have no idea what goes on out of it."

"What made you leave South Norwood?"

"Don's stomach. The doctor said the air would do him good."

"Speaking of that, doesn't the sea go too far out? We went down on the beach before dinner, but couldn't see it anywhere."

On the other side of the fire, the Commandant turned his eyes from Phrynne and looked at Gerald.

"I wouldn't know," said Mrs. Pascoe. "I never have time to look from one year's end to the other." It was a customary enough answer, but Gerald felt that it did not disclose the whole truth. He noticed that Mrs. Pascoe glanced uneasily at the Commandant, who by now was staring neither at Phrynne nor at Gerald but at the toppling citadels in the fire.

"And now I must get on with my work," continued Mrs. Pascoe, "I only came in for a minute." She looked Gerald in the face. "Thank you," she said, and rose.

"Please stay a little longer," said Gerald. "Wait till my wife wakes up." As he spoke, Phrynne slightly shifted.

"Can't be done," said Mrs. Pascoe, her lips smiling. Gerald noticed that all the time she was watching the Commandant from under her lids, and knew that were he not there, she would have stayed.

As it was, she went. "I'll probably see you later to say good-night. Sorry the water's not very hot. It's having no porter."

The bells showed no sign of flagging.

When Mrs. Pascoe had closed the door, the Commandant spoke.

"He was a fine man once. Don't think otherwise."

"You mean Pascoe?"

The Commandant nodded seriously.

"Not my type," said Gerald.

"DSO and bar. DFC and bar."

"And now bar only. Why?"

"You heard what she said. It was a lie. They didn't leave South Norwood for the sea air."

"So I supposed."

"He got into trouble. He was fixed. He wasn't the kind of man to know about human nature and all its rottenness."

"A pity," said Gerald. "But perhaps, even so, this isn't the best place for him?"

"It's the worst," said the Commandant, a dark flame in his eyes. "For him or anyone else."

Again Phrynne shifted in her sleep: this time more convulsively, so that she nearly woke. For some reason the two men remained speechless and motionless until she was again breathing steadily. Against the silence within, the bells sounded louder than ever. It was as if the tumult were tearing holes in the roof.

"It's certainly a very noisy place," said Gerald, still in an undertone.

"Why did you have to come tonight of all nights?" The Commandant spoke in the same undertone, but his vehemence was extreme.

"This doesn't happen often?"

"Once every year."

"They should have told us."

"They don't usually accept bookings. They've no right to accept them. When Pascoe was in charge they never did."

"I expect that Mrs. Pascoe felt they were in no position to turn away business."

"It's not a matter that should be left to a woman."

"Not much alternative surely?"

"At heart, women are creatures of darkness all the time." The Commandant's seriousness and bitterness left Gerald without a reply.

"My wife doesn't mind the bells," he said after a moment. "In fact she rather likes them." The Commandant really was converting a nuisance, though an acute one, into a melodrama.

The Commandant turned and gazed at him. It struck Gerald that what he had just said in some way, for the Commandant, placed Phrynne also in a category of the lost.

"Take her away, man," said the Commandant, with scornful ferocity.

"In a day or two perhaps," said Gerald, patiently polite. "I admit that we are disappointed with Holihaven."

"Now. While there's still time. This *instant*."

There was an intensity of conviction about the Commandant which was alarming.

Gerald considered. Even the empty lounge, with its dreary decorations and commonplace furniture, seemed inimical. "They can hardly go on practising all night," he said. But now it was fear that hushed his voice.

"Practising!" The Commandant's scorn flickered coldly through the overheated room.

"What else?"

"They're ringing to wake the dead."

A tremor of wind in the flue momentarily drew on the already roaring fire. Gerald had turned very pale.

"That's a figure of speech," he said, hardly to be heard.

"Not in Holihaven." The Commandant's gaze had returned to the fire.

Gerald looked at Phrynne. She was breathing less heavily. His voice dropped to a whisper. "What happens?"

The Commandant also was nearly whispering. "No one can tell how long they have to go on ringing. It varies from year to year. I don't know why. You should be all right up to midnight. Probably for some while after. In the end the dead awake. First one or two, then all of them. Tonight even the sea draws back. You have seen that for yourself. In a place like this there are always several drowned each year. This year there've been more than several. But even so that's only a few. Most of them come not from the water but from the earth. It is not a pretty sight."

"Where do they go?"

"I've never followed them to see. I'm not stark staring mad." The red of the fire reflected in the Commandant's eyes. There was a long pause.

"I don't believe in the resurrection of the body," said Gerald. As the hour grew later, the bells grew louder. "Not of the body."

"What other kind of resurrection is possible? Everything else is only theory. You can't even imagine it. No one can."

Gerald had not argued such a thing for twenty years. "So," he said, "you advise me to go. Where?"

"Where doesn't matter."

"I have no car."

"Then you'd better walk."

"With her?" He indicated Phrynne only with his eyes.

"She's young and strong." A forlorn tenderness lay within the Commandant's words. "She's twenty years younger than you and therefore twenty years more important."

"Yes," said Gerald. "I agree... What about you? What will you do?"

"I've lived here some time now. I know what to do."

"And the Pascoes?"

"He's drunk. There is nothing in the world to fear if you're thoroughly drunk. DSO and bar. DFC and bar."

"But you're not drinking yourself?"

"Not since I came to Holihaven. I lost the knack."

Suddenly Phrynne sat up. "Hallo," she said to the Commandant; not yet fully awake. Then she said, "What fun! The bells are still ringing."

The Commandant rose, his eyes averted. "I don't think there's anything more to say," he remarked, addressing Gerald. "You've still got time." He nodded slightly to Phrynne, and walked out of the lounge.

"What have you still got time for?" asked Phrynne, stretching. "Was he trying to convert you? I'm sure he's an Anabaptist."

"Something like that," said Gerald, trying to think.

"Shall we go to bed? Sorry, I'm so sleepy."

"Nothing to be sorry about."

"Or shall we go for another walk? That would wake me up. Besides, the tide might have come in."

Gerald, although he half despised himself for it, found it impossible to explain to her that they should leave at once; without transport or a destination; walk all night if necessary. He said to himself that probably he would not go even were he alone.

"If you're sleepy, it's probably a *good* thing."

"Darling!"

"I mean with these bells. God knows when they will stop." Instantly he felt a new pang of fear at what he had said.

Mrs. Pascoe had appeared at the door leading to the bar, and opposite to that from which the Commandant had departed. She bore two steaming glasses on a tray. She looked about, possibly to confirm that the Commandant had really gone.

"I thought you might both like a nightcap. Ovaltine, with something in it."

"Thank you," said Phrynne. "I can't think of anything nicer."

Gerald set the glasses on a wicker table, and quickly finished his cognac.

Mrs. Pascoe began to move chairs and slap cushions. She looked very haggard.

"Is the Commandant an Anabaptist?" asked Phrynne over her shoulder. She was proud of her ability to outdistance Gerald in beginning to consume a hot drink.

Mrs. Pascoe stopped slapping for a moment. "I don't know what that is," she said.

"He's left his book," said Phrynne, on a new tack.

"I wonder what he's reading," continued Phrynne. "Foxe's *Lives of the Martyrs*, I expect." A small unusual devil seemed to have entered into her.

But Mrs. Pascoe knew the answer. "It's always the same," she said contemptuously. "He only reads one. It's called *Fifteen Decisive Battles of the World*. He's been reading it ever since he came here. When he gets to the end, he starts again."

"Should I take it up to him?" asked Gerald. It was neither courtesy nor inclination, but rather a fear lest the Commandant return to the lounge: a desire, after those few minutes of reflection, to cross-examine.

"Thanks very much," said Mrs. Pascoe, as if relieved of a similar apprehension. "Room One. Next to the suit of Japanese armour." She went on tipping and banging. To Gerald's inflamed nerves, her behaviour seemed too consciously normal.

He collected the book and made his way upstairs. The volume was bound in real leather, and the top of its pages were gilded: apparently a presentation copy. Outside the lounge, Gerald looked at the fly-leaf: in a very large hand was written "To my dear Son, Raglan, on his being honoured by the Queen. From his proud Father, B. Shotcroft, Major-General." Beneath the inscription a very ugly military crest had been appended by a stamper of primitive type.

The suit of Japanese armour lurked in a dark corner as the Commandant himself had done when Gerald had first encountered him. The wide brim of the helmet concealed the black eyeholes in the headpiece; the moustache bristled realistically. It was exactly as if the figure stood guard over the door behind it. On this door was no number, but, there being no other in sight, Gerald took it to be the door of Number One. A short way down the dim, empty passage was a window, the ancient sashes of which shook in the din and blast of the bells. Gerald knocked sharply.

If there was a reply, the bells drowned it; and he knocked again. When to the third knocking there was still no answer, he gently opened the door. He really had to know whether all would or could be well if Phrynne, and doubtless he also, were at all costs to remain in their room until it was dawn. He looked into the room and caught his breath.

There was no artificial light, but the curtains, if there were any, had been drawn back from the single window, and the bottom sash forced up as far as it would go. On the floor by the dusky void, a maelstrom of sound, knelt the Commandant, his cropped white hair faintly catching the moonless glimmer, as his head lay on the sill, like that of a man about to be guillotined. His face was in his hands, but slightly sideways, so that Gerald received a shadowy distorted idea of his expression. Some might have called it ecstatic, but Gerald found it agonised. It frightened him more than anything which had yet happened. Inside the room the bells were like plunging, roaring lions.

He stood for some considerable time quite unable to move. He could not determine whether or not the Commandant knew he was there. The Commandant gave no direct sign of it, but more than once he writhed and shuddered in Gerald's direction, like an unquiet sleeper made more unquiet by an interloper. It was a matter of doubt whether Gerald should leave the book; and he decided to do so mainly because the thought of further contact with it displeased him. He crept into the room and softly laid it on a hardly visible wooden trunk at the foot of the plain metal bedstead. There seemed no other furniture in the room. Outside the door, the hanging mailed fingers of the Japanese figure touched his wrist.

He had not been away from the lounge for long, but it was long enough for Mrs. Pascoe to have begun to drink again. She had left the tidying up half-completed, or rather the room half-disarranged; and was leaning against the overmantel, drawing heavily on a dark tumbler of whisky. Phrynne had not yet finished her Ovaltine.

"How long before the bells stop?" asked Gerald as soon as he opened the lounge door. Now he was resolved that, come what might, they must go. The impossibility of sleep should serve as an excuse.

"I don't expect Mrs. Pascoe can know any more than we can," said Phrynne.

"You should have told us about this—this annual event before accepting our booking."

Mrs. Pascoe drank some more whisky. Gerald suspected that it was neat. "It's not always the same night," she said throatily, looking at the floor.

"We're not staying," said Gerald wildly.

"Darling!" Phrynne caught him by the arm.

"Leave this to me, Phrynne." He addressed Mrs. Pascoe. "We'll pay for the room, of course. Please order me a car."

Mrs. Pascoe was now regarding him stonily. When he asked for a car, she gave a very short laugh. Then her face changed, she made an effort, and she said, "You mustn't take the Commandant so seriously, you know."

Phrynne glanced quickly at her husband.

The whisky was finished. Mrs. Pascoe placed the empty glass on the plastic overmantel with too much of a thud. "No one takes Commandant Shotcroft seriously," she said. "Not even his nearest and dearest."

"Has he any?" asked Phrynne. "He seemed so lonely and pathetic."

"He's Don and I's mascot," she said, the drink interfering with her grammar. But not even the drink could leave any doubt about her rancour.

"I thought he had personality," said Phrynne.

"That and a lot more, no doubt," said Mrs. Pascoe. "But they pushed him out, all the same."

"Out of what?"

"Cashiered, court-martialled, badges of rank stripped off, sword broken in half, muffled drums, the works."

"Poor old man. I'm sure it was a miscarriage of justice."

"That's because you don't know him."

Mrs. Pascoe looked as if she were waiting for Gerald to offer her another whisky.

"It's a thing he could never live down," said Phrynne, brooding to herself, and tucking her legs beneath her. "No wonder he's so queer if all the time it was a mistake."

"I just told you it was not a mistake," said Mrs. Pascoe insolently.

"How can we possibly know?"

"*You* can't. *I* can. No one better." She was at once aggressive and tearful.

"If you want to be paid," cried Gerald, forcing himself in, "make out your bill. Phrynne, come upstairs and pack." If only he hadn't made her unpack between their walk and dinner.

Slowly Phrynne uncoiled and rose to her feet. She had no intention of either packing or departing, but nor was she going to argue. "I shall need your help," she said, softly. "If I'm going to pack."

In Mrs. Pascoe there was another change. Now she looked terrified. "Don't go. Please don't go. Not now. It's too late."

Gerald confronted her. "Too late for what?" he asked harshly.

Mrs. Pascoe looked paler than ever. "You said you wanted a car," she faltered. "You're too late." Her voice trailed away.

Gerald took Phrynne by the arm. "Come on up."

Before they reached the door, Mrs. Pascoe made a further attempt. "You'll be all right if you stay. Really you will." Her voice, normally somewhat strident, was so feeble that the bells obliterated it. Gerald observed that from somewhere she had produced the whisky bottle and was refilling her tumbler.

With Phrynne on his arm he went first to the stout front door. To his surprise it was neither locked nor bolted, but opened at a half-turn of the handle. Outside the building the whole sky was full of bells, the air an inferno of ringing.

He thought that for the first time Phrynne's face also seemed strained and crestfallen. "They've been ringing too long," she said, drawing close to him. "I wish they'd stop."

"We're packing and going. I needed to know whether we could get out this way. We must shut the door quietly."

It creaked a bit on its hinges, and he hesitated with it half-shut, uncertain whether to rush the creak or to ease it. Suddenly, something dark and shapeless, with its arm seeming to hold a black vesture over its head, flitted, all sharp angles, like a bat, down the narrow ill-lighted street, the sound of its passage audible to none. It was the first being that either of them had seen in the streets of Holihaven; and Gerald was acutely relieved that he alone had set eyes upon it. With his hand trembling, he shut the door much too sharply.

But no one could possibly have heard, although he stopped for a second outside the lounge. He could hear Mrs. Pascoe now weeping hysterically; and again was glad that Phrynne was a step or two ahead of him. Upstairs the Commandant's door lay straight before them: they had to pass close beside the Japanese figure, in order to take the passage to the left of it.

But soon they were in their room, with the key turned in the big rim lock.

"Oh God," cried Gerald, sinking on the double bed. "It's pandemonium." Not for the first time that evening he was instantly more frightened than ever by the unintended appositeness of his own words.

"It's pandemonium all right," said Phrynne, almost calmly. "And we're not going out in it."

He was at a loss to divine how much she knew, guessed, or imagined; and any word of enlightenment from him might be inconceivably dangerous. But he was conscious of the strength of her resistance, and lacked the reserves to battle with it.

She was looking out of the window into the main street. "We might *will* them to stop," she suggested wearily.

Gerald was now far less frightened of the bells continuing than of their ceasing. But that they should go on ringing until day broke seemed hopelessly impossible.

Then one peal stopped. There could be no other explanation for the obvious diminution in sound.

"You see!" said Phrynne.

Gerald sat up straight on the side of the bed.

Almost at once further sections of sound subsided, quickly one after the other, until only a single peal was left, that which had begun the ringing. Then the single peal tapered off into a single bell. The single bell tolled on its own, disjointedly, five or six or seven times. Then it stopped, and there was nothing.

Gerald's head was a cave of echoes, mountingly muffled by the noisy current of his blood.

"Oh goodness," said Phrynne, turning from the window and stretching her arms above her head. "Let's go somewhere else tomorrow." She began to take off her dress.

Sooner than usual they were in bed, and in one another's arms. Gerald had carefully not looked out of the window, and neither of them suggested that it should be opened, as they usually did.

"As it's a four-poster, shouldn't we draw the curtains?" asked Phrynne. "And be really snug? After those damned bells?"

"We should suffocate."

"They only drew the curtains when people were likely to pass through the room."

"Darling, you're shivering. I think we *should* draw them."

"Lie still instead, and love me."

But all his nerves were straining out into the silence. There was no sound of any kind, beyond the hotel or within it; not a creaking floorboard or a prowling cat or a distant owl. He had been afraid to look at his watch when the bells stopped, or since: the number of the dark hours before they could leave Holihaven weighed on him. The vision of the Commandant kneeling in the dark window was clear before his eyes, as if the intervening panelled walls were made of stage gauze; and the thing he had seen in the street darted on its angular way back and forth through memory.

Then passion began to open its petals within him, layer upon slow layer; like an illusionist's red flower which, without soil or sun or sap, grows as it is watched. The languor of tenderness began to fill the musty room with its texture and perfume. The transparent walls became again opaque, the old man's vaticinations mere obsession. The street must have been empty, as it was now; the eye deceived.

But perhaps rather it was the boundless sequacity of love that deceived, and most of all in the matter of the time which had passed since the bells stopped ringing; for suddenly Phrynne drew very close to him, and he heard steps in the thoroughfare outside, and a voice calling. These were loud steps, audible from afar even through the shut window; and the voice had the possessed stridency of the street evangelist.

"The dead are awake!"

Not even the thick bucolic accent, the guttural vibrato of emotion, could twist or mask the meaning. At first Gerald lay listening with all his body, and concentrating the more as the noise grew; then he sprang from the bed and ran to the window.

A burly, long-limbed man in a seaman's jersey was running down the street, coming clearly into view for a second at each lamp, and between them lapsing into a swaying lumpy wraith. As he shouted his joyous message, he crossed from side to side and waved his arms frantically. By flashes, Gerald could see that his weatherworn face was transfigured.

"The dead are awake!"

Already, behind him, people were coming out of their houses, and descending from the rooms above shops. There were men, women, and children. Most of them were fully dressed, and must have been waiting in silence and darkness for the call; but a few were dishevelled in night attire or the first garments which had come to hand. Some formed themselves into groups, and advanced arm in arm, as if towards the conclusion of a Blackpool beano. More came singly, ecstatic and waving their arms above their heads, as the first man had done. All cried out, again and again, with no cohesion or harmony. "The dead are awake! The dead are awake!"

Gerald became aware that Phrynne was standing behind him.

"The Commandant warned me," he said brokenly. "We should have gone."

Phrynne shook her head and took his arm. "Nowhere to go," she said. But her voice was soft with fear, and her eyes blank. "I don't expect they'll trouble *us*."

Swiftly Gerald drew the thick plush curtains, leaving them in complete darkness. "We'll sit it out," he said, slightly histrionic in his fear. "No matter what happens."

He scrambled across to the switch. But when he pressed it, light did not come. "The current's gone. We must get back into bed."

"Gerald! Come and help me." He remembered that she was curiously vulnerable in the dark. He found his way to her, and guided her to the bed.

"No more love," she said ruefully and affectionately, her teeth chattering.

He kissed her lips with what gentleness the total night made possible.

"They were going towards the sea," she said timidly.

"We must think of something else."

But the noise was still growing. The whole community seemed to be passing down the street, yelling the same dreadful words again and again.

"Do you think we can?"

"Yes," said Gerald. "It's only until tomorrow."

"They can't be actually dangerous," said Phrynne. "Or it would be stopped."

"Yes, of course."

By now, as always happens, the crowd had amalgamated their utterances and were beginning to shout in unison. They were like agitators bawling a slogan, or massed troublemakers at a football match. But at the same time the noise was beginning to draw away. Gerald suspected that the entire population of the place was on the march.

Soon it was apparent that a processional route was being followed. The tumult could be heard winding about from quarter to quarter; sometimes drawing near, so that Gerald and Phrynne were once more seized by the first chill of panic, then again almost fading away. It was possibly this great variability in the volume of the sound which led Gerald to believe that there were distinct pauses in the massed shouting; periods when it was superseded by far, disorderly cheering. Certainly it began also to seem that the thing shouted had changed; but he could not make out the new cry, although unwillingly he strained to do so.

"It's extraordinary how frightened one can be," said Phrynne, "even when one is not directly menaced. It must prove that we all belong to one another, or whatever it is, after all."

In many similar remarks they discussed the thing at one remove. Experience showed that this was better than not discussing it at all.

In the end there could be no doubt that the shouting had stopped, and that now the crowd was singing. It was no song that Gerald had ever heard, but something about the way it was sung convinced him that it was a hymn or psalm set to an out-of-date popular tune. Once more the crowd was approaching; this time steadily, but with strange, interminable slowness.

"What the hell are they doing now?" asked Gerald of the blackness, his nerves wound so tight that the foolish question was forced out of them.

Palpably the crowd had completed its peregrination, and was returning up the main street from the sea. The singers seemed to gasp and fluctuate, as if worn out with gay exercise, like children at a party. There was a steady undertow of scraping and scuffling. Time passed and more time.

Phrynne spoke. "I believe they're *dancing*."

She moved slightly, as if she thought of going to see.

"No, no," said Gerald, and clutched her fiercely.

There was a tremendous concussion on the ground floor below them. The front door had been violently thrown back. They could hear the hotel filling with a stamping, singing mob.

Doors banged everywhere, and furniture was overturned, as the beatic throng surged and stumbled through the involved darkness of the old building. Glasses went and china and Birmingham brass warming pans. In a moment, Gerald heard the Japanese armour crash to the boards. Phrynne screamed. Then a mighty shoulder, made strong by the sea's assault, rammed at the panelling and their door was down.

> "The living and the dead dance together.
> Now's the time. Now's the place. Now's the weather."

At last Gerald could make out the words.

The stresses in the song were heavily beaten down by much repetition.

Hand in hand, through the dim grey gap of the doorway, the dancers lumbered and shambled in, singing frenziedly and brokenly;

ecstatic but exhausted. Through the stuffy blackness they swayed and shambled, more and more of them, until the room must have been packed tight with them.

Phrynne screamed again. "The smell. Oh, God, the smell."

It was the smell they had encountered on the beach; in the congested room, no longer merely offensive, but obscene, unspeakable.

Phrynne was hysterical. All self-control gone, she was scratching and tearing, and screaming again and again. Gerald tried to hold her, but one of the dancers struck him so hard in the darkness that she was jolted out of his arms. Instantly it seemed that she was no longer there at all.

The dancers were thronging everywhere, their limbs whirling, their lungs bursting with the rhythm of the song. It was difficult for Gerald even to call out. He tried to struggle after Phrynne, but immediately a blow from a massive elbow knocked him to the floor, an abyss of invisible trampling feet.

But soon the dancers were going again: not only from the room, but, it seemed, from the building also. Crushed and tormented though he was, Gerald could hear the song being resumed in the street, as the various frenzied groups debouched and reunited. Within, before long there was nothing but the chaos, the darkness, and the putrescent odour. Gerald felt so sick that he had to battle with unconsciousness. He could not think or move, despite the desperate need.

Then he struggled into a sitting position, and sank his head on the torn sheets of the bed. For an uncertain period he was insensible to everything: but in the end he heard steps approaching down the dark passage. His door was pushed back, and the Commandant entered gripping a lighted candle. He seemed to disregard the flow of hot wax which had already congealed on much of his knotted hand.

"She's safe. Small thanks to you."

The Commandant stared icily at Gerald's undignified figure. Gerald tried to stand. He was terribly bruised, and so giddy that he wondered if this could be concussion. But relief rallied him.

"Is it thanks to *you*?"

"She was caught up in it. Dancing with the rest." The Commandant's eyes glowed in the candlelight. The singing and the dancing had almost died away.

Still Gerald could do no more than sit upon the bed. His voice was low and indistinct, as if coming from outside his body. "Were they... were some of them..."

The Commandant replied, more scornful than ever of his weakness. "She was between two of them. Each had one of her hands."

Gerald could not look at him. "What did you do?" he asked in the same remote voice.

"I did what had to be done. I hope I was in time." After the slightest possible pause he continued. "You'll find her downstairs."

"I'm grateful. Such a silly thing to say, but what else is there?"

"Can you walk?"

"I think so."

"I'll light you down." The Commandant's tone was as uncompromising as always.

There were two more candles in the lounge, and Phrynne, wearing a woman's belted overcoat which was not hers, sat between them, drinking. Mrs. Pascoe, fully dressed but with eyes averted, pottered about the wreckage. It seemed hardly more than as if she were completing the task which earlier she had left unfinished.

"Darling, look at you!" Phrynne's words were still hysterical, but her voice was as gentle as it usually was.

Gerald, bruises and thoughts of concussion forgotten, dragged her into his arms. They embraced silently for a long time; then he looked into her eyes.

"Here I am," she said, and looked away. "Not to worry."

Silently and unnoticed, the Commandant had already retreated.

Without returning his gaze, Phrynne finished her drink as she stood there. Gerald supposed that it was one of Mrs. Pascoe's concoctions.

It was so dark where Mrs. Pascoe was working that her labours could have been achieving little; but she said nothing to her visitors, nor they to her. At the door Phrynne unexpectedly stripped off the overcoat and threw it on a chair. Her nightdress was so torn that she stood almost naked. Dark though it was, Gerald saw Mrs. Pascoe regarding Phrynne's pretty body with a stare of animosity.

"May we take one of the candles?" he said, normal standards reasserting themselves in him.

But Mrs. Pascoe continued to stand silently staring; and they lighted themselves through the wilderness of broken furniture to the ruins of their bedroom. The Japanese figure was still prostrate, and the Commandant's door shut. And the smell had almost gone.

Even by seven o'clock the next morning surprisingly much had been done to restore order. But no one seemed to be about, and Gerald and Phrynne departed without a word.

In Wrack Street a milkman was delivering, but Gerald noticed that his cart bore the name of another town. A minute boy whom they encountered later on an obscure purposeful errand might, however, have been indigenous; and when they reached Station Road, they saw a small plot of land on which already men were silently at work with spades in their hands. They were as thick as flies on a wound, and as black. In the darkness of the previous evening, Gerald and Phrynne had missed the place. A board named it the New Municipal Cemetery.

In the mild light of an autumn morning the sight of the black and silent toilers was horrible; but Phrynne did not seem to find it so. On the contrary, her cheeks reddened and her soft mouth became fleetingly more voluptuous still.

She seemed to have forgotten Gerald, so that he was able to examine her closely for a moment. It was the first time he had done so since the night before. Then, once more, she became herself. In those previous seconds Gerald had become aware of something dividing them which neither of them would ever mention or ever forget.

1984

IF SHE BENDS, SHE BREAKS

John Gordon

John Gordon (1925–2017), was known to his friends and family as Jack. He was born in Jarrow, Tyne and Wear, in the industrial heartland of England's north-east, before moving in 1937 as a 12-year-old outsider to Wisbech in the Cambridgeshire Fens (close to the county's confluence with Lincolnshire and Norfolk). In his memoir he recalled his arrival in the inland port: "A full tide from the Wash had lifted the river's face to within a foot or two of the roadway and we seemed to be riding through a flood." In many regards the place appeared magical to the young Jack, far removed from the abject poverty of post-Depression Jarrow. Later, after a stint in the navy at the end of the Second World War, he returned and became a newspaper reporter for the *Isle of Ely and Wisbech Advertiser*, where he furthered his knowledge of the town and its surroundings. This familiarity shows in his fiction, in which the unsettling flatness of the landscape is virtually omnipresent. "It's the loneliness and absolute clarity of the line between the land and the sky where you can see for miles that always strikes me with a feeling of magic and mystery," he said in a 2009 interview about his last novel, *Fen Runners*.

The House on the Brink (one of my favourite young adult novels—comparable to Alan Garner's *The Owl Service*) was Gordon's second work of fiction, following on two years after 1968's *The Giant Under the Snow*, a highly regarded children's fantasy that centres on the legend of the Green Man. Both were conceived in Norwich, where he had relocated in 1962; he wrote his early books while working on the city's *Evening News*, and went on to publish another fourteen novels. In addition, he was a fine craftsman of spooky short stories, with "If She Bends, She Breaks", which I give you here, perfectly capturing the wintry strangeness of his adopted Fens.

Ben had felt strange ever since the snow started falling. He looked out of the classroom window and saw that it had come again, sweeping across like a curtain. That was exactly what it seemed to be, a curtain. The snow had come down like a blank sheet in his mind, and he could remember nothing beyond it. He could not even remember getting up this morning or walking to school; yesterday was only a haze, and last week did not exist. And now, at this moment, he did not know whether it was morning or afternoon. He began to get to his feet, but dizziness made him sit down.

"I know it's been freezing hard." Miss Carter's voice from the front of the class seemed distant. He wanted to tell her he felt unwell, but just for the moment he did not have the energy. She had her back to the stove as usual, and the eyes behind her glasses stared like a frightened horse's as they always did when she was in a passion. "It's been freezing hard," she repeated, "but the ice is still far too dangerous, and nobody is to go anywhere near it. Do you understand?"

Tommy Drake, in the next desk to Ben, murmured something and grinned at somebody on Ben's other side. But he ignored Ben completely.

"Tommy Drake!" Miss Carter had missed nothing. "What did you say?"

"Nothing, Miss."

"Then why are you grinning like a jackass? If there's a joke, we all want to hear it. On your feet."

As Tommy pushed back his chair, Ben smiled at him, weakly, but Tommy seemed to be in no mood for him and winked at somebody else as though Ben himself was not there.

"Well?" Miss Carter was waiting.

Tommy stood in silence.

"Very well. If you are not going to share your thoughts with the rest of us, perhaps you will remind me of what I was saying a moment ago."

"About the ice, Miss?"

"And what about the ice?"

"That it's dangerous, Miss." Then Tommy, who did not lack courage, went on, "What I was saying was that you can always tell if it's safe."

"Oh you can, can you?" Miss Carter pursed her lips, and again waited.

"If she cracks, she bears," said Tommy. "If she bends, she breaks." It was a lesson they all knew in the flat Fenland where everybody skated in winter. A solid cracking sound in the ice was better than a soft bending. But it meant nothing to Miss Carter.

"Stuff and nonsense!" she cried.

"But everybody knows it's true." Tommy had justice on his side and his round face was getting red.

"Old wives' tales!" Miss Carter was not going to listen to reason. "Sit down."

Ben saw that Tommy was going to argue, and the sudden urge to back him up made him forget his dizziness. He got to his feet. "It's quite true, Miss," he said. "I've tried it out."

She paid no attention to him. She glared at Tommy. "Sit down!"

Tommy obeyed, and Miss Carter pulled her cardigan tighter over her dumpy figure.

"Listen to me, all of you." Her voice was shrill. "I don't care what anybody says in the village; I won't have any of you go anywhere near that ice. Do you hear? Nobody!" She paused, and then added softly, "You all know what can happen."

She had succeeded in silencing the classroom, and as she turned away to her own desk she muttered something to the front row who began putting their books away. It was time for Break.

Ben was still standing. In her passion she seemed not to have seen him. "What's up with her?" he said, but Tommy was on his feet and heading towards the cloakroom with the rest.

The dizziness came over Ben again. Could nobody see that he was unwell? Or was his illness something so terrible that everybody wanted to ignore it? The classroom had emptied, and Miss Carter was wiping her nose on a crumpled paper handkerchief. He would tell her how he felt, and perhaps she would get his sister to walk home with him. He watched her head swing towards him and he opened his mouth to speak, but her glance swept over him and she turned to follow the others.

A movement outside one of the classroom's tall, narrow windows made him look out. One boy was already in the yard, and the snow was thick and inviting. Beyond the railings there was the village, and through a gap in the houses he could see the flat fens, stretching away in a desert of whiteness. He knew it all. He had not lost his memory. The stuffiness of the classroom was to blame—and outside there was delicious coolness, and space. Without bothering to follow the others to the cloakroom for his coat, he went out.

There was still only the boy in the playground; a new kid kicking up snow. He was finding the soft patches, not already trodden, and as he ploughed into them he made the snow smoke around his ankles so that he almost seemed to lack feet.

Ben went across to him and said, "They let you out early, did they?"

The new kid raised his head and looked at the others who were now crowding out through the door. "I reckon," he said.

"Me an' all," said Ben. It wasn't strictly true, but he didn't mind bending the truth a bit as he had been feeling ill. But not any more. "Where d'you come from?" he asked.

"Over yonder." The new kid nodded vaguely beyond the railings and then went back to kicking snow. "It's warm, ain't it?" he said, watching the powder drift around his knees. "When you get used to it."

"What do your dad do?"

"Horseman," said the kid, and that was enough to tell Ben where he lived and where his father worked. Only one farm for miles had working horses. Tommy's family, the Drakes, had always had horses and were rich enough to have them working alongside tractors, as a kind of hobby.

"You live along Pingle Bank, then," said Ben. The horseman had a cottage there near the edge of the big drainage canal, the Pingle, that cut a straight, deep channel across the flat fens.

"That's right," said the kid, and looked up at the sky. "More of it comin'."

The clouds had thickened over the winter sun and, in the grey light, snow had begun to fall again. The kid held his face up to it. "Best time o' the year, winter. Brings you out into the open, don't it?"

"Reckon," Ben agreed. "If them clouds was in summer we should be gettin' soaked."

"I hate gettin' wet." The kid's face was pale, and snow was resting on his eyelashes.

"Me an' all."

They stood side by side and let the snow fall on them. The kid was quite right; it seemed warm.

Then the snowball fight rolled right up to them, and charging through the middle of it came Tommy pulling Ben's sister on her sledge. Just like him to have taken over the sledge and Jenny and barge into the new kid as though he was nobody. Ben stooped, rammed snow into two hard fistfuls and hurled them with all his force at Tommy's red face. He was usually a good shot but he missed, and Tommy was yelling at Jenny as she laboured to make snowballs and pile them on the sledge.

"They ain't no good! Look, they're fallin' apart." Tommy crouched and swept them all back into the snow.

Jenny had no height but a lot of temper. She was on her feet, her face as red as his, and yanked her sledge away.

"Bring that back!" he yelled, but Ben was already charging at him.

Tommy must have been off-balance because it took no more than a touch to push him sideways and send him into the snow flat on his back.

"You want to leave my sister alone." Ben sat on his chest with his knees on Tommy's arms. "Tell her you're sorry."

He and Tommy were the same size, both strong, and sometimes they banged their heads together just to see who would be the first to back off. But this time, without any effort or even bothering to answer him Tommy sat up and spilled Ben off his chest as though he had no weight at all. And as he tilted back helplessly, Ben saw the new kid standing by, watching.

"Hi!" he shouted. "Snowball fight. You're on my side."

The kid looked pretty useful; pale, but solid. And Ben needed help.

"You done it wrong," the new kid said to Ben, and without hurrying he stepped forward.

The kid reached out to where Tommy was still sitting and put a hand over his face, spreading out pale, cold fingers across his mouth and eyes. He seemed merely to stroke him, but Tommy fell backwards.

"You don't need no pressure," said the kid. "All you got to do is let 'em know you're there."

"You got him!" Ben had rolled away to let the kid tackle Tommy alone. "Show us your stuff!"

The kid seemed to be in no hurry, and Tommy lay where he was, one startled eye showing between the pallid fingers. Any second now and there would be a quick thrust of limbs and Tommy would send the kid flying. It was stupid to wait for it; Ben started forward to stop the massacre.

But then the kid looked up. The snow was still in his eyelashes, and a crust of it was at the corners of his mouth, like ice.

"Want me to do any more?" he asked.

In the rest of the playground, shouts of snowfights echoed against the high windows and dark walls of the old school building, but in this corner the grey clouds seemed to hang lower as if to deaden the kid's voice.

"I asked you," he said. "You want to see me do some more?"

Tommy stirred, gathering himself to push. In a moment the boy would pay for being so careless, unless he had some trick and was pressing on a nerve. Ben wanted to see what would happen. He nodded.

The kid did not look away from Ben, but his hand left Tommy's face. And Tommy did not get up. He simply lay there with his eyes and mouth wide open. He looked scared.

The kid, still crouching, began to stroke the snow. He curved his fingers and raked it, dusting the white powder into Tommy's hair, then over his brow and his eyes, and then the kid's hand, so pale it could not be seen in the snow, was over Tommy's lips, and snow was being thrust into the gaping mouth. The kid leant over him and Tommy was terrified. He tried to shout, but more snow was driven into his mouth. He rolled over, thrashing helplessly.

The kid paused as though waiting for instructions. But Ben, curious to see what Tommy would do, waited.

It was then that the brittle little sound of a handbell reached them. It came from the porch where Miss Carter was calling them in. But suddenly the sound ceased, and even the shouting of the snowfights died. The whole playground had seen her drop the bell.

She started forward, pushing her way through the crowds, and then, caught up in her anxiety, they came with her like black snowflakes on the wind.

It was Tommy, jerking and choking on the ground, that drew them. It was no natural fooling in the snow. He was fighting to breathe. And the new kid stood over him, looking down.

"Tommy, what have you done!" Miss Carter was stooping over him, crying out at the sight of his mouth wide open and full of whiteness. "Oh my God!"

Ben stared across her bent back at the new kid. He simply stood where he was, a sprinkle of white in the short crop of his black hair, and gazed back at him.

"Who did this to you?" Miss Carter had thrust her fingers into the snow-gape in Tommy's face, and rolled him over so that he was coughing, gasping, and heaving all at once. "How did it happen?"

But he could not answer and she helped him to his feet and began walking with him.

"Who saw it? Which of you did this?" She had snow in her fur-lined boots and her grey hair was untidy. Her little red nose was sharp with the cold and she pointed it round the ring that had gathered, sniffing out the guilty one. "You?" Her eyes were on Ben but had passed by almost before he had shaken his head. "What about you?" The new kid was at the back of the crowd and did not even have to answer.

Denials came from every side, and the chattering crowd followed her into school.

Ben and the kid hung back, and were alone in the porch when the door closed and shut them out. Neither had said a word, and Ben turned towards him. The kid stood quite still gazing straight ahead as though the door was the open page of a book and he was reading it. He wore a long black jacket, and a grey scarf was wound once around his neck and hung down his back. Ben noticed for the first time that the kid's black trousers were knee-length and were tucked into long, thick socks. They looked like riding breeches, and he thought the kid must help his father with the horses. But his boots were big and clumsy, not elegant like a horseman's. There was something gawky about him; he looked poor and old-fashioned.

"You done all right," said Ben. "Tommy ain't bad in a fight."

The kid turned towards him. There was still unmelted snow on his cheeks, and his eyelashes were tinged with white. His dark eyes were liquid as though he was on the verge of crying, but that was false. They had no expression at all. "He ain't as good as he reckon," said the kid, and left it at that.

"What class you in?" Ben asked.

"Same as you."

"Didn't notice you."

"I were by the stove."

"Miss Carter always keep her bum to that, that's why it don't throw out no heat," said Ben, but the kid did not smile. He led the way inside.

They had not been missed. Miss Carter was still fussing around Tommy. She had pulled the fireguard back from the stove so that he could go to the front of the class and sit close to it. But she was still angry. "I'm going to catch whoever did that to you, and when I do..." She pinched in her little mouth until it was lipless and her eyes needled round the room.

Ben had taken his usual place at the back, and suddenly he realised the new kid had wandered off. He searched and found him. He was sitting at a desk no more than two paces from Miss Carter and Tommy. He had one arm over the desk lid, and the other resting loosely on the back of his chair. He was quite untroubled.

"Stand up, Tommy," Miss Carter ordered. "Now turn round and point out who did this terrible thing."

Tommy, a hero now, was enjoying himself. He faced the class. Ben could see the pale curve of the new kid's cheek and guessed at the deep-water look of the eyes that were turned on Tommy.

"Tommy!" said Miss Carter, and obediently Tommy looked round the room. He smirked at several people but not at Ben. He ignored him as though angry with him for what had happened yet not prepared to betray him. But there was a real risk he would get his revenge on the kid. Yet again his glance went by as though the boy's desk was empty, and he said, "Nobody done it. I just fell over, that's all."

The girl next to Ben whispered to her friend, "Maybe he had a fit. That looked like it with his mouth all white. Like he was foaming."

"Be quiet!" Miss Carter had lost her patience. "Sit down!" she ordered Tommy, and for the rest of the afternoon she was savage, even with him.

From time to time Ben looked towards the new kid, but he kept his head bowed over his work and Ben saw no more than the black bristles of his cropped hair. Nobody attempted to speak to him because whenever anybody moved, Miss Carter snapped.

The last half-hour dragged, but then, with a rattle of pencils and a banging of desk lids, the afternoon ended. The new kid wasted no time. He was out of the door ahead of everybody else, and Ben did not catch him until he was halfway across the playground.

"Where you going?" he asked.

"The Pingle."

"We ain't supposed to. Because of the ice."

"I live there."

Then Ben remembered the horseman's cottage on the bank, but he said, "Ain't you going to hang around here a bit? We got some good slides in the yard."

"Ice is better."

The others, charging out at the door, prevented Ben saying more. Jenny, with her sledge, was being chased by Tommy. He was himself again and was telling her, "Your sledge will go great on the Pingle."

"I don't want to go," she said.

A bigger girl butted in. "You heard what Miss Carter said, Tommy Drake. Ain't you got no sense?"

Tommy paid no attention. "Come on, Jenny. I ain't got time to go home and fetch me skates, or else I would. I'll bring 'em tomorrow and you can have a go. Promise."

She was tempted, but she said, "I don't want to go there. And you know why."

"I won't take a step on it unless it's rock hard," said Tommy.

"I ain't going," said Jenny.

At the school gate, the kid moved his feet impatiently on the step. It had been cleared of snow and the metal studs on his boots rattled.

Tommy had also lost his patience. "If she cracks she bears, if she bends she breaks. Everybody know that's true, no matter what old Carter say. And I won't budge away from the bank unless it's safe."

"No," said Jenny.

Suddenly the kid kicked at the steps and made sparks fly from the sole of his boot, and Tommy looked up. The wind dived over the school roof in a howl and a plunge of snow, and the kid's voice merged with it as he yelled, "Come on!"

He and Ben ran together, and Tommy grabbed at the sledge and made for the gate. Several others came with him.

Ben and the boy kept ahead of the rest as they rounded the corner into the lane. Traffic had failed to churn up the snow and had packed it hard, almost icy, so it would have been as good as anywhere for Jenny's sledge, but Ben ran with the boy between hedges humped and white, and the others followed.

They left the road just before it climbed to the bridge across the Pingle, and they stood at the top of the bank, looking down. They were the first to come here. The grass blades, slowly arching as the snow had added petal after petal through the day, supported an unbroken roof just clear of the ground. Below them, the straight, wide channel stretched away to left and right through the flat, white land. The water had become a frozen road, and the wind had swept it almost clear, piling the snow in an endless, smooth drift on the far side.

Tommy had come up alongside them. "You could go for miles!" he shouted.

But Jenny hung back. "I don't like it." The air was grey and cold and it almost smothered her small voice. "I want to go home."

"It ain't dark yet." His voice yelped as though it came from the lonely seagull that angled up on a frozen gust far out over the white plain. He began to move forward. "Let's get down there."

"She doesn't want to go." Ben was close to him, but Tommy paid no heed. "Nobody's going down that bank, Tommy." Ben stepped forward, blocking his way. "Nobody!"

Tommy came straight on. His eyes met Ben's but their expression did not change. His whole attention was focused on the ice below and his gaze seemed to go through Ben as though he was not there.

In a sudden cold anger Ben lowered his head and lunged with both arms. He thrust at Tommy's chest with all his force. His fingers touched, but in the instant of touching they lost their grip. He thrust with all his power, but it was air alone that slid along his arms and fingers, and Tommy was past and through and plunging down the bank.

The kid, watching him, said, "You still don't do it right."

Tommy had taken Jenny's sledge with him, and at the ice edge he turned and shouted to them up the bank. "Come on, all of you!"

"No!" Ben stood in front of them. "Don't go!" He opened his arms, but they came in a group straight for him. "Stop!" They did not answer. Their eyes did not look directly at him. They pushed into him, like a crush of cattle, pretending he was not there. He clutched at one after another but the strange weakness he had felt earlier made him too flimsy to stop anything and they were beyond him and going down to join Tommy.

"I got to teach you a few things," said the kid.

"I don't feel too good," said Ben. "I think I ought to go home."

The boy gazed at him for a moment with eyes that again seemed to be rimmed with frost, and shook his head. "There's them down there to see to," he said.

Slowly, Ben nodded. He had to think of Jenny.

They went down together and found Tommy still on the bank. Frozen reeds stood up through the ice and there was a seepage of water at the edge that made them all hesitate. All except the new kid. He put one foot on it, testing.

"If she cracks she bears," he said.

Ben watched. The boy had plenty of courage. He was leaning forward now, putting all his weight on the ice.

"She cracks," he said.

But Ben had heard nothing. "No," he called out. "She bends."

He was too late. The boy had stepped out on to the ice. Then Ben heard the crack under his boots, and the echo of it ringing from bank to bank and away along the endless ice in thin winter music.

The boy moved out until he was a figure in black in the middle of the channel. "She bears," he called out, and Ben, who knew he could never stop the others now, stepped out to be with him.

There was no crack this time, but the ice held. He could feel the gentle pulse of it as he walked towards the middle. There was something almost like a smile on the new kid's face. "Both of us done it," he said, and Ben nodded.

On the bank there was a squabble. The big girl, protecting Jenny, was trying to pull the sledge rope from Tommy. "Let her have her sledge," she said. "You didn't ought to have brung her here."

"It's safe enough."

"I don't care whether it's safe or not, you didn't ought to have brung her. Not Jenny, of all people."

"Why all the fuss about Jenny?" said Ben to the kid. "I don't know what they're going on about."

"Don't you?" The kid's eyes, darkening as the day dwindled, rested on him. Far away along the length of the frozen channel, snow and sky and darkness joined.

"Why don't they come out here?" said Ben. "They can see us."

"We can go and fetch 'em," said the kid.

"How?"

"Get hold of that sledge. They'll follow."

Ben hesitated. Perhaps he was too weak to do even that.

The kid saw his doubt, and said, "You've pulled a sledge before, ain't you?" Ben nodded. "Well all you got to do is remember what it feel like. That's all."

Ben had to rely on him. Everything he had tried himself had gone wrong. He walked across to where Tommy was still arguing.

"See what you done to her," the girl was saying. She had her arm around Jenny's shoulder and Jenny was crying, snuffling into her gloves. "Ain't you got no feelings, Tommy Drake?"

"Well just because it happened once," said Tommy, "that ain't to say it's going to happen again."

"Wasn't just once!" The girl thrust her head forward, accusing him. "There was another time." She lifted her arm from Jenny's shoulder and pointed up the bank behind her. "There was a boy lived up there, along Pingle Bank; he came down here and went through the ice one winter time, and they never found him till it thawed."

"That were a long time ago," said Tommy. "Years before any of us was born."

"You ought to know about that if anybody do, Tommy Drake. That boy's father worked on your farm. Everybody know about that even if it was all them years ago. His father were a horseman and lived along the bank."

"Hey!" Ben was close to Tommy. "Just like the new kid."

But even that did not make Tommy turn his way. Ben reached for the sledge rope and jerked it. He felt the rope in his fingers just before it slipped through and fell, but he had tugged it from Tommy's grasp and the sledge ran out on to the ice.

"Come on, Tommy," he said. "Come with me and the new kid."

The girl was watching the sledge and accusing Tommy. "What did you want to do that for?"

"I didn't," he said.

"I did it," said Ben, but nobody looked towards him.

The girl was furious with Tommy. "Just look what you done. Now you'll have to leave it."

Tommy had put one foot on the ice, testing it. "I ain't frit," he said. "I reckon it'll hold."

"Of course it will." Ben encouraged him. "We're both out here, ain't we?" He paused and looked over his shoulder to make sure, but the kid was still there, watching. "Two of us. Me and him."

Tommy had both feet on the ice and had taken another step. "See," he called to the others on the bank. "Nothing to it."

"Don't you make a parade out there by yourself any longer, Tommy Drake." The girl pulled Jenny's face tighter into her shoulder and made an effort to muffle Jenny's ears. She leant forward as far as she could, keeping her voice low so that Jenny should not hear. "Can't you see what you're doing to her? This were just the place where Ben went through the ice last winter."

Tommy, stamping to make the ice ring beneath him, kept his back to her. "If she cracks," he said, "she bears. If she bends, she breaks."

"Can't you hear?" said the girl. "This is just the place where Ben were drowned!"

The snow came in a sudden flurry, putting a streaked curtain between Ben and the rest of them. It was then that he remembered. He remembered everything. The kid had come up to stand beside him, and they stood together and watched.

The ice under Tommy sagged as they knew it would. They heard the soft rending as it split, and they saw its broken edge rear up. They heard the yell and the slither, and remembered the cold gulp of the black water that, with years between, had swallowed each of them. But now it was somebody else who slid under.

Then Jenny's scream reached Ben through the wind that was pushing down the channel as the night came on. She should be at home; not out here watching this. He stooped to the sledge and pushed. On the bank they saw nothing but a tight spiral of snow whipped up from the ice, but the sledge slid into the water beside Tommy and floated. He grabbed at it.

From out on the ice they saw the girl, held by the others, reach from the bank and grasp the rope, and then Tommy, soaking and freezing, crawled into the white snow and made it black. They watched as the whole group, sobbing and murmuring, climbed the bank, showed for a few moments against the darkening sky and were gone.

In the empty channel the two figures stood motionless. Their eyes gazed unblinking through the swirl as the snow came again, hissing as it blew between the frozen reeds.

1990

DR. MATTHEWS' GHOST STORY

Penelope Fitzgerald

Penelope Mary Fitzgerald (*née* Knox, 1916–2000) was a biographer and one of the great British novelists of the twentieth century. The granddaughter of two bishops, her father was a poet and the editor of *Punch* magazine. Her earliest years were spent in Sussex, before her father's editorship took the family to the capital. She went to school in Buckinghamshire and earned a scholarship to Somerville College, Oxford, where she received a first in English in 1938. She married Desmond Fitzgerald in 1942, with whom she had three children. After the war, the pair co-edited the *World Review*, a cultural and literary magazine, until it folded in 1953. She later worked for a time as a bookseller in Southwold, Suffolk, before becoming a teacher.

Fitzgerald's first book did not come until 1975, when she was aged 58: a biography of the Pre-Raphaelite artist Edward Burne-Jones. *The Golden Child*, her debut novel, followed two years after but it was *The Bookshop* (1978), drawing on her experiences in Southwold, that brought the first of her four Booker Prize nominations; she was to win it the following year with *Offshore*. Perhaps her greatest work—and my personal favourite—is her last, *The Blue Flower*, which explores the life of the eighteenth-century German poet "Novalis". Even so, of all her books it is *The Gate of Angels* (1990), set in the Cambridge of 1912 with its portrayal of an imagined, but accurate, simulacra of M. R. James—Dr. Matthews, the Provost of "St James"—that I most wish I had written. She even manages to include within the novel a wonderful standalone pastiche of a Jamesian story that's terrifying in its own right; I present that to you here.

When I was a young man, I took part in any dig that was going, whether it was likely to lead to anything or not. You see, I was set in my bent very early, I mean the discoveries that can be made from old texts, and the discoveries that can be coaxed out of the earth itself and even more from brick and stone. One would say, a peaceful occupation enough. Anyway, it happened that our summer expedition of 1869 was, of all places, to the fields opposite what is now Mr. Turner's farm—only there was no house near it then, and no Mr. Turner—(the name at the farm was Hinton)—and, instead of the present road there was a cart-track across the fields which had been raised where it passed the farm gates into something like a bridge. It had been strengthened at that point with brickwork; after a summer storm, you could watch the sandmartins sliding in and out of the drainage holes, and I don't think I have ever seen so many swifts.

The bricks were very old, certainly mediæval. It had been established by the man in charge of our little expedition, Edward Nisbet—(you will not remember him)—that between the second half of the thirteenth century and 1427 there had been a small nunnery at this unlikely spot. The nuns were Sisters of the Seven Sorrows. The dedication had been to St. Salomé, the Virgin Mary's midwife. The farm, at the time, may well have been connected with the nunnery. All four of us stayed there, sleeping two and two in the four-posters in the garrets. The farmer's wife was pleased enough to have our custom. Selling eggs and poultry, and taking in passing guests, were the only extra money she could hope for, and how many people were likely to pass there in those days before the road was made?

"I hope you young gentlemen slept sound," she asked us the first morning. We hastened to reassure her, except for Nisbet, who, while scrupulously polite, cared very much for accuracy.

"Nothing of great importance, but you and your friends were singing and talking very late, Mrs. Hinton."

—"You mean me and Hinton? We're never late retiring. We work too hard for that."

The rest of us, discerning a little resentment, or self-righteousness, here, said that we had heard nothing. I had slept in the same room as Nisbet, and I had certainly heard nothing.

We had paid Hinton to have the top-soil turned over before we came so that we could start our measurements and drawings at once. We had also hired two farmworkers, who gave it as their opinion that the site looked like nothing so much as a couple of rows of piggeries. The ground plan of the convent, to tell the truth, seemed likely to turn out to be nothing very particular. The only real interest of the place lay in an account given in 1426 of a special visitation ordered by the Bishop of Ely. At that time things were in an unsatisfactory state. There were only two very old women there who still wore the habit, though both were dirty and neglected, and a third who, though also old, was said to be of immoral life. The roof was described as "not sufficient to keep out the rain". The Bishop seems to have sent a second commissioner, empowered if necessary to evict the women and rehouse them in the convent of St. Radegund. But the place was unimportant, and no further records survive. If the Bishop's visitor arrived, there is no means of knowing what happened to him. By the time the road was built there had been nothing for some three hundred years to show where once the nunnery stood. The grass covered it, the cattle moved over it.

Nisbet was no better the following night, when he actually woke me by dashing cold water in my face and told me that he could not only hear the voices but, quite distinctly, what was said.

"In, in, in", again and again, and once, "in with him. Under, under, under." The voices rose very high, higher than a woman's, he thought. They had been terrible to him.

The idea of some kind of joke on the part of Mrs. Hinton arose, but to be rejected at once. Mrs. Hinton laughed once and only once during one short stay, when one of our party tripped over the worn front doorstep of the farm kitchen and measured his length on the floor. Then she did laugh, in fact wept and wheezed with laughter. She didn't, she said, in the usual run, see anything like that from one year's end to the other, and it had done her good.

"One must be glad to have done our hostess good," said Nisbet. "I suppose, by the way, she can't be susceptible to rheumatism."

"I suppose the whole Fen country is agueish," I said.

"You don't feel a touch of it, Matthews?"—Did he? I asked.

"I'm in pain," he answered, and now that I looked at him (it being a feature of living closely with anyone that you cease looking at them attentively) I saw that there was a leaden paleness, a darkness round his eyes and nostrils, which would normally be a symptom of the very ill.

"What sort of pain?"

"There is a pressure. I feel constricted."

"That's in your mind, Nisbet."

"It's not in my mind."

"Let us get some fresh air."

We went down to the diggings, although it was only just light.

Nisbet at once suggested that we ought to open up the brickwork and the culverts in the ditch.

I have already referred to the culverts as being certainly as old as the convent. The field, of course, no longer relied on them for its drainage. Still, if they were dismantled, they would have to be put back, and neither of our farmworkers seemed very confident about being able to do this. To our astonishment, they both expressed the opinion that it was a bad thing to meddle about with old drainage work, and that there was no telling what was underneath it.

"But that's exactly what we're here for," I said. "That's what we're paying you for. We particularly want to know what is underneath it."

They said they'd known jobs like that before, which had ended with the ground caving in and collapsing altogether. Pressed, they could not give the exact details. I am sure, however, that we should not have persisted with the idea if Nisbet had not shown such a sickly eagerness and a disposition, while the rest of us were at our surveying and note-taking, to linger round the culvert.

"Hang it," the others said. "He's nosing about like a dog round a sewer."

He went out before we did, and came back later. Hoping to lighten the atmosphere, I asked him if he had seen anything in particular? To my surprise, he said he thought he had.

"Well, what, or whom?"

Reluctantly, he told me that it was an old woman, who had opened her mouth at him, as though gaping or gobbling. She was quite toothless. Now, forty years ago, old women without teeth were more common than not. If they were poor, they had no remedy. I asked him why he should care about that? He answered that he had been afraid she would touch him. I would have felt like laughing if he hadn't looked as he did.

"Where was she going?" I asked.

"To Guestingley, I suppose. There was nowhere else she could go." He repeated, "I was afraid she was going to touch me."

I forget whether I mentioned that the other two members of our party were medical students. Although that by no means proved they knew anything very much, I decided to ask them something about the effects of strain, and whether we oughtn't to advise, or persuade, Nisbet to go home as soon as possible. Before I had the opportunity to do this, however, Nisbet told me that the night before, during which I must admit I had been sleeping soundly, he had got up and gone down to the ditch again to examine the brickwork in the bright moonlight.

"Well, and was your old woman there?"

He had seen three women, he said. They were down on hands and knees, poring at something large and dark which they had brought with them. It was the naked body of a man. The man was not dead, because there was some movement of the legs and feet. Then, by a process which Nisbet could not see, the man, whose bones must have been crushed and collapsed and his body distorted into a shape of grotesque length and thinness, was being inserted inch by inch into the culvert. He never made a sound, but the feet still moved.

—"And what did they say, these women?"

—"They said 'in', 'in', and then 'under'."

"There'll be a moon tonight," I said. "I can't help feeling that it's a good deal easier to observe things by day, but if you want to do this night walking again, I shall come with you."

He looked at me as if he couldn't remember exactly who I was. I should have said that by this time he was eating almost nothing, whereas the rest of us, after working all day in the open air, had very large appetites. We could not, of course, ask him not to sit at table with us, but it would have been much more pleasant if he had not. Mrs. Hinton's feeling obviously was that he had paid for his board, so he ought to be given it. She put down great platefuls in front of him and took them away untouched without a word.

We went to our rooms and to bed.

"What the blazes are you doing?" I shouted, waking up suddenly. I had gone to sleep, and Nisbet, who had not undressed, was just going out of the room. I put on my Norfolk jacket and followed. Once outside the house, although normally Nisbet never ran, he began to run. I caught up with him at the same wretched place. He was lying down on the ditch, still damp and full of long weeds and grasses in the height of summer.

"I was waiting for you, Matthews."

"Waiting for what? Have you found anything?"

"I wasn't looking for anything. I know what's there. My point is—have you got a sharp knife?"

"What for? I daresay I could fetch one from the kitchen."

"All this should have been done in silence. You must cut my tongue out. That will be the work for you to do."

I was determined to get him back to the farm. His mind seemed to have given way, which was a relief rather than otherwise. At that age I was reasonably strong. Rather stronger than Nisbet, perhaps. They talk about dragging people away, but how can you do it unless you can get hold of an arm or a leg? We were wrestling, both covered with grass and dirt. Nisbet repeated again and again, with an unpleasant tone of voice, "In, in, sweetheart. In, in!"

—"This won't do, old fellow," I said. His "in, in" made my flesh creep. I wasn't getting the better of him, and suddenly he reached over and stuck his right hand and half his arm in the culvert. It was a night of broken cloud and I could hardly see what I was doing. I got down and lay shoulder to shoulder with him, putting my left arm under his left armpit. Then I began to heave. It wasn't simply a question of his being caught or being stuck in the drain tunnel. Someone was hauling against me, stroke by stroke, to get him away.

"Pull together, Nisbet," I shouted in his ear. "Imagine we're both back at school. The tug-of-war, Nisbet, think of that. Heave!" I did not know where Nisbet had been at school, but I couldn't think of any other appeal to make. From what I could see, he was not looking much like a schoolboy. He was doing nothing to help me. He was doing his frantic best, in fact, to get free from me. Still "in, in, in". The only chance I had was when (as at last he did, lolling sideways) he fainted. Now the arm came out free, like a recoil. The hand had not gone, it was still joined at the wrist, but it was bones and tendons only. All the flesh had been dragged or sucked off to the last shreds. They had it all. I said aloud, "He'll bleed to death." But my shouting—"Pull together", I suppose, and so forth,—must have been much louder than I knew and the other two fellows were running in their nightshirts down from the farm. I did not think of what they would feel when they saw poor Nisbet.

Neither of them had dealt before with a major haemorrhage, still, once he was on the kitchen table, they were able to manage a tourniquet. I fetched the doctor myself. I have forgotten now what explanation I gave. "We are just on a quiet little expedition," I said. "During the summer vacation." The doctor said he had never, in all his experience, been called in to an accident like this, particularly as the result of a quiet little expedition.

I do not know that you are ever likely to hear much more about this story. Certainly, Nisbet, although he recovered, was always very unwilling to talk about it. Because of his disability, he never took orders, for which he had been intended. Apart from the loss of his arm up to the elbow, there was some impairment to the brain. I believe he went to live abroad, I think in Belgium; yes, it was Belgium.

You will ask, what of the excavations? They were never taken in hand again, although there was necessarily some digging when the road was built. I made it my business at that time to find out whether anything worth noticing had been turned up. Yes, an ancient male skeleton, a curiosity, and rather a horrible one. It appeared to have been crushed and rolled up and then stretched or elongated. It was difficult to see how such a thing could have been carried out, particularly if it was done before the man was dead. There were a few rags of flesh, rather like the leather tongues of shoes; cured, you see, by the damp. To historians, much the most interesting items were some scraps of parchment which had been thrust or stuffed at some point, in a quite unseemly way, into the corpse. The few letters (there were no complete words) which could be deciphered made it almost certain that these scraps were part of a *quoniam igitur*—a writ of eviction issued by the Bishop, following on a second visit and inspection. You must remember that although there are more than ten thousand mediæval writs of *significavit* in the Public Record Office, there was, up to that time, not a single example of a *quoniam igitur*. You will understand, therefore, the historians' excitement. But it must be said that historians, in my experience, are excitable people.

2008

POSSUM

Matthew Holness

Matthew Holness (b. 1975) is a writer, actor and director who wrote and starred in the 1980s-horror spoof *Garth Marenghi's Darkplace* from 2004 (its earlier stage incarnation won the 2001 Edinburgh Comedy Award). The Channel 4 six-parter remains a cult favourite and, for me, one of the great comedy series of this century. Matthew's debut feature-length work as a director came in 2018 with *Possum*, a hugely atmospheric and disturbing psychological horror movie set in Norfolk, the county where he's lived for more than fifteen years.

Away from film and television, Matthew has written several anthologised eerie tales, and two successful novels, *Garth Marenghi's TerrorTome* (2022) and *Garth Marenghi's Incarcerat* (2023). He also contributed the introduction to Swan River Press's 2019 edition of Sheridan Le Fanu's "Green Tea", Matthew's own favourite literary work of the genre.

"Possum", which you're about to read here, was written in 2008, the year Matthew moved to Norfolk. "The initial idea came to me while walking a stretch of the north Kent coastline close to where I grew up—but much of its territory was informed by my watching of Lawrence Gordon Clark's BBC adaptation of *A Warning to the Curious*," Matthew says. "I remember listening to the soundtrack music while writing the story, so I think East Anglia was always in my mind. With the screen version, I fully shifted the locale to Norfolk and created a fictional town called Fallmarsh."

Many of the movie's most-striking scenes were shot at Stiffkey, just a few miles from the pine-littered dunes and empty sands that haunt the climax of Clark's seminal 1972 adaptation. And the thing that is Possum itself presents a similarly terrifying apparition, both on the page and on the screen, to the earlier film's William Ager ("No diggin' 'ere!"). Given a choice, I really couldn't say which of the two I'd rather be confronted by under those endless, lonely skies...

I picked it up by the head, which had grown clammy inside the bag, drawing to it a fair amount of fluff and dirt, and pushed the obscene tongue back into its mouth. Then I blew away the black fibres from its eyes and lifted out the stiff, furry body, attached to its neck with rusted nails. The paws had been retracted by means of a small rotating mechanism contained within the bag handle itself, and I detached the connecting wires from the small circuit pad drilled into its back. Forcing my hand through the hole in its rear, around which in recent months I had positioned a number of small razor blades, I felt within for the concealed wooden handle. Locating it, and ignoring the pain along my forearm, I swerved the head slowly left and right, supporting the main body with my free hand while holding it up against my grubby mirror.

I'd come home to bury it, which was as good a place as any, despite my growing dislike of the mild southern winters. Yet, having stepped from the train carriage earlier that afternoon and sensed, by association I suppose, the stretch of abandoned line passing close behind my old primary school, up towards the beach and the marshes beyond, I'd elected to burn it instead; on one of Christie's stupid bonfires, if he was still up to building them.

Despite my intentions, I'd felt inclined to unveil Possum midjourney and hold what was left up against the compartment window as we passed through stations; my own head concealed, naturally. But I'd thought better of that; I dare say rightly. In any case, the bag concealing him drew inevitable attention when, entering the underpass on my way back to the house, one of his legs shot out, startling two small boys who were attempting to hurry past. Several adjustments to the internal mechanism in recent years had enabled the puppet's limbs to extend outward at alarming speeds, so that when operated in the presence of suggestible onlookers, it looked as if the legs of some demonic creature, coarse and furred, had darted suddenly from an unseen crevice. Then, as happened rather beautifully on this occasion, the perturbed children, or child, more often than not would catch sight of a second, larger hole, carefully positioned at the rear of the bag to capture their peripheral vision, and glimpse, within, an eye following them home. The effect, I must say, was rather stunning, yet had, like any great performance, taken years to perfect.

Christie had not been at home when I'd arrived, although as usual the front door had been left ajar and the kitchen table crammed with large piles of rubbish awaiting destruction. Stacked among the old comics and clothes I'd found the familiar contents of my bedroom drawer, along with an old tube of my skin cream and a skull fragment I'd once dug up at the beach. Having retrieved these, I'd drunk a large measure of his cheap whiskey, tried the lounge door, which, as expected, was locked, then taken my bag up to the bedroom. The walls had been re-papered again with spare rolls from the loft, familiar cartoon faces from either my sixth or seventh year. The boards were still damp, the floor slimy, and a strong odour of paste hung heavily in the cramped room. I'd opened a window—the weather was indeed horribly mild—and switched the overhead bulb off, favouring darkness for what I was about to do.

Although the body was that of a dog, Possum's head was made of wax and shaped like a human's, and I could not have wished for a more convincing likeness. Capturing even my old acne scars, yet with hair less neat and a gaunt quality reminiscent of the physical state I had embodied when the mould was made, the eyes were its greatest feature. Belonging to what had once been a bull terrier, both were former lab specimens, heavily diseased, preserved together for years in an old jar of formaldehyde. Several minor adjustments and refinements made by a former colleague, a long-dead teacher of science to whom my work had strangely appealed, had turned them into hard, bright, unique-looking decorations for Possum's face. Deceptively cloudy until caught in the appropriate light, these two vaguely transparent orbs were the key to Possum's success, and, despite patent similarities in our appearance, evidence of his own unique personality.

My most recent addition to his appearance, nevertheless, had also proved extremely effective. At the beginning of summer I had attached coloured flypaper to the tongue, which, like the body, was canine in origin, and over several months the mouth had accrued a large cluster of dead insects that dropped abruptly into view whenever the puppet licked or swallowed, invariably scattering one or two dried bluebottles into my spellbound and horrified audience. This proved to be a striking accessory, particularly as a tiny battery-powered mechanism in the concealed handle allowed me to control rudimentary facial movements, although I had never bothered learning how to throw my voice. Possum's wide-eyed, open-mouthed stare penetrated well enough during his sudden intrusions, without the need of vocal embellishment. Only ever unleashing him at points in my dramas when his presence was a complete surprise, his unnerving silence merely served to exacerbate his chaotic misbehaviour. Whether devouring other characters without warning, usually the hero or heroine, or bursting through walls and destroying with unrestrained violence my neat but tedious endings, Possum's soundless, unpredictable presence captivated my young audiences like no other puppet I'd ever built. He was a law unto himself, and was now even challenging my own authority.

I leaned closer toward the mirror, reflecting on my most recent performance, and watched the sinking sun darken Possum's face with shadow. I observed how his head continued to stir subtly of its own accord as my body's natural rhythms gradually made their way through into his, and I tried in vain to freeze his movements. Before it was fully dark I took Possum outside.

There was no hint of a winter frost, and the earth was suitably wet. I dropped him in the stagnant water tank behind the old shed, where he couldn't get out, and hurled mud and stones down at him from my vantage point at the rim. I pulled faces at him until I could no longer discern anything below, then went back into the house. I considered waiting up for Christie's return, but instead went straight to bed.

I awoke to find Possum beside me, his long tongue hanging out like a vulgar child's. The head had been turned to face me in my sleep, and the eyes in the dawn light were a pale, milky yellow. As I sat up to scratch the tiny bites covering my legs and ankles, several dry houseflies dropped from the pillow onto my bed sheet. Later I found a dead wasp tucked inside my pyjama pocket. I pushed Possum to the floor, noting that his head had been wiped clean and his body scrubbed. Sensing that the parlour games had begun, I dressed quickly. I could hear Christie clattering about in the kitchen below, and I took the puppet with me when I went downstairs.

"Good morning and thank you," I said, dumping Possum on the table. "Now please burn all your hard work."

Christie, moving slowly with the aid of a stick, handed me a mug of strong tea and the ancient cake tin.

"Good morning," he said, smiling under his thick, nicotine-stained beard. "The head is expertly made."

"As are the legs," I said, sipping my drink. "A perfect job."

"*You* wired them in?" he asked.

I looked out at the garden. A huge bonfire had been piled ready.

"I want it burned," I said. "That's why I threw it out. You wasted your whole night. Now that's funny."

Christie laughed, which made me laugh.

"I'm going for a walk," I added. "What will you do?"

The old man hobbled slowly across the room, into the hallway.

"I'm going to bed," he said, and began climbing the stairs. I waited until he was halfway up, then called out loudly.

"Wasn't your best."

I interpreted his prolonged silence as a subtle joke and went out into the garden. I inspected Christie's mammoth bonfire, rummaging through the piles of ragged clothes and compost until I located some more of my old possessions buried underneath. I wasn't upset to see my gloves there, but I rescued an old watch my father had given me on my sixth birthday and decided that I would try and mend it. Deep within the piled rubbish was the inevitable roadkill, the largest of which was a mangled fox. I dragged it out by its tail, and as I passed back through the house on my way to the front door, slung it halfway up the stairs, hoping Christie might fall when he bent down to remove it. Then I sealed Possum up in my black bag and walked to the school.

I didn't stop once along the lane, although I saw enough to know that my old classroom, the scene of Christie's infamous stunt, had long since disappeared. An extension to the central building almost blocked my view of the playground, where the brick wall, over which I'd escaped, had been painted over with a large smiling face. I passed the second of two remote mobile classrooms, decorated with tiresome nativity displays, and carried on towards the familiar stone steps leading down to the abandoned station. I followed these onto the empty platform, examining the shelter on the opposite side of the track. Despite an abundance of thick spray-paint and several smashed windows, the place was abandoned. I dropped down silently onto the disused line. The metal tracks had been ripped up long before I was born, and the banks on each side of the route, beyond the declining platform, were heavily overgrown. The ancient trail turned sharply to the left before reaching a small, concealed footpath that snaked off into the trees. I brushed aside overhanging branches as I forced myself along it, pausing several times to pinpoint precisely where I'd once built my secret camp. Further along I located the old tree I'd climbed to impress friends, and the small slope we'd raced down. Beyond these, hidden beneath the thickest trees, was the place I was looking for.

I crouched down on the approaching path and located a suitable vantage point. I made my way over to a dense row of bushes and knelt behind the leaves. The ground around me was littered with empty crisp packets and crushed tins. Nearby lay scattered the feathers of a dead bird. Sooner than I had expected to I developed cramp, and, making as little movement as possible, shifted weight to my hands. Then I settled down to wait, keeping absolutely still.

When I finally heard someone approaching, I opened the bag. Possum's face stared up at me as I drew back the leather, eyes whitening in the overhead sun. I gave him some muddy leaves to eat and was in the process of extricating the rest of his body when I heard someone else approaching at speed from behind. I barely had time to conceal Possum before a tall man appeared from within the trees. He wore walking shoes and a short winter coat, and carried a school rucksack under one arm. His face was hostile and suspicious.

"Good morning," I said. Without replying, he moved off swiftly in the direction of the approaching child, calling loudly. I stood up, finding myself unable to move due to the numbness in my legs, and grabbed the handle of my bag. I waited, suspecting that I might require the use of Possum's limbs in order to effect a diversion worthy of pantomime. But no-one else appeared, and the man did not return. As soon I could, I walked home through a great many winding streets.

"Tell me again about the fox," Christie said.

"We were in the woods one day and saw a fox. It was panting at the mouth and its whole body was shaking. We thought it had swallowed something bad. When we came back later it was dead. So we played with it a while... stuck things in it. Then, as we left for home, the fox stood up. It had been playing with us."

"I mean the fox you dropped on my stairs," Christie replied, smugly. Another game won. And putting the dead animal in my bed and laying it out on the kitchen table before me as I ate my breakfast equalled three victories already that morning.

"You shouldn't have stolen from my bonfire," he said. "That was misbehaviour."

I sipped my tea and ate his stale cake. "Merry Christmas."

"Not yet, it isn't."

Christie rose slowly from the table and put on the jacket he'd hung over the back of his chair.

"Not staying?" I said, examining the local paper spread out before me.

"Places to go. The house is your own."

"I know it is," I countered. "And don't you forget it." One parlour game to me.

"I'll be back at six to start my bonfire."

I followed him out into the hall, trying the handle of the locked lounge door as I passed, loudly enough for him to hear.

"What happened to our decorations?" I asked. "We used to have several boxes."

The old man was struggling with his shoe-laces. I didn't help him.

"And what's this with the old caravan site?" I said, indicating the article I'd read.

"Deconstruction," he replied, eyes focused on his feet.

"It's hideous. What are they putting in its place?"

He stood up, wheezing, and limped forward into mild sunshine.

"Nothing."

I followed, handing him his walking stick.

"Nothing at all?"

"Not if they find things." He unearthed a strange-looking plant from the ground, exposing a huddle of pink, swollen tubers.

"These shouldn't be ready this time of year."

I stepped back inside the house.

"I'll have something else for you to burn later. My puppet."

"Not working any more?" he said, over his shoulder.

"Retired," I replied, and shut the door on him.

The bleak monotony of the muddy shoreline was lifted only by the distant dance of little red Wellingtons far behind. Echoes of light laughter overtook me on the breeze as someone closer, concealed on the far side of the approaching breaker, kicked pebbles repeatedly against the wooden barrier. I refrained from operating the bag in this exposed area, progressing instead along the coastal path toward the strange sunken mast that bordered the marshes. This tall concrete post stood out bleakly against the horizon, as it had done ever since I was a boy, a rusted sign nailed to its front stating "Keep Out". I was still unsure what purpose it had once served, but thought perhaps it could have formed part of an electrical generator servicing the nearby caravan site. Unchanged, it stood grim and obsolete while I leaned against it and watched the trail behind, cradling my cigarette from the wind.

Ahead, the path grew slippery as it rose toward the crest of a wide ridge overlooking a large, artificial crater. Formed by a jettisoned wartime bomb, this enclosed ravine was broken only by the slow progress of a shallow, man-made stream through its centre. The path, dipping sharply as I continued toward a low wooden bridge, crossed the green and stagnant water, disappearing again over the opposite rim.

The bridge itself retained most of its original slats, yet one or two had fallen away over the years, exposing a pool of foul silt below. I stepped across, looking down at the clay bank rising from the water's edge, noticing several holes in the mud that looked like the work of small animals. I considered planting Possum inside one so that my half-buried likeness could surprise the unwary children following behind, but then I thought of a better plan.

Removing Possum from the bag, I left the bridge and stepped down with him into the stream below, my feet sinking deep into the thick, oily mud. Using the roll of tape I always carried with me, I manoeuvred myself beneath the bridge and fastened Possum's body securely to the rotting planks, directing his face so that the eyes stared back up through the slats. Returning to the top, I was pleased to discover that the effect was quite disarming, and would prove so, I hoped, to my approaching billy goats.

I left Possum to do his work and moved onward, out of the ravine and across an expanse of wet marsh towards the abandoned caravan site beyond. As I approached, cleansing the mud from my boots in deep puddles, I heard the resounding thud of electrical machinery. The approach to the site involved crossing a stile situated half way along an elongated hedge, concealing the cabins beyond from view. I was surprised to find, however, that this had now disappeared, along with many of the caravans I had expected to see on the far side. Some distance away, a slow mechanical digger was shifting piles of rubble toward a larger mound. Across what remained of the park stood a few of the oldest cabins, built decades before to capitalise on the town's short-lived tourist trade. Many were blackened by what must have been a recent fire on the site, their walls and doors plastered with offensive graffiti. On one, a small naked doll had been tied to the remains of a twisted television aerial.

As I walked around the edge of the site, away from the digger, I encountered a "No Trespassing" sign posted up by the local council. Rain began to fall in large, heavy droplets, and the ground grew rapidly sodden. I sat down on an old tyre and watched as the man operating the digger shut off its engine and wandered over to a small truck parked at the far edge of the site. The vehicle moved off into the main road and headed back towards town, leaving the site deserted.

I felt around in my bag for my tool case. Opening it, I removed a small chisel I kept with me for repairs and began to sift through the mud around my feet, smelling the yellow earth caught on its metal blade. I carved a large smiling face into the muddy ground and watched as the rain slowly destroyed its features, then walked back to collect Possum.

At first I thought the tape must have worked loose in the rain, but then I saw how far the puppet had moved from the vicinity of the bridge, and decided that a real dog must have dragged it there. It couldn't have been one of the children, and closer examination of the muddy bank behind Possum revealed small paw marks, almost completely eroded by the recent downfall. Possum's head had been mauled at the ears, and one of the eyes was protruding slightly more prominently than usual. I kicked him around in the wet for a while and stamped hard on his face, wondering whether it was worth burying him permanently beneath the mud at the caravan site. Then I remembered the digger, packed him up in my bag and walked home.

"I'd like a demonstration before I burn him," said Christie, opening two tins of cheap lager for us. "Nothing special, but I want to see how the legs work."

"Trade secret," I replied, lighting the candles. When this was done he finally removed our meals from the oven.

"What other puppets do you use?"

"Several, but I want this one burned."

He served me the larger dish, which I realised was the dead fox.

"I heard about your last performance," he said, popping his half-smoked cigarette in Possum's mouth, whom I'd sat in the guest's chair between us. "One of my old teaching colleagues wrote to me about it. An unpredictable affair, by all accounts."

I ignored the comment and jabbed at the sticky burnt carcass staring up at me from my plate.

"I don't like this," I said. "Care to swap?"

Grinning, my host tucked greedily into what appeared to be a small bird.

"You forgot party crackers," I said, sipping from my tin.

"And grace," he replied, removing a small shred of bone from his upper lip.

"They'll take me back," I said, poking my fork at Possum, "once *he's* gone."

"We'll need gloves to get rid of it," Christie said. "It's diseased."

I examined my hands, which I sensed were peeling terribly and starting to bleed, and felt my face. I was covered.

"Eczema," I said, hiding what I could of me beneath the table.
"Remember," said Christie, his mouth full. "A demonstration."

The front half of the cabin was severely smoke-damaged, although in places I could still make out graffiti beneath the blackened panelling. The place stank of urine and petrol, and I sat at the back with my bag, near to where the bathroom had once been, and watched the remains of the site through a charred breach in the van opposite.

It was about midday when I crouched down on my knees so that I could not see out and crawled across the cabin floor. I examined where the cupboard used to be and touched the far side of the rear wall with my hands, feeling for the faint words scratched somewhere upon its surface. I leaned closer, sniffing at the floor, then gasped suddenly and withdrew. I stood up, returned to the seat, and opened my black bag.

I pulled Possum out and sat him on my lap. His body felt softer on one side. When I pressed my fingers against the fur, the insides gave a little, and I assumed they must be damaged in some way. His protruding eye, too, had broken open. A crack to the outer shell had caused a small leakage that ran down Possum's face, looking like dried egg yolk and smelling vaguely of chemicals.

I pulled his tongue down and tucked stray hairs behind his mauled ears. The wiring mechanism now broken, I extended, manually, each of his legs, until he sat astride me. I lay back against the seat, stretching my body lengthways, pulling him on top of me so that his face rested inches from my own. I slung his two front paws over my shoulders, opened my own mouth to mirror his, and stared back into his contaminated eyes. Then, with my tongue, I removed one of the dead flies from his.

"Don't," I said, and swallowed it. One by one, I ate them all. When Possum's mouth was clear, I lifted him from me, very gently, and sat myself up. I resisted the urge to retch and removed the tool case from my black bag. Having selected a blade, I picked up Possum, bit his ear without warning and threw him roughly to the floor. I knelt down on top of him and sawed at his nose, slowly and methodically, until I had sliced off its tip. I stuffed the severed segment inside his mouth and angled his limbs against the floor. With my boot I snapped each joint in turn and threw the broken legs out of the open window. I seized Possum's torso and thrust my arm inside. Crying out as the razors cut deeply into my wounds, I smashed the puppet hard against the wall, rocking the unstable cabin, before scraping the mutilated face against every sharp and jagged surface I could see. I removed my arm then, which was bleeding heavily, and took the scissors from my tool bag. I snipped off Possum's hair and jammed the tattered clumps between his teeth. I stabbed his eyes repeatedly with both blades until the weak one gave way entirely, spurting a glob of liquid over my fingers and up the scissor blade. I spat back at him, attempting to gouge a channel from one eyehole to the other, across his nose. The wax proved too strong, and instead I cut my own fingers. Grabbing a blunt wooden pole from my bag, I struck his head several times before shoving the blunt end of the pole into his mouth. When I'd finished thrusting, his head pinned and useless against the cabin wall, I gathered what was left of him beneath my arm and threw him into the corner. I kicked his stomach repeatedly until it caved in, exposing the stained wooden handle inside. I stuffed the belly with junk and threw Possum through the broken doorway, out into the yard beyond. Then I sucked the blood from my fingers, picked up my bag and left the cabin.

I stood as close to the flames as I could bear, hoping that my clothes would retain the smell of smoke. Christie shovelled in another heap of rubbish, momentarily stifling the blaze. I opened my bag and pulled out Possum's head, which I'd severed from his body with a spade while Christie had ransacked the last of my bedroom cupboards.

"Season's greetings," I said, tossing it across the grass towards him. "Too late for a demonstration."

"You should let me fix it," he said. "I like fixing things."

I lifted up the headless remains and threw them on the bonfire. Smoke curled around the bent, twisted nails wrenched incompletely from the neck as a sharp, sulphurous odour burned my nostrils. Flames snapped loudly against the coarse, brown fur as Christie held up the decapitated head and laughed.

"A broken toy," he said. "You shouldn't have."

"I saw it and thought of you," I replied, which made him laugh even more. I lit us both cigarettes while Christie perched what remained of Possum on an old wooden stool. He stuck his own inside the puppet's mouth and begged another. When we'd finished, he lifted up the head ceremoniously and dropped it on the bonfire, along with my watch, smiling to himself as he jammed them deep into the blazing compost with his pitchfork.

"How will you spend your Christmas day?" he asked.

"Exercising," I replied.

"Exorcising?"

"Past the school, if you must know."

"The school." Christie's face was a mischievous grin. "I taught you there once."

"I know. You died reading us a story."

"I came especially, the day after that business with the fox. To teach you all a lesson."

I watched Possum's face blacken and bubble, collapsing gradually into soft clear rivers of molten wax.

"Now that was a game to remember," Christie continued. "The looks on your faces. You should have seen yourselves."

"I'll be out all day," I said, zipping up my coat.

"Children talk such rot." The flames began to rise again as he turned over a pile of burning rags. "When there's no-one there to reassure them."

The eyes fell out together, exposing two pallid-looking sockets. I went inside and tried, without success, to force open the lounge door.

I had meant to purchase my return ticket, but realised upon reaching the station that there would be no trains leaving until the following day. I wandered for an hour or so until I gathered enough courage to enter one of the few pubs that were open. There I stomached a strong whiskey and some fatty sandwiches as the sun went down, before heading out once more, away from insufferable partygoers, into the darkness of the surrounding streets.

I gazed into people's houses through open blinds as I passed. The gaudy house-fronts, plastered with coloured lights and cheap decorations, one after another, left me feeling lost, so I sought darker avenues as I fled the town centre in the direction of my old school.

The ground through the adjacent lane was slippery, as if many people had been rushing along it during the day, and I found myself slowing involuntarily and glancing across at the disparate group of buildings that made up the school. A single lamp lit the area of the playground, exposing the large painted face that marked the area where Christie had chased us, full of life having feigned his terrifying heart attack. Someone, I assumed a janitor, was watching television in a small hut on the far side of the concrete field. I stopped for a moment to stare at the small alley in which I had sat alone many times during that final year, attempting to make sense of all that had happened to me. When I heard something enter the lane behind me, I moved on, quickening my pace.

I raced down the stone steps, crossed the old platform and dropped down into the abandoned line, pausing only to adjust my vision once more to the surrounding darkness. I moved off carefully, the noise of my footfalls interrupted only by the soft rush of wind moving through the nearby treetops. It took me longer than usual, but I eventually found the small hidden pathway into the trees and walked along it, noting that the ground here, like the school lane, was wetter and more broken up than before.

I found the place again instinctively, clear as the event still was in my memory, and stood up straight upon the spot, making sure I didn't slouch or bend my back in any way. I unzipped my coat and drew out the small lunch box I'd filled secretly after Christie had left the house. I removed the lid and, one by one, thrust my peeling hands into Possum's ashes, noting the sharp, unpleasant smell my skin now emitted. Once I was satisfied that the remains were truly soiled, I tipped the powdered mess onto the ground where the man had first shown himself to me, and smeared what was left into the earth, tossing the empty box into a nearby bush, near where he'd dragged me.

It was while I was wiping my hands clean with my handkerchief that I heard the dog. It had followed me through the empty station and was nosing through the bushes behind, tracking my scent. I thought of playing dead, but then strode out into the footpath, holding out my diseased hands that he'd hated touching. I screamed loudly at the top of my voice and this time the dirty creature stalking me ran a mile.

I mouthed words into the telephone receiver as my fingers tapped nervously on the dull, metallic surface of the rotary dial, flashing blue lights from the distant caravan site reflected against it. When

I looked up again, the policeman who'd walked over to watch me hadn't moved.

"He put me in his bag," I said aloud, to the faint, hypnotic hum of the dial tone. "Then he carried me to his caravan."

The rain had returned. I peered out across the grass slope, trying to look preoccupied, as the policeman made his decision and moved toward me.

"He always covered his face," I said, suddenly desperate for air. I nudged the door ajar.

"…he never took it off."

I hung up. Foolishly, as the officer reached me, I smiled.

"On your way," he ordered, studying my features. As I walked back to town, one of their cars followed me home.

Christie was drunk when he opened the door, and laughed openly at the state of my hands.

"That won't help you."

I snatched the bottle from him and wandered through into the kitchen, swigging heavily from it. The linoleum floor stuck to the soles of my shoes.

"I'm leaving tomorrow," I said.

"Are you?" he replied.

"Thanks for putting me up."

"Always a pleasure." He grinned inanely, performing an awkward, drunken dance. "Always was."

He began to sing an obscene song.

"Why don't you go to bed?" I snapped, taking another swig from the bottle. Swaying, I leant down and put what was left back in the cupboard under the sink.

"Your present's in the lounge," he said.

I lost balance, then, and dropped to the floor. My hands touched his dirt as I crawled towards the corner of the room.

"Sorry everything's so late." He stopped moving long enough to light a cigarette. He seemed younger to me.

"I'll have a car collect you tomorrow."

"They've found something up at the site," I said, eventually.

Christie inhaled deeply, knelt down and blew his smoke in my face.

"They have indeed."

Suddenly sheepish, he giggled pathetically, stood and stumbled off in the direction of the stairs, moving up them much faster than I'd thought he was capable of.

I didn't go in there immediately, as the whiskey had made me feel nauseous. I smoked a couple more cigarettes and listened for a while to Christie breaking my things in the room above.

When I did finally enter our lounge, unlocked for the first time in decades, I saw that nothing had changed since the day Christie first appeared with news of my bereavement. The tree was still there, its branches bare since the night of their funeral when he'd got me drunk for the first time and burned our decorations in front of me. I looked up to the top, where my Daddy had once lifted me to place our fairy, and saw something else I recognised.

It was the man's dog mask, and although now I could see only the wall behind through its cruel eyeholes, I realised it had belonged to Christie after all, and he'd worn it here beside me all these years, waiting for my courage to awaken.

Below, beneath the tree, was my present, wrapped up in newspapers and tied at the top with an ancient ribbon. It was a large, odd-looking object, bearing an old gift tag addressed to me that hung, quite still, from a small thread of dull, red cotton.

As I crawled toward the parcel, it twitched suddenly and a faint rustling sounded from the wrapping where the taut sheets began to bulge rapidly back and forth, as though something trapped beneath them were trying to breathe. When its long leg burst through the paper and pawed violently at the carpet in front, teeming with life, I reached out eagerly to unwrap my Possum.

2016

BLOOD RITES

Daisy Johnson

Daisy Johnson (b. 1990) has written two novels: *Everything Under* (2018), for which she became the youngest shortlisted author for the Booker Prize, and *Sisters* (2020). She grew up in the East Anglian Fens, which she refers to as "this strange flat land between Cambridge and the coast"; in interviews Daisy has described her vivid childhood memories of driving to school across the endless level fields, and of sleeping in an attic room that looked out over Ely Cathedral. The sense of the landscape's inherent otherness permeates her debut book, *Fen* (2016), which won the prestigious Edge Hill Short Story Prize. This fabulous collection of unsettling tales follows the lives of women and girls living in an anonymous Fen town and its surroundings—a liminal place where uncanny things happen: a teenager transforms into an eel, foxes begin to talk and, here in "Blood Rites", a trio of vampiric young women leave Paris for this harsh, flat world, unwittingly discovering the smallness and ugliness in the hearts of the local men they come to consume…

Daisy has a new collection of Fen-haunted short stories, *The Hotel*, coming out in late 2024.

When we were younger we learnt men the way other people learnt languages or the violin. We did not care for their words, their mouths moving on the television, the sound of them out of radios, the echo chamber of them from telephones and computers. We did not care for their thoughts; they could think on philosophy and literature and science if they wanted, they could grow opinions inside them if they wanted. We did not care for their creed or religion or type; for the choices they made and the ones they missed. We cared only for what they wanted so much it ruined them. Men could pretend they were otherwise, could enact the illusion of self-control, but we knew the running stress of their minds.

We left Paris one morning knowing we would never go back. English was the language of breaking and bending and it would suit our mouths better. None of us would ever fall in love in English. We would be safe from that.

Moving did not suit us; we were out of sync, out of time with ourselves. We rented a big, wrecked house out by the canal. Tampons swelled the drainage system; our palms were crisscrossed with promise scars barely healed before the next one. We promised we would never let it happen again. What had happened in Paris. None of us would let our food ruin our lives. The old walls of the house grew stained, dark swells of rustish wash across the sagging ceilings.

Greta came back most nights mournful; she'd been hunting roadkill. Arabella grew purposeful with unease, raided the butchers and spent the long days cooking up a storm of meat pies, of roasted birds inside birds and thick, heavy, unidentified stews. I was swept along by their disorientation, found myself lying in wait for the large, unafraid mice that populated the kitchen, found myself obsessed with daytime television, endless hours watching old quiz shows or the shopping channel.

We settled. Eventually. Greta, dancing the way she used to, bare feet tapping along the corridors, said it was a stupendous house, a house that knew how to feel. I laid down mouse traps and culled whole colonies in a day. We ate the leftovers of Arabella's cooking obsession in one long, sluggish evening and then emptied everything in the fridge into the bin. There was nothing in there we needed more than what we would have.

Arabella invested in a pair of wellington boots, put on one of the mouldy raincoats we'd found in a cupboard and went out on a reconnaissance mission. Came back talking, without pause, on seed-planting schedules and wind direction. She'd been, she said, in the local pub and she'd met men there who she thought would taste like the earth, like potatoes buried until they were done, like roots and tree bark. English men never really said what they were thinking: all that pressure inside, fermenting. We could imagine it easily enough.

She held out her hand, told us to taste it, told us she'd been able to smell their salt-of-the-earth insides across the barren winter fields. We sucked until we could: fen dirt heavy enough to grow new life in it.

Later Arabella broke into seriousness: we would have to be careful, pick carefully. We'd have to share. She changed the Bob Dylan record with her long white toes.

We shaved all the hair off our legs and underarms, plucked until we were smooth, coating the white bathtub in drag lines of dark;

moisturised until we shone white and slick through the dim; painted crimson "yes" markers on our mouths.

We looked the way hunters must do. We looked the way we'd looked in Paris, half-glimpsed shards and shadows of skin, the meaningful line of stocking or bra.

This isn't going to work, Greta said, pulling at her hair.

We raided the backs of the wardrobes; hunted in the dressing-up boxes we'd saved for bored days, snuck out to pillage washing lines. Regrouped and stood silently at the sight of ourselves: jodhpurs and polo necks and gilets.

Greta said, dreamily, that we looked like child catchers.

Arabella said we looked fierce.

She got the money and we pushed into boots and wellingtons at the door and went out, Greta trailing behind to catch her fingers on the blackberry bushes and kick at the frozen puddles. At the door to the pub Arabella turned to look at us for one final check: wiping her thumb at the blood Greta had used to darken her lips, straightening my carefully knotted scarf, mussing her hair with both hands. The Fox and Hound. We went in. Lined up at the bar. Listened to the quiet that spread the way a spool unravelled.

Arabella leant over on both elbows and smiled the way she did and said we would really quite like three gin and tonics if that was all right.

We were hungry but we took our time. Greta liked the school kids, drunk already, though it was barely eight o'clock, and rowdy on it. She bought them drinks because they were too young to do it themselves, laughed at their under-the-table shot taking. We heard her telling them that drinking would only ever get better, that they would spend their lives lying to their doctor about the number of pints they consumed. They looked at her as if she were a thing summoned up, formed from everything they'd never even known they wanted.

Arabella liked the old men in their corners or sat at the bar alone, talking in strange, weathered code to the barman about different ales. She liked the veined alcoholism of them, the implicit watching. She knew enough about the World Cup to get by.

It didn't matter who they liked. The one we would take had raw hands from the cold and narrow, glass-covered eyes. I knew before I went to him the sort of girl he'd want, one shy enough to look as though she shouldn't be there, one quiet enough to look as though she had something to hide. He did not respond in much more than monosyllables to my questions. I liked the dull return of his voice, the way he looked at his glass rather than at my face. He was, he said, a vet. When he was drunker he would tell me it was a bad time to be someone who cared about animals. He told me about the foxes being gassed in their earths. I told him everything has to die somewhere.

I finished my drink and he bought me another, bought one for himself, did not clink the glass I held up, only held his up too: a salute. He spoke about animals as if I knew them too and remembered them well. He worried about the land, thought he would move on when he had half a chance. Less than half.

It's not the way it used to be, he said.

When it was flooded? I said, half joking, and he looked at me as if this were a thing you could not mention, were not allowed to mention.

He was not married, had no children, was on his own the way someone was when they knew no different. I did not ask his name.

We left together. He said he was too drunk to drive and I said I was walking anyway. On the long, straight, dark road I sucked his bottom lip into my mouth and he made a startled sound as if someone had broken something sharp into him. At the onset of headlights coming over the flats I pulled him to the hedge line, forced the gasp from him again. He was afraid of me though not for the reason he should have been. When I took out one breast, he would not touch it, only stood a safe distance and looked until we carried on.

At the house I saw it as he must have done and wondered if he knew what was coming. It smelt of feathers and iron kettles. I took him to the kitchen. There were broken wine glasses on the table; our discarded clothes were in piles. The fur hat on the draining board looked sentinel, only dozing. I made him a whisky and water strong enough he puffed his cheeks out, shook his head.

He seemed unsurprised to find them in the sitting room, dressed in their nighties, Greta's head on Arabella's lap, a Leonard Cohen vinyl turning slowly next to them. I sat close enough to him on the sofa I could see the ice in his glass shaking. He sat and looked around at the rows of records, the 1965 Van Hurst guitar taken from a travelling musician, the signed January Hargrave posters.

Are you in a band? he asked. Arabella called him a lovely man and offered him her hand to kiss. Greta laughed like a child, told him we were groupies and—because she'd been hungry the longest—she got the first try. We asked her if he had the flavour of love and she only smiled a scarlet smile and said he tasted the way burrowing into the earth, mouth whaling open, would taste.

It was not the occasion for leftovers. We buried the little that was left in the big back garden, toasted our success with a whole bottle of something local Arabella had stolen. There wasn't enough of him remaining to merit a burning, though I think that would have been best: a sacrificial fire to warn the rest of our coming.

The next day we woke with a strangeness inside us we could not identify. Tried to stave it off with our favourite songs, our best dresses, opened all the windows to air the house through.

I feel—Greta started to say and Arabella gave her a look good and hard enough to silence her. Said: I'll paint your nails.

I lay watching them. I felt heavy, ached through. Not full—rather bored, weary.

I feel—Greta started again.

Stop it, Greta, Arabella said. It's fine.

I sat up, rigid. I did not know where it had come from but there were things I wanted to tell them right now; there were things they needed to know. About the giving-in the earth was doing, about the dying foxes and the flood water. The globe was comprised of bone and organ, the mandible of the sea, the larynx and thyroid, the scapula and vertebrae that held it all together. I bit my tongue until the feeling passed.

It was not the first time we'd eaten something we shouldn't.

For a week or so the vet pressed out from inside us. I caught Arabella in the kitchen, weeping over a plucked chicken. Greta began speaking in clipped monosyllables. I caught myself counting the bones in their bodies.

Still, soon we were hungry again. Arabella said that we needed to be careful; this was not Paris. She took up cooking once more and we ate well and often. Sometimes she went to the butchers, came back with quails and woodcock and whole pigs. Mostly she went hunting in the thin spinneys that separated the farms, came back with rabbits and pheasants. Then we got bored of this and we did not eat at all.

When the time came we decided we could not risk picking up another man in the pub. We made a profile on some dating websites, spent long evenings sitting around the computer, pushing one another's hands away. We found a man who, in his picture, showed only his chest, one hand holding up a phone to take the photo. His profile said that he enjoyed drinking and working out. He wrote that he'd been a sailor but didn't do that any more.

Men like that, Arabella said, no one is ever surprised when they go missing.

We sent him a message and he replied quickly. He used the words cock and cunt and fuck and hard with a regularity which dried them meaningless. Occasionally he'd, typing drunk perhaps, talk about a girl and a baby and a twin brother and how he'd lost the lot of them. The next day he'd regain his composure, write that he wanted to do this to us and he wanted us to do that to him. And when we were done he was going to do this. We said all right, sent him photos of Greta in her underwear, arranged an evening for him to come to the house.

We dressed Greta. This was not the occasion for polo shirts or wellington boots. We painted her mouth a red church.

When the doorbell went, Greta climbed into her heels. The smell of aftershave was palpable through the door. He looked older than he'd said on the Internet, thin at the cheeks, dressed up the way someone pretending to be younger might do. He looked her up and down with a slowness, said his name was Marco and he was ready. Greta giggled. Stepped backwards to let him in. The big hallway was dark. He stumbled on something, an abandoned book or rolling wine bottle. Greta led the way to the kitchen. We closed the front door behind him.

The next day the feeling that had come after the vet was back and worse. Arabella went out to get rid of the car. Greta and I sat in silence in the sitting room. Arabella must have been thinking about it on the drive: it's because we haven't eaten for a while, she said as she marched in, tracking mud. We're just full.

We took turns in the bath. The nail varnish Arabella was using to paint her nails overturned, spilt a thin blue splash over the wooden floor.

Fucking Jesus, Arabella said matter-of-factly and then looked around as if to see where the words had come from. Greta laughed and then fell silent, dipping her head beneath the water line.

When I woke that night Arabella was shifting beneath the heavy blanket, her hands doing fast work out of sight, her eyes on the revealed white of Greta's shoulder and neck. I lay and watched her until she turned to me, poked out a concentrating tongue, said: I'd like a piece of that. I want a piece of that. Roared when I reached out to pinch the skin on her arm, called me words I did not think I knew: except, then, I did.

At breakfast I tried to confront them. Arabella was buttering her toast with violent, angry motions.

I think they are inside us, I said.

What do you mean? What the fuck do you mean? Arabella's knife went through her toast and squealed over the plate.

Greta looked a little pained across from me. I wondered if perhaps she was not quite lost yet, if there were syllables she retained that were still her own; if she felt, at times, her own language pressing back.

You're both talking like that boy we ate the other night, I said. The rude one.

Bollocks, Arabella said. Greta got up and went and turned the radio on loud.

I wanted to tell them I knew the truth. The truth was fen men were not the same as the men we'd had before. They lingered in you the way a bad smell did; their language stayed with you.

I locked myself in the pantry, waited to see if I could feel it coming before it got there. I watched out for hints of violence in words that came to mind. I hunted for a thickness in the sentences that formed silently. I was looking so hard for the man that I did not see his predecessor climbing up in my belly again until it was too late.

There was the smell of spice and meat. I dozed off on the warm floorboards, dreamt I was swimming from the inside of one animal to another, moving organs aside with my hands. Often, as I passed from the gut of a horse to one of a dog to a small, angry cat, I could see the sickness beating in them, reached out with my fingers to try and fend it away. It was not until I woke up, Greta banging on the door with both hands and asking what the fuck was I doing she needed to eat some fucking food, that I realised I knew the names for the parts of all the animals I'd dreamt of. It was not a light knowledge, not a thing I could carry with me without noticing or caring any: it was rock heavy, a heated weight. I opened my mouth and heard the words spilling out in a stream I could not see the end of: adrenal, abdominal, abrin, antipyretic, aortic, arrhythmia—

1936

A VIGNETTE

M. R. James

M. R. James, worn down by the toll the Great War had taken on Cambridge life and the loss of so many of his former students at King's—including several to whom he was close—returned to Eton shortly before the Armistice to become provost at the school he had himself so fondly attended. It was a role he was to hold until his death on 12 June 1936. He is buried in Eton Town Cemetery.

A few months after his passing, James was to give us a poignant, final depiction of the East Anglian landscape of his youth. Written in 1935 and printed posthumously in 1936, "A Vignette" is the only one of James's works to reference Great Livermere and his childhood home directly. The apparently autobiographical tale tells of a malevolent, haunting face glimpsed through an opening in the rectory's garden wall, and may, in itself, lay to rest the question he was so frequently asked: "Do I believe in ghosts? To which I answer that I am prepared to consider evidence and accept it if it satisfies me."

"A Vignette" would seem strongly to suggest that, in the end, he had indeed accepted the evidence. Or, at the very least—like Parkins in "'Oh, Whistle, and I'll Come to You, My Lad'"—that his views on certain points were now "less clear cut than they used to be"…

You are asked to think of the spacious garden of a country rectory, adjacent to a park of many acres, and separated therefrom by a belt of trees of some age which we knew as the Plantation. It is but about thirty or forty yards broad. A close gate of split oak leads to it from the path encircling the garden, and when you enter it from that side you put your hand through a square hole cut in it and lift the hook to pass along to the iron gate which admits to the park from the Plantation. It has further to be added that from some windows of the rectory, which stands on a somewhat lower level than the Plantation, parts of the path leading thereto, and the oak gate itself can be seen. Some of the trees, Scotch firs and others, which form a backing and a surrounding, are of considerable size, but there is nothing that diffuses a mysterious gloom or imparts a sinister flavour—nothing of melancholy or funereal associations. The place is well clad, and there are secret nooks and retreats among the bushes, but there is neither offensive bleakness nor oppressive darkness. It is, indeed, a matter for some surprise when one thinks it over, that any cause for misgivings of a nervous sort have attached itself to so normal and cheerful a spot, the more so, since neither our childish mind when we lived there nor the more inquisitive years that came later ever nosed out any legend or reminiscence of old or recent unhappy things.

Yet to me they came, even to me, leading an exceptionally happy wholesome existence, and guarded—not strictly but as carefully as was any way necessary—from uncanny fancies and fear. Not that such guarding avails to close up all gates. I should be puzzled to fix the date at which any sort of misgiving about the Plantation gate first visited me. Possibly it was in the years just before I went to school, possibly on one later summer afternoon of which I have a faint memory, when I was coming back after solitary roaming in the park, or, as I bethink me, from tea at the Hall: anyhow, alone, and fell in with one of the villagers also homeward bound just as I was about to turn off the road on to the track leading to the Plantation. We broke off our talk with "good nights", and when I looked back at him after a minute or so I was just a little surprised to see him standing still and looking after me. But no remark passed, and on I went. By the time I was within the iron gate and outside the park, dusk had undoubtedly come on; but there was no lack yet of light, and I could not account to myself for the questionings which certainly did rise as to the presence of anyone else among the trees, questionings to which I could not very certainly say "No", nor, I was glad to feel, "Yes", because if there were anyone they could not well have any business there. To be sure, it is difficult, in anything like a grove, to be quite certain that nobody is making a screen out of a tree trunk and keeping it between you and him as he moves round it and you walk on. All I can say is that if such an one was there he was no neighbour or acquaintance of mine, and there was some indication about him of being cloaked or hooded. But I think I may have moved at a rather quicker pace than before, and have been particular about shutting the gate. I think, too, that after that evening something of what Hamlet calls a "gain-giving" may have been present in my mind when I thought of the Plantation, I do seem to remember looking out of a window which gave in that direction, and questioning whether there was or was not any appearance of a moving form among the trees. If I did, and perhaps I did, hint a suspicion to the nurse the only answer to it will have been "the hidea of such a thing!" and an injunction to make haste and get into my bed.

Whether it was on that night or a later one that I seem to see myself again in the small hours gazing out of the window across moonlit grass and hoping I was mistaken in fancying any movement in that half-hidden corner of the garden, I cannot now be sure. But it was certainly within a short while that I began to be visited by dreams which I would much rather not have had—which, in fact, I came to dread acutely; and the point round which they centred was the Plantation gate.

As years go on it but seldom happens that a dream is disturbing. Awkward it may be, as when, while I am drying myself after a bath, I open the bedroom door and step out on to a populous railway platform and have to invent rapid and flimsy excuses for the deplorable deshabille. But such a vision is not alarming, though it may make one despair of ever holding up one's head again. But in the times of which I am thinking, it did happen, not often, but oftener than I liked, that the moment a dream set in I knew that it was going to turn out ill, and that there was nothing I could do to keep it on cheerful lines.

Ellis the gardener might be wholesomely employed with rake and spade as I watched at the window; other familiar figures might pass and repass on harmless errands; but I was not deceived. I could see that the time was coming when the gardener and the rest would be gathering up their properties and setting off on paths that led homeward or into some safe outer world, and the garden would be left—to itself, shall we say, or to denizens who did not desire quite ordinary company and were only waiting for the word "all clear" to slip into their posts of vantage.

Now, too, was the moment near when the surroundings began to take on a threatening look; that the sunlight lost power and a quality of light replaced it which, though I did not know it at the time my memory years after told me was the lifeless pallor of an eclipse. The effect of all this was to intensify the foreboding that had begun to possess me, and to make me look anxiously about, dreading that in some quarter my fear would take a visible shape. I had not much doubt which way to look. Surely behind those bushes, among those trees, there was motion, yes, and surely—and more quickly than seemed possible—there was motion, not now among the trees, but on the very path towards the house. I was still at the window, and before I could adjust myself to the new fear there came the impression of a tread on the stairs and a hand on the door. That was as far as the dream got, at first; and for me it was far enough. I had no notion what would have been the next development, more than that it was bound to be horrifying.

That is enough in all conscience about the beginning of my dreams. A beginning it was only, for something like it came again and again; how often I can't tell, but often enough to give me an acute distaste for being left alone in that region of the garden. I came to fancy that I could see in the behaviour of the village people whose work took them that way an anxiety to be past a certain point, and moreover a welcoming of company as they approached that corner of the park. But on this it will not do to lay overmuch stress, for, as I have said, I could never glean any kind of story bound up with the place.

However, the strong probability that there had been one once I cannot deny.

I must not by the way give the impression that the whole of the Plantation was haunted ground. There were trees there most admirably devised for climbing and reading in; there was a wall, along the top of which you could walk for many hundred yards and reach a frequented road, passing farmyard and familiar houses; and once in the park, which had its own delights of wood and water, you were well out of range of anything suspicious—or, if that is too much to say, of anything that suggested the Plantation gate.

But I am reminded, as I look on these pages, that so far we have had only preamble, and that there is very little in the way of actual incident to come, and that the criticism attributed to the devil when he sheared the sow is like to be justified. What, after all, was the outcome of the dreams to which without saying a word about them I was liable during a good space of time? Well, it presents itself to me thus. One afternoon—the day being neither overcast nor threatening—I was at my window in the upper floor of the house. All the family were out. From some obscure shelf in a disused room I had worried out a book, not very recondite: it was, in fact, a bound volume of a magazine in which were contained parts of a novel. I know now what novel it was, but I did not then, and a sentence struck and arrested me. Someone was walking at dusk up a solitary lane by an old mansion in Ireland, and being a man of imagination he was suddenly forcibly impressed by what he calls "the aerial image of the old house, with its peculiar malign, scared, and skulking aspect" peering out of the shade of its neglected old trees. The words were quite enough to set my own fancy on a bleak track. Inevitably I looked and looked with apprehension, to the Plantation gate. As was but right it was shut, and nobody was upon the path that led to it or from it. But as I said a while ago, there was in it a square hole giving access to the fastening; and through that hole, I could see—and it struck like a blow on the diaphragm—something white or partly white. Now this I could not bear, and with an access of something like courage—only it was more like desperation, like determining that I must know the worst—I did steal down and, quite uselessly, of course, taking cover behind bushes as I went, I made progress until I was within range of the gate and the hole. Things were, alas! worse than I had feared; through that hole a face was looking my way. It was not monstrous, not pale, fleshless, spectral. Malevolent I thought and think it was; at any rate the eyes were large and open and fixed. It was pink and, I thought, hot, and just above the eyes the border of a white linen drapery hung down from the brows.

There is something horrifying in the sight of a face looking at one out of a frame as this did; more particularly if its gaze is unmistakably fixed upon you. Nor does it make the matter any better if the expression gives no clue to what is to come next. I said just now that I took this face to be malevolent, and so I did, but not in regard of any positive dislike or fierceness which it expressed. It was, indeed, quite without emotion: I was only conscious that I could see the whites of the eyes all round the pupil, and that, we know, has a glamour of madness about it. The immovable face was enough for me. I fled, but at what I thought must be a safe distance inside my own precincts I could not but halt and look back. There was no white thing framed in the hole of the gate, but there was a draped form shambling away among the trees.

Do not press me with questions as to how I bore myself when it became necessary to face my family again. That I was upset by something I had seen must have been pretty clear, but I am very sure that I fought off all attempts to describe it. Why I make a lame effort to do it now I cannot very well explain: it undoubtedly has had some formidable power of clinging through many years to my imagination. I feel that even now I should be circumspect in passing that Plantation gate; and every now and again the query haunts me: Are there here and there sequestered places which some curious creatures still frequent, whom once on a time anybody could see and speak to as they went about on their daily occasions, whereas now only at rare intervals in a series of years does one cross their paths and become aware of them; and perhaps that is just as well for the peace of mind of simple people.

ALSO AVAILABLE

Like any other boy I expected ghost stories at Christmas, that was the time for them. What I had not expected, and now feared, was that such things should actually become real.

Strange things happen on the dark wintry nights of December. Welcome to a new collection of haunting Christmas tales, ranging from traditional Victorian chillers to weird and uncanny episodes by twentieth-century horror masters including Daphne du Maurier and Robert Aickman.

Lurking in the blizzard are menacing cat spirits, vengeful trees, malignant forces on the mountainside and a skater skirting the line between the mortal and spiritual realms. Wrap up warm—and prepare for the longest nights of all.

ALSO AVAILABLE

> ... and then the music was so loud, so beautiful that I couldn't think of anything else. I was completely lost to the music, enveloped by melody which was part of Pan.

In 1894, Arthur Machen's landmark novella *The Great God Pan* was published, sparking the sinister resurgence of the pagan goat god. Writers of the late-nineteenth to mid-twentieth centuries, such as Oscar Wilde, E. M. Forster and Margery Lawrence, took the god's rebellious influence as inspiration to spin beguiling tales of social norms turned upside down and ancient ecological forces compelling their protagonists to ecstatic heights or bizarre dooms.

Assembling ten tales and six poems—along with Machen's novella—from the boom years of Pan-centric literature, this new collection revels in themes of queer awakening, transgression against societal bonds and the bewitching power of the wild as it explores a rapturous and culturally significant chapter in the history of weird fiction.

ALSO AVAILABLE

But foliage surrounded him, branches blocked the way; the trees stood close and still; and the sun dipped that moment behind a great black cloud. The entire wood turned dark and silent. It watched him.

Woods play a crucial and recurring role in horror, fantasy, the gothic and the weird. They are places in which strange things happen, where it is easy to lose your way. Supernatural creatures thrive in the thickets. Trees reach into underworlds of pagan myth and magic. Forests are full of ghosts.

Lining the path through this realm of folklore and fear are twelve stories from across Britain, telling tales of whispering voices and maddening sights from deep in the Yorkshire Dales to the ancient hills of Gwent and the eerie quiet of the forests of Dartmoor. Immerse yourself in this collection of classic tales celebrating the enduring power of our natural spaces to enthral and terrorise our senses.

ALSO AVAILABLE

*There was a faint rustling sound, like some small silk thing
blown in a gentle breeze. He sat up straight, stark and
scared, and a small wooden voice spoke in the stillness.
'Pa-pa,' it said, with a break between the syllables.*

From living dolls to spirits wandering in search of solace or vengeance, the ghostly youth is one of the most enduring phenomena of supernatural fiction, its roots stretching back into the realms of folklore and superstition. In this spine-tingling new collection Jen Baker gathers a selection of the most chilling hauntings and encounters with ghostly children, expertly paired with notes and extracts from the folklore and legends which inspired them.

Reviving obscure stories from Victorian periodicals alongside nail-biting episodes from master storytellers such as Elizabeth Gaskell, M. R. James and Margery Lawrence, this is a collection by turns enchanting, moving and thoroughly frightening.

For more Tales of the Weird titles
visit the British Library Shop (shop.bl.uk)

We welcome any suggestions, corrections or feedback you may have, and will aim to respond to all items addressed to the following:

The Editor (Tales of the Weird), British Library Publishing,
The British Library, 96 Euston Road, London NW1 2DB

We also welcome enquiries through our X (Twitter) account, @BL_Publishing.